Praise for the

# LAUREN BARATZ-LOGSTED

### THE THIN PINK LINE
"Wonderfully funny...a fine sense of the absurd and
a flair for comic characterization."
—*Kirkus* (starred review)

"Proves c
half-pregr
and
—Karen Karbo, author of *Motherhood Made a Man Out of Me*

"It's impossible to put this debut novel down without knowing
how Jane is going to end this charade after her ninth month."
—*Pittsburgh Post-Gazette*

10-08

CROSSING THE LINE

about b

"Baratz-Loc

# Baby Needs a New Pair of Shoes

# LAUREN BARATZ-LOGSTED

RED
DRESS
I N K
TM

10-08
14-

BABY NEEDS A NEW PAIR OF SHOES

A Red Dress Ink novel

ISBN-13: 978-0-373-89576-2
ISBN-10:    0-373-89576-3

www.RedDressInk.com

**Printed in U.S.A.**

For Laura Wininger:
with love and thirty years of friendship,
this one's for you.

## ACKNOWLEDGMENTS

Thank you to Pamela Harty for being my agent and friend.

Thank you to my editor, Margaret O'Neill Marbury, and her assistant, Rebecca Soukis, for their hard work on this book. Special thanks to Adam Wilson for services above and beyond.

Thank you to the Friday Night Writing Group—Jerry Brooker, Andrea Schicke Hirsch, Greg Logsted, Robert Mayette, Kristi Peterson, and Lauren Catherine Simpson—for being there.

Thank you to Kaethe Douglas and Sue Estabrook for being amazing first readers and friends.

Thank you to all my family and friends and, especially, my great mother, Lucille Baratz.

Thank you to my husband Greg Logsted and our daughter Jackie—no writer has the words to describe how wonderful you are.

## AUTHOR'S NOTE

If you look for the particular Jimmy Choo shoes mentioned
in this book, you won't find them, except perhaps in resale
outlets. Jimmy Choo did in fact make all these shoes, exactly
as described, but this book was written in fall of 2005 and,
since then, many catalogue seasons have come and gone,
and many Choos have passed into the realm of fashion legend.

# Prologue

It was a hand dealt straight out of a dream: two Aces.

*What to do, what to do…*

Easy answer: the dealer had just shuffled right before dealing, so there were nearly six full decks left in the chute, all of those beautiful Jacks, Queens and Kings. Even the Tens would be beautiful and a person didn't need to be a pro at counting cards to realize that the game, for once, was strongly in the player's favor.

So, very easy answer: split the Aces.

The next decision, if not as easy, relied totally on the player's instincts: double down, or let the original bet ride? The original bet represented half of the player's holdings, but the player was feeling cocky, riding high. Besides, the dealer was showing a Seven.

Big deal.

The player looked at the dealer, a face that had become so familiar. The player looked over one shoulder, at the man standing just behind, a man who gave a slight nod of his head: approval.

Giving the matter no further thought, the player pushed the rest of the chips forward, hitting the table limit. Those chips, tens of thousands of dollars worth of chips, represented everything the player had in the world.

Whatever two cards the dealer turned over next would decide the future fate of the player.

And so, let the real game begin...

# 1

Everything I learned in life, I learned from Shakespeare; about comedy and tragedy, about the reversal of expectations and fortune. Oh, and from my dad, Black Jack Sampson—I learned a lot from him, too.

I woke up that morning, brushed my teeth, ate breakfast.

I've read enough books in my life that I do realize it goes against wisdom to tell a story about a person waking up in the morning and then following them step-by-step until the storyteller puts them to bed at night. But the way I figure it, no wild journey ever began without someone waking up in the morning. I mean, if I never woke up in the morning, there'd be no story at all.

So, getting back to the beginning: I woke up in the morning, had breakfast. The stamp-sized kitchen was a natural light–deprived airless room, its walls perversely painted dark purple-red on a whim by me and my roommate right after we'd moved in. The paint wasn't even dried when we realized that we mutually hated the color, which gave the room the air of a minuscule bordello plus four-bagel toaster (hers), but it would have taken more home-improvement initiative than either of us had to correct the *Architectural Digest* error of our ways. If we were going to revamp the place, we'd also need to replace the light blue-and-white tiled floor, turned yellowish with age, and the ceiling light fixture, behind which an extraordinary number of bugs gravitated to die. But this would have entailed more visits to Home Depot for just one room than I ever intended to make in my entire life. Let the ugliness ride.

I opened up one of the lower kitchen cabinets, pulled out an opened box of Cocoa Krispies, next to which were three more boxes—insurance—and poured some into a bowl. Then I reached into one of two dorm-sized fridges stacked on top of each other in the tiny kitchen, took out a fresh carton and poured milk into a glass. I always ate my cereal dry, had done so since I was a child, a fact that had made more than one previous boyfriend feel all squicky.

At present, I had no boyfriend. Maybe it was the cereal.

My dry-cereal habit also made my roommate, Hillary, feel squicky—the other fridge belonged to her—so it was a good thing she only had to watch me eat it on weekends, her job as a psychologist causing her to leave earlier in the morning than me.

Then I sat down to do the same thing I did during break-fast every morning: watch The Weather Channel, listening with half an ear as the forecast for Danbury played three times during the half-hour loop, while going through the *New York Times*—front page, editorials and crossword puzzle, always in exactly that order—all while crunching my dry cereal. When the last forecast was broadcast on the screen and I was finally convinced that it would indeed be sunny and dry with a high of ninety-two degrees Fahrenheit, I pushed the paper aside, so that now it was bumping newsprint with my roommate's newspaper of choice, the *New York Post;* considering my roommate had a more highbrow job than mine, her news tastes were lower, but she claimed the jumble puzzles were fun. Then I turned the TV to one of the morning news-talk shows and commenced packing my lunch.

As one of the TV anchors, pretending to be a serious jour-nalist, droned on about the importance of doing the Back to School shopping thing before the last minute (still a month away), I opened the freezer and took out my lunch: an Amy's Cheese Pizza Pocket, carbon copies of which filled half the freezer—the other half of which was filled with what I would have for dinner, the same thing I had for dinner every night when I was at home: Michael Angelo's Four Cheese Lasagna.

I have a confession to make here: I am an addictive per-sonality.

Like my father before me, like a rat repeatedly hitting a lever to get at a piece of cheese, for most of my life, when

I liked something, I kept hitting that lever even after I was no longer hungry, even after I'd started to hate cheese. This single-minded stick-to-itiveness had served me well in some regards. Back in college, my refusal to let a thing go until I was done with it had led to me reading not just the eight plays assigned in my Shakespeare I class, but *all* of Shakespeare's plays plus the sonnets. True, *Titus Andronicus* sucked, but I was glad to have cried through Lear's *Cordelia, Cordelia! Stay a little* speech, empathized with Macbeth's shattering *tomorrow, and tomorrow, and tomorrow,* and would have given my eyeteeth to have been Ariel listening to Prospero as Prologue clapped Shakespeare into retirement. But the same obsessiveness that had led me to bardolatry also meant that, once the next semester started, my discovery of Singapore Slings resulted in my drinking them every night at the pub, missing most of my classes and flunking just enough courses to forfeit my student loan. Sometimes my behavior is comic, sometimes it's tragic, and it's only the final outcome of each individual story that determines which one it really is. So that's who I am—a rat repeatedly pushing a lever for cheese—and this is my story.

Of course, like many obsessives, I wasn't always this way. My obsessions started when I was eight, the year my mom first got sick. I used to tell myself: *If I just fold the towels the exact same way every time, if I knock on the door two and never three times each time I want to enter her room, if I eat the same foods at every meal, she won't get sicker. She won't die.* But, of course, she did get sicker. She did die. The process took ten years from start to finish. And, true, my bargaining with the Devil of Obsessive Behavior hadn't saved her. But, by the time she was dead, I was too used to the security of my obsessiveness to let it go.

While I waited the two minutes and thirty seconds for my pizza pocket to heat up in the microwave, I got out my purple insulated lunch bag and threw in an Igloo ice pack and two cans of my latest drinking obsession: Diet Pepsi Lime. There was a case of it in the fridge and a spare case in the stairwell. When I got home after work, when I had my dinner, I'd drink my other favorite drink with it: Jake's Fault Shiraz, of which there were a half-dozen bottles in the fridge. I liked my wine red and cold, and I liked Jake's Fault a lot, but despite my obsessiveness, I'd limited myself to one or two glasses at a sitting, despite the near overwhelming compulsion to drink the whole bottle.

Hey, if my daily diet lacked nutritional variety, if there was never a piece of fruit or a real vegetable in sight—not in my fridge, at any rate—at least I took a daily multivitamin. So, okay, so maybe that multivitamin was Flintstones, but still… There were plenty of fruits and vegetables in my roommate's, just as there was a wider variety of food in the lower cabinets that were earmarked as hers.

I read a book once that said many people don't like having overnight guests, not because they're inhospitable or worried that the guests will be a nuisance, but because of a fear of having others see how intensely weird they really are in their own habits. That's me, a woman intensely weird in her own habits, afraid to let the rest of the world see in.

As I zipped my purple lunch bag shut, the morning talk show switched over to commercial and suddenly *he* was there again: the man of my dreams.

I guess that bears explaining and really he wasn't the man of my dreams, since the man of my dreams was faceless, but certainly he'd inspired a lot of my recent dreams.

The man in question was The Yo-Yo Man.

I mean, it wasn't like he wore a streaming superhero red cape with a giant yellow *Y* emblazoned on his chest, but I thought of him as The Yo-Yo Man. And the commercials he starred in had been airing for about a month.

There was a new yo-yo manufacturer, Ball & String, which had been trying to unseat Duncan as *the* manufacturer of yo-yos for some time now. Their latest gambit involved a commercial campaign where this incredibly talented yo-yoist—yes, I did just say *yo-yoist* like it was an actual word—did things that were, well, downright amazing. I guess the theory behind making these commercials was that it wasn't enough for one company to try to say in print ads that they were better than another; when a medium was so visual, they needed to actually *show,* not just tell. The things that The Yo-Yo Man could do were amazing, and yet he made it look so effortless, as if anyone, including the viewer at home, could potentially do the same, if only they used the Ball & String. He could spin two yo-yos simultaneously, he could juggle fire in one hand while doing Round the World

with his other and, man, let me tell you, he could walk my
dog any day.

Not that I have a dog. I don't even particularly *like* dogs.
But, really, The Yo-Yo Man could walk my dog any day.

And he was cute. Did I mention that The Yo-Yo Man was
cute? Not that you could tell height from a TV commercial, but I still guessed him to be about six feet even to my
own five feet even. His hair was the opposite of mine, his
being long, curly and blond. And his eyes were a crystal blue-
green where mine were somewhere between the light and
dark chocolates in a box of Russell Stover. So he was the
opposite of me, plus he was cool.

He was certainly cooler than his backup yo-yoists, for of
course the commercial did have a supporting cast. How
better to get the message across that the Ball & String yo-
yo was the best device ever invented to aid someone in their
journey to becoming as cool as The Yo-Yo Man than to
surround him with also-rans, less cool men and women
dropping their own yo-yos, setting their hair on fire, because
they were not as talented just yet, because they did not have
the right yo-yo.

What, I ask you, is sadder than being an also-ran to The
Yo-Yo Man?

I particularly felt sorry for the guy furthest in the background. Furthest Guy, as I thought of him, was kind of
geeky-looking, with short-cropped brown hair and uncool
clothes; I couldn't make out his eye color. And I guess that
was part of the point: to even rate eye color in the commer-

cial, to be as cool as The Yo-Yo Man, a guy needed Ball &
String.

And ever since this commercial started airing, nearly
every night I had a dream about a man with a yo-yo. The
man in my dream was faceless, so it was hard to tell if he
was supposed to be The Yo-Yo Man or not, but whoever he
was, he was just as amazing with his tricks as The Yo-Yo Man.
I don't want you thinking I was *obsessed* or anything and it
wasn't as though I dreamed of him all night long, but, as I
say, he haunted me often enough.

As soon as the commercial ended, the strains of The Yo-
Yo Man theme song abruptly cut short, I switched off the
TV.

I grabbed my lunch bag and looked down at my attire: a
black Coldplay T-shirt that had seen better days, faded khaki
shorts, scuffed Nikes.

Sighing at the underachieving squalor that was me, I
grabbed the last Ernest Hemingway book I needed to read
to make my tour of him complete and my yellow bucket,
in which were my squeegee, a shammy, a paint scraper and
two rolls of paper towels.

My employer? Squeaky Qlean Window Washing.

Yes, I wash windows.

# 2

Even if I hated the name Squeaky Qlean—the name dreamed up by the business's proprietor, Stella Davis, a woman who had yet to realize that there were misuses for the letter Q—window washing was the perfect job for me. The repetitive motions fit the internal rhythms of my obsessive personality, plus, although there was not a whole lot of prestige involved—precisely, none—at least my mind was my own. I'd had jobs where I was actually required to *think* on someone else's time clock and I found the lack of opportunity for free association to be just too mentally confining.

"You're twenty-eight years old now, Delilah." Hillary would attempt to grow me up from time to time. "Isn't it time you thought about getting a *real* job?"

Those words always rankled some, but it was hard for me to get mad at Hillary or if I did get mad, to stay mad for too long, because Hillary Clinton was the best friend I'd ever had. She was not only my best friend, though, my mother long dead, she was like a mother to me, too. We may have squabbled like family members constantly, but I loved her. She was my favorite living woman in the world.

And, yes, her name really was Hillary Clinton.

But this was no time to be thinking about Hillary Clinton, or the fact that she was my best friend, or the fact that she'd remained my friend even though I was not much of an achiever and she was a huge one, or the fact that maybe I was something of a charity case for her, her continued friendship toward me making me something akin to her more lost-cause clients—Hillary always said that my obsessions were both a comfort to me and what victimized me most, making it a perfect vicious circle—because Stella Davis, my boss, was pulling up in the Squeaky Qlean van outside my condo, South Park. The van was pristine white, with a picture of a tuxedo-wearing penguin cleaning a window on it, the window having those little sparkly star thingies all over it, not unlike on a Windex bottle, in order to symbolize the acme of window-cleaning perfection.

South Park always seemed to me to be a silly name for a condo in Danbury, since Connecticut is north and there was no park in sight, but we at least had a stamp-sized balcony—fraternal twin to the minuscule kitchen—off the living room of our unit that afforded a view of the pool down below, so I tried to suck it up about the nonsensical name.

Another thing that impressed me as silly, as it did every workday, was Stella's appearance and attire. Stella had her blond hair in an honest-to-God bouffant style, her green eyes highlighted by full makeup, her buxom top encased in a faux tuxedo T-shirt that had tails down the back, her perky bottom in pristine white shorts, with black socks on her feet and white leather sneakers over those that she polished every day. When we picked up Stella's two other employees, Conchita and Rivera, both from Brazil, they would be similarly dressed, sans the hooker makeup.

"If we look better than the competition," Stella was fond of saying, "people will want to use us instead. After all, who would you rather hire, a window washer that looks like she's ready to accept an Academy Award or one who's dressed sloppy like, well, *you?*"

I'd pointed out to Stella, repeatedly, that while penguins were my favorite non-cat animal, loving penguins and wanting to look like a penguin were two very different things and that with my shortness, I couldn't help but look like a waddling refugee from Antarctica in one of her getups. If I were any other member of the crew, undoubtedly Stella would have fought me on this—Stella was big on fighting— but she grudgingly acknowledged that I was the best worker she'd ever had. My nickname among the crew, The Golden Squeegee, ensured that I'd have a job with Stella for as long as I wanted one. And, besides, the pristine white shorts they all wore always wound up splattered with gray window sploodge by the end of the day anyway, kind of spoiling Stella's desired effect of bucket-carrying Hollywood stars on the red carpet.

As for Conchita and Rivera, and the all–girl crew, Stella was also fond of saying, "I don't hire men anymore. The EOE people can sue me if they want to, but have you ever hired a man to do hard work? What a bunch of whiners. 'It's too hot out here.' 'When do we get off work?' 'I have a second job to get to.' 'That ladder's too high.' 'I'm taking my break now.' I swear to God, I always thought it was just me. But then I talked to a colleague who owns a landscaping service and he said the exact same thing. 'Ask a 100-pound girl to pull a tree out of the ground with her bare hands and she gets right to it. Ask a 200-pound man and before he's even touched the damn thing, he's calling Worker's Comp on his cell phone to verbally file papers for his bad back. Give me a six-pack of chicks any day.' Naturally, I poked him in the gut with my pool cue for saying 'chicks,' but, believe you me, I know from whence he speaks."

"So what did you do last night?" Stella asked, snapping her omnipresent gum as she keyed up the ignition. "What're you reading today? Not that Hemingway guy again. Isn't he the one who hated chicks?"

I knew that the barrage of questions—Stella was a relent-less talker—would continue until we picked up Conchita and Rivera, at which point Stella's attentions would focus solely on them. Unlike me, but very much like Stella, Conchita and Rivera were big talkers.

Like me, Conchita and Rivera were short and dark. But unlike me, where in Stella's uniform I would have looked like a reject extra from *March of the Penguins,* Conchita and Rivera looked hot hot hot, like maybe they worked at an upscale Hooters or something.

"Stel-*la!*" Conchita and Rivera jointly trilled as they hopped into the van.

Conchita and Rivera lived in a neighborhood that would have depressed me, one of Danbury's few rough neighborhoods, but they never seemed to mind, greeting each day of being alive with an exuberance I could only envy. Of their former home in Brazil, obviously worse, all they would ever say was, "You don't even want to *know,* Delilah. Better for us here."

The Girls From Brazil, as Stella and I referred to them, were illegal aliens. But I was sure not going to be the one to turn them in. If their situation here wasn't scary enough, the tone they got in their voice when they told me I didn't even want to *know* what it was like where they came from. During the three years I'd been working for her, whenever Stella had put ads in the paper prior to hiring them, despite the fact that Stella offered a generous hourly wage, the only people to apply were other Brazilians. The way I figured it, they weren't stealing jobs from legal people, because no one legal wanted their jobs; no one except me, that is.

The Girls From Brazil also always greeted Stella as though

they were trying to pick her up, *in that way,* which was not far from the truth since Conchita and Rivera were free-living lesbians, always willing to expand their circle of love. But while they incessantly flirted with Stella, they never once flirted with me, making me feel somehow pathetic in the extreme: my hot meter was turned so low, I wasn't even hot enough to be desirable to free-living lesbians.

Oh, well. At least I owned the title of The Golden Squeegee.

And I did love the women I worked with, if for their sheer vibrancy alone, even if they did have a tendency to pick on me.

"Stel-*la.*" Conchita poked her head between the front seats. "How come *she* always gets to sit in front?"

"She" was their name for me.

"Because she gets carsick," Stella explained for the umpteenth time. "And I don't want her vomiting in my hair."

"Sounds pretty flimsy to me," said Rivera. "Have you actually ever *seen* her get carsick?"

"Well, no," Stella conceded. "But do any of us really want to?"

A valid argument, I thought, even as I muttered, "'Fire burn, and cauldron bubble.'" Honestly, did there have to be three of them to devil me?

"What did she say?" Conchita asked.

"Something about fire and bubbles," Rivera said. "I don't know. Maybe she's singing some kind of dumb-ass song?"

"Where are we working today?" Conchita asked.

"First job, a big house in Westport," Stella said. "Movie star."

Westport and the towns around it had more movie stars per square mile than anywhere else outside of Hollywood and it seemed that they were all clients of Squeaky Qlean. In fact, we did so many homes belonging to famous people that Stella occasionally flirted with the idea of adding "Window washers to the stars!" to her business cards but worried that her upscale clientele would find that too presumptuous.

"So no salsa dancing on the ladders," Stella cautioned. "You girls need to act like professionals today. The job is way overpriced and I'm hoping to talk them into having us back each month."

Monthly window cleaning might seem like a ridiculous expense for a private homeowner, but Stella had secured one such client already, a famous record producer who lived out on the water. When we first did his house, he hadn't had it done in ten years and he spent the whole morning following me from room to room—I was always the inside person—stoned out of his mind, laughing and muttering, "Clean windows. Way cool. I can see. I can *see!*" Mister Famous Record Producer had moved in around the time of the Clinton impeachment, something he still hadn't gotten over all these years later. "The man got impeached for a blow job—a blow job! If people in the music business got fired for that, there'd be no music left anywhere in *the world*." Stella had actually needed to talk him out of having us come every week, which was what he originally wanted, and, good as the money was, none of us wanted to listen to him do his "I can *see!*" number that often or listen to him whine about how Bubba had gotten treated, even those of us who agreed with him. If every window washer lost their job over a…

If traffic was kind and Rte 7 wasn't one long parking lot, Westport was a good thirty-five minutes from Conchita and Rivera's apartment, so I pulled out my book and went back to my Hemingway, figuring on getting some reading in. A few more chapters—I'd started the book the night before—and I would have read everything Papa'd ever written.

"What you reading today?" Conchita asked.

I held up the book, showed them the cover.

"No shit, *chica,*" Rivera said, "but the sun also sets, too, you know, every damn day."

Indeed.

Stella had not been whistling Windex when she said the client we were doing was a movie star. Elizabeth Hepburn, star of stage and screen, may have been as old as television, but even I, who preferred pages to celluloid, knew who she was. She had two Academy Awards on her mantel—I was tempted to dance with them when she went down for her morning nap, book in hand, but resisted the urge—and had starred in my all-time favorite movie, *A Bitter Pill,* about a starlet who overcomes her strumpet past only to be taken out by brain cancer on the night of the Oscars. "Did someone turn the lights out in here?" was a line that always made me bawl like a baby and always made Hillary laugh at me for bawling like a baby.

Due to my fear of heights, I was always the inside person. Still, even though there were three of them outside and only one of me inside, despite Stella's earlier admonitions to take this job seriously, they all goofed around so much that I was done long before they would finish.

Hey, they don't call me The Golden Squeegee for nothing.

So I grabbed my lunch bag from the van and sat out on a far corner of the fieldstone terrace, figuring no one in the house could object to that too much so long as I cleaned up after myself, and pulled out my now-cold Amy's Cheese Pizza Pocket, popped open my Diet Pepsi Lime and polished off my Hemingway.

Food done; drink done; book, and therefore all of Hemingway, done. Crap, I hadn't thought to bring a backup book. What was taking the other three so long?

"Miss?" The voice was tentative and a bit shaky, as though the speaker was recovering from something. And yet somehow the voice was confident as well, as though the speaker was also sure that whoever her audience was, that audience would immediately burst into applause. "Oh, miss?"

I looked up to see Elizabeth Hepburn, wearing a plush pink satin bathrobe despite the warmth of the day, standing in the sliding-glass doorway. She may have been close to ninety, but she was still a stunner, with blue eyes like a chip from the sky, hair as white as a new Kleenex tissue and a perfect smile that defied the viewer to claim those teeth weren't real; poking out from the bottom of her robe, she had white fur mules on her pedicured feet. If I hadn't worried it might be taken amiss, I really might have applauded for her.

But from doing other stars' homes with Stella, I'd come to realize that stars could be, well, *strange*. It was like they didn't know what they wanted. On the one hand, they wanted you to know who they were—"I am important!"—but on the other, they didn't want you to acknowledge who they were, as if somehow that acknowledgment might be an intrusion.

I jumped up from where I'd been sitting, wiped my hands off on my khakis.

"I'm sorry," I started to say. "I shouldn't have—"

"Of course you should have." She pooh-poohed my concerns away. "I just looked out the windows—they're so clean! I can *see!*—and saw you sitting out here while you waited for the others to finish and I thought you maybe could use some company."

There was something lonely-looking about her, making me think that maybe *she* was the one who could use some company, but I couldn't say that. So I merely accepted the seat she indicated at the white-painted wrought-iron table.

"Here," she said. "You sit here and I'll go inside and get dessert. I baked cookies last night," she added proudly.

Elizabeth Hepburn baked her own cookies?

She was back in a flash, cookies and fresh lemonade on a tray, and damn if those cookies weren't good. The rest of the crew didn't know what they were missing, being such slow workers. Of course, if the rest of the crew were fast workers, I probably would never have gotten to taste those cookies, so there was that.

"What were you reading?" she asked.

Why did everyone always ask me that? It seemed like it was a question I answered several times a day.

Like I'd done with Stella, Conchita and Rivera earlier, I flashed the book's cover.

*"Ernie?"* she said. "People still read *Ernie?*"

Ernie?

"Once I start reading an author, I read everything they ever wrote," I said. "This is the last and I don't know what to read next. Why? Did you know—?"

"Oh, my, yes. When I was a lot younger, I hooked up with Ernie—is that how you say it these days, 'hooked up'?—in Key West."

"Really?" I found this amazing. For while some people might be thrilled to talk to a movie star, I was even more thrilled to be talking to someone who had met a writer.

"Yes, really."

For the first time, she seemed miffed at something, maybe miffed that I had doubted her. But then I realized it was something else that had her going.

"Pfft." She dismissed Papa with a wave of her manicured

hand. "Ernie wasn't such a big deal. All he used to do was go on and on and *on* about that goddamned fish."

Before I knew it, Elizabeth Hepburn was telling all, everything about Ernie and everything about several of the other famous people she'd ever met or been with over the years. This might have seemed strange to some and I guess it was strange, but I was kind of used to it. I don't know if it was that I was a former Psych major who had flunked out, or that Hillary's own psychologist instincts had rubbed off on me by association, but whenever I found myself in similar situations, whenever I was done before the rest of the crew, whoever's house we were doing wound up spilling the beans to me like I was Delilah Freud.

And, yes, it did turn out that Elizabeth Hepburn's biggest problem was that she was lonely....

"There's almost no one left in the world," she said, "who shares the memories I do, nobody who can testify that the things I remember really happened or not. Why, when Ernie and I—"

"Yo, *chica,* get the lead—" Rivera skidded around the corner of the house but stopped talking abruptly when she saw me sitting, eating cookies with the client.

"Oops," she said, "sorry to interrupt. But we're all finished and we need to get to the next—"

"That's quite all right," Elizabeth Hepburn said, rising. "I'll just go get my checkbook."

A moment later, we were still packing up the van and tying down the ladders, when Elizabeth Hepburn met us out on the gravel drive. That drive was so perfect, I'd have bet money someone regularly raked the gray-and-white pebbles.

"For you." She handed a check to Stella. "And for you." She handed one crisp ten-dollar bill each to Conchita and Rivera. *"Gracias."*

I wondered if the girls were going to hit her. Anytime someone tried to speak Spanish to them they got all hot under their penguin collars. "We're *Brazilian*, you know? What do you think, that everyone who speaks with a certain kind of accent comes from the same country or speaks the same language? We speak *Portuguese* in Brazil, not *Spanish*. If you want to thank us, say *obrigado*, none of that *gracias* shit, *obrigado* very much."

I found their reaction a bit extreme, especially in relation to me but also because it was often Stella's customers they were going off on and it seemed like the people were just trying to be polite. I know I was. But then I would think how I would like it if someone came to America from, say, Germany, and started talking to me with a Texan accent because that's what they mostly heard on TV, and I wouldn't like that at all.

But perhaps they saw the same vulnerability in Elizabeth Hepburn that I'd seen earlier, because they let the ostensible insult pass, merely muttering *"Gracias"* in return.

Elizabeth Hepburn turned to me. "And for you." She handed me a large paperback book.

"What's this?" I asked.

"Well," she said, "you said you were out of reading material."

"But what is it?" I asked.

I'd never heard of the author, Shelby Macallister, nor the title, *High Heels and Hand Trucks: My Life Among the Books.* And the cover, on which was one perfect blue-green stiletto, was pink pink pink.

Elizabeth Hepburn's famous blue eyes twinkled as she answered, "Chick Lit."

"*Chick Lit?* But I've never—"

"Go on," she said, "treat yourself. They're tons of fun. Myself, I'm addicted to them."

Addiction was something I could well understand…

"Go on." Elizabeth Hepburn nodded her chin, as if she were trying to persuade me to try crack cocaine rather than just a book outside of my normal realm of reading. "Try it. I swear to God, you're going to love it and want more and more. And, oh—" she put her hand to her face in awe "—those Choos."

"Choos?" I said. "Did you say 'Choos'? Don't you mean to say 'shoes'?"

"Oh, no," she said, awe still in her eyes, "those Choos, those Jimmy Choos."

I had no idea what she was talking about and my expression must have said as much, because she reached out a hand, placed it reassuringly on my arm.

"A girl needs more than a fish in her life for fun, Delilah. Now don't forget to come back and visit me sometime—"

oddly enough, she was not the first customer to thusly invite me "—and don't forget to tell me what you think of those Choos. I'd bet both my Academy Awards you're going to love them!"

# 3

"How's that Michael Angelo's Four Cheese Lasagna working out for you?"

Startled, I dropped my fork, causing some of the red sauce to splash up, speckling my wrist and the open pages of the book I was reading. I'd been so engrossed in *High Heels and Hand Trucks: My Life Among the Books,* which was about an underachieving independent bookseller who takes a job as the lapdog to a publishing bigwig, that I hadn't even heard Hillary come in.

"What's that you're reading?" she asked.

See what I mean? People always ask me that question.

Before I could answer, Hillary flipped the book over to the jacket to look for herself as I wiped at the red speckles on my wrist.

Hillary sniffed. "Not exactly Hemingway, is it?"

"It's better than Hemingway!" I enthused.

Hillary cocked one perfect blond eyebrow in my general direction, an eyebrow that was waxed and sculpted regularly by the nice Asian ladies at Nail Euphorium, a place I'd never set foot in but heard tell of from Hillary.

"Okay," I conceded, "maybe it's not Hemingway, but this book is *fun!*"

She still looked skeptical as she opened her refrigerator, the one on top, and removed fresh vegetables. I had no doubt she was going to make some kind of amazing homemade sauce, but my Michael Angelo's really was working for me just fine.

"As a matter of fact—" I enthused on "—after I finish this one, I'm going to—"

"Don't say it." Hillary stopped me cold, brandishing a sharp knife. "You're going to go down to the bookstore and buy everything else this woman, this *Shelby Macallister* has ever written, right?"

"Wrong," I said, a touch snottily, but it was so nice to uncover someone else's wrongness for a change. "You are so wrong."

"Oh?"

"Shelby Macallister hasn't written any other books before, meaning I can't get any more of hers until she writes them. So there."

Hillary shrugged, contrite, and went back to chopping. "Then I stand corrected."

It was a good thing her back was to me, so she couldn't see my blush when I said, "But I am going to go to the bookstore and buy a stack more of this kind of book."

"I *knew* it!" She slammed the knife home so hard that poor little green pepper didn't stand a chance. "Every time you get going on something—"

"Hi, honey—" it was my turn to cut her off "—how was your day?"

This was how Hillary and I plugged along in our merrily dysfunctional way, had done so since back in our college days, at least before I flunked out: I was wacky, she called me on my wackiness, I sidetracked that call by being solic- itous, and on we went.

Hard as it was to tear myself away from *High Heels,* I put the book down and reaching behind me—the eat-in kitchen was that small—opened the door to the lower fridge.

"May I interest you in a libation?" I asked, going all waiterly on her. "Tonight we have Jake's Fault Shiraz, Jake's Fault Shiraz and, hmm, let's see, Jake's Fault Shiraz."

Hillary tried to be stern, but before long she started to laugh, which was just fine, that was the way it always was with us.

"Oh, I don't know." She rolled her eyes. "I guess I'll take the Jake's Fault Shiraz."

"Good choice, madam." I rifled in the utility drawer for the rabbit-ears corkscrew. "Why don't you go change out of your work clothes while I pour you a glass." Hillary wore the pants in our family and had a great selection of spiffy suits that didn't deserve to get ruined. "I'll even finish chopping your vegetables for you."

"Thanks, it has been a day."

Sure, she should change so as not to get anything messy on her nice suit, but I really wanted her out of the room so she wouldn't see what I was about to do with that corkscrew. Hillary had given it to me in my holiday stocking the winter before because I always had trouble opening bottles with the old-fashioned, cheap, blue, plastic corkscrew I'd been using for years. But what she did not yet know was that even with the high-tech marvel she had given me, a corkscrew so wonderful it could make a sommelier out of a five-year-old, I still had problems with the damn thing, always pushing down on the ears too prematurely so that the cork only rose partway out and I wound up mangling it as I twisted it between my legs, trying to uncork it the rest of the way.

The cork came out almost without incident, meaning it snapped a bit at the bottom and I had to press that snapped part through into the wine down below. I poured us each a glass, but Hillary must have decided to indulge in a second shower and by the time she emerged, I was too deep into *High Heels and Hand Trucks* again to make polite conversation while she ate and did whatever else she did, only taking in her words in the most peripheral way. The written word being the way I connected with the world, my imagination caught up in the mere prose descriptions of all those Choos.

Her: "Do you want more of this wine?"

Me: (stretching out glass without looking) "You wouldn't believe these shoes."

Her: "Want to watch *American Idol 25* with me?"

Me: "You would not believe these shoes."

Her: "How about Jon Stewart?"

Me: "You would *not* believe these shoes."

Her: "I guess I might as well hit the—"

Me: "You *would* not—"

Her: "Oh, stuff it, Delilah. 'Night."

Well, that was rude.

But here was the thing: you would not believe these shoes, no one would, unless you read about them yourself, I thought, shutting the book after the last page.

Damn! It was after midnight. I'd need to wait until after work the next day, technically that day, to go to the bookstore and pick up more books like *High Heels*. I was definitely going to be reading more books like *High Heels*.

But then I realized something else: *reading* about the shoes, which the author constantly described as "architectural marvels" as if there were no other words for them, was a far cry from actually *seeing* the shoes. I mean it's always show, don't tell, right? And as good as the author was at describing the shoes—there were so many of them!—I suddenly was struck by an overwhelming urge: I needed to *see* those shoes.

But what to do, what to do…

I had no idea who in Danbury might actually sell Jimmy Choos, probably nobody, and even if I took the last train into Manhattan, all the shops there would be closed at one in the morning.

What to do, what to do…

There was only one computer in our apartment and it wasn't mine.

I gently turned the knob on the door to Hillary's bedroom, tiptoed over toward her computer, tried not to trip over anything in the dark—"Ouch!"—and shushed myself, silently cursed my own clumsiness and immediately thanked my stars I hadn't woken her, sat down in her desk chair, turned on the monitor and Googled the obvious.

The PDF file for all things Jimmy Choo was on the screen before me—the Asha, the Asha, I really wanted the Asha!—when…

"Delilah, just what the *hell* do you think you're doing?"

But I was too caught up in the pretty images on the screen before me to feel as appropriately guilty, snagged and embarrassed as I might otherwise have felt.

"Oh, never mind that." I pooh-poohed her. "Look. *Look!*"

"I don't want to look," Hillary said, totally peeved and sporting quite a case of bed head, I must say. "I want my sleep." She grabbed the mouse and moved it toward the shut-down menu. "And I want you to—"

"No!" I stopped her hand. Then, feeling totally contrite, I wheedled, "Please look."

"Oh, all *right.*"

At first, she just looked annoyed, but as I ceded control of the mouse and she started to click on the images of the shoes and boots and sandals, enlarging some of the images as I had done earlier…

"Well—" she was still resisting the pull "—I'm not crazy about some of the red ones."

"Oh, me, neither," I said quickly, trying to sound agreeable. And it really wasn't much of a stretch since, despite red being one of my favorite colors, the red pairs didn't grab me as much as the others.

I saw her eyes stray back toward the comfort of her rumpled sheets. Thinking I couldn't let her get away, since I really did need a cohort here, if for nothing else than to keep me from being so lonely in the midst of my own obsessions, I grabbed the mouse back and quickly clicked on a different image.

"Look at this," I said eagerly.

It was the Asha.

"Oh, my!" Hillary said, her eyes going all glittery, as my own had no doubt done a short time ago.

"And this," I said, clicking again.

It was the Ghost, which was maybe even more spectacular than the Asha, if such a thing were possible.

"Oh, *my!*" Hillary said again.

"And this." I clicked one last time.

It was the Parson Flat.

"*I* would buy that shoe!" she trumpeted.

I knew the Parson Flat would get her.

"How much…?" she started to ask.

In another second, she'd be racing for her Dooney & Bourke bag to fish out her Amex.

"But that's the whole problem!" I all but whined.

"What?" Hillary said. "Are they too much money?"

"I don't *know*," I said. "I keep clicking around, but I don't see *any* prices here."

"Oh, dear," Hillary said. "That's never good."

"What do you mean?"

"Have you ever eaten in a restaurant where they don't list the prices on the menu?"

"Um, *no*. Who do you think I am, *you?*"

"Trust me, it's never cheap when they don't list the prices."

We both stared at the screen.

I tried on a nonchalant shrug.

"So?" I said. "How expensive can a little bit of leather and maybe some glitter be?"

"Who knows?" Hillary said. "But I'm guessing very."

"There's only one way to find out," I said.

"Hmm?" She was still transfixed by the Parson Flats.

"Road trip!"

"Oh, no," she said, successfully tearing her gaze away. "This is your insanity, not mine."

"Please." I was back in wheedle mode. "Wouldn't you like to at least see if you could afford them?"

Before she could answer, I clicked to the part of the catalog where boutique locations were listed. I didn't think I'd ever persuade her to go to London or Dublin or Milan or Moscow or Kuwait City or Hong Kong, Korea, Bangkok or even São Paulo to shop for shoes, although I suppose Paris might have been nice. Hillary always said she wanted to see Paris. But at least I could try...

"There are two stores right in Manhattan," I said. "One in the Olympic Tower on Fifth Avenue, the other on Madison. We could each use a day off from work. Come on, just one day. Nobody says we have to buy anything..."

"If I say yes, can I go back to sleep?"

"Yes."

"Yes."

Five minutes later...

"And turn off that computer!"

"Sorry."

Still, for good measure and so that I'd have something to remind her with should she change her mind, I printed pictures of our three favorites: the Asha, the Ghost and the Parson Flats.

"And stop using my printer!"

"Sorry."

Then I went to sleep, too.

And all night long, I dreamt of the faceless Yo-Yo Man. I was in his arms, on my feet a pair of Ashas.

I was dancing in my Jimmy Choos.

# 4

But getting a day off from Squeaky Qlean was not as easy as I thought.

"If you absolutely need to be sick," Stella said when I called her up with my lie, "then be sick tomorrow. We've got four jobs today and I need all squeegees on deck. Tomorrow there's only one."

This turned out to be not such a bad thing because, while eating my cold Amy's Cheese Pizza Pocket in the van after I'd finished the inside of the second job, I was struck by inspiration.

On the bench between the driver's seat and where I was sitting, feet propped up on the dash, lay Stella's bible: her scheduling book. In it, were listed the names, addresses and phone numbers of the jobs for each day we worked. She usually left the prices out, perhaps for fear that if we ever actually knew how much she was bringing in, The Girls From Brazil and I—The Golden Squeegee, I might add!— would demand a higher hourly wage.

Quickly, feeling very Nancy Drew, I flipped through Stella's bible. She always tore off the corner of the page once the day was done, so it was easy work for me to find the page from the day before, on which was listed Elizabeth Hepburn's name, her address and her no-doubt unlisted phone number.

I found a pen on the seat and grabbed a parking ticket Stella was never going to pay anyway out of the glove compartment, and was just shoving the piece of paper into the pocket of my khakis when Rivera sauntered up.

"Yo, *chica*," she said.

From time to time, I wondered if *chica* was actually a Portuguese word or if they just liked to play with me. A part of me was tempted to sneak onto Hillary's computer that night and look it up on Babel Fish but then I decided I really did not want to know.

"What's The Golden Squeegee doing now," Rivera asked, "looking through Stella's book to see what time we might get off today? Damn, it's a hot one."

"Heh," I nervously laughed. "That's exactly what I was doing. Heh."

Five hours later, home, grimy, exhausted, I picked up the phone, punched in the number on the parking ticket.

It didn't take more than a brief description, certainly

there was no persuading required on my part, and Elizabeth Hepburn was on board.

"Are you sure?" I said. "We'll be taking the train and no one said we're actually going to *buy* anything."

"Are you kidding?" she laughed. "I've been waiting for an offer like this for *years*—road trip!"


"Tell me again why we're taking Elizabeth Hepburn to Jimmy Choo's with us?" Hillary asked the next day just prior to pulling her red Jeep into Elizabeth Hepburn's circular driveway.

"Because she's old," I said, "and we'll be old one day, if we're lucky, and we'll hope to be invited out. Because she's lonely and she's fun."

"Good enough."

But, apparently, there was something about me that was no longer good enough for Elizabeth Hepburn.

"Tsk, tsk, tsk." She tsked as I got out of the car.

It would have been annoying but it had been a long time since anyone had cared enough to tsk-tsk me. My late mother had been a great tsker, but since then...

"What's wrong?" I asked.

"You don't want to go into the city looking like a...*ragamuffin,* do you?"

"That's exactly what I told her!" Hillary said.

"Who are you?" Elizabeth Hepburn demanded.

"Hillary Clinton."

A slow smile rose on Elizabeth Hepburn's soft features. "Of course," she said.

"What's wrong with the way I look?" I asked again.

But before they could answer, I could see it for myself. Hillary, as always, was dressed impeccably. Riding the rails into the city on a hot summer day, she had on a sleeveless peach sundress with a wide-brimmed straw hat and flat gold sandals that were pretty damn attractive, even if they weren't Jimmy Choos. As for Ms. Hepburn, she had a slightly more modest aqua sundress on that brought out the color of her eyes, a straw hat with a big floral band à la the late Princess Diana and open-toed spectator pumps that matched her dress. For an octogenarian, she had a great set of wheels.

While I had on...

"All right already!" I said. "I get the point! But isn't it true these days that so long as you can afford the price tag or pay the restaurant tab, no one cares how casual you look?"

"I care," Elizabeth Hepburn said, drawing her spine up to its full acceptance-speech glory.

"Well, it's a little late for me to go home and change," I said.

Besides, I was thinking, what's so wrong about jean shorts, a T-shirt and my Nikes? With ten million people or so in the city, there would be plenty of people who looked like me, probably be a lot more people looking like me than like these two garden-party missies. And, hey, my T-shirt was clean.

"I can fix this," Elizabeth Hepburn said. Then she crooked a finger at me. "Come."

Five minutes later, I was back on the gravel drive. Gone were my shorts and T, replaced by a fairly pretty peasant blouse and long skirt.

"What we wore back in the sixties," Elizabeth Hepburn said, "it's all come back again."

The amazing thing was, having caught a glimpse of myself in the mirror on the way out, I didn't look half-bad. It was a bittersweet pill to swallow, the idea that I looked better in an old lady's clothes than my own.

"Sorry about the shoes." Elizabeth Hepburn directed her apology to Hillary as though I wasn't there. "But mine are all too small for her. I did always have such tiny feet. It was one of the things Rudolf Nureyev used to say he loved about me."

Rudolf Nureyev? Wasn't he—?

"That's okay." Hillary shrugged as she studied the tips of my Nikes as they peeked out from under the long dress. "We'll just tell the salesgirls at Jimmy Choo's that she's our country cousin and that's why we brought her in, because she needs their help…*bad*."

"Gee, thanks," I said. "Maybe you two should just go on without me."

"Now, now." Elizabeth Hepburn rubbed my arm. "Where would we be without you? You're the glue, Delilah, you are definitely the balls of the operation."

A short time later, as we boarded the train, Hillary tossed

over her shoulder, "Will you be able to manage a day without Amy's Cheese Pizza Pockets for lunch?"

"Very funny," I groused.

But, of course, I had my own doubts.

Later, as we exited Grand Central Station, she said, "We never did decide which Jimmy Choo's we should go to, the one on Fifth or the one on Madison?"

"Oh, definitely the one on Madison," Elizabeth Hepburn put in quickly. "It always reminds me of the time I slept with the president."

"Which president?" I asked.

"Why, President Madison, of course," she said huffily.

*"She thinks she slept with President Madison?"* Hillary and I mouthed at one another behind her back.

It suddenly occurred to me that maybe Elizabeth Hepburn had never slept with Ernie Hemingway after all.

"Besides," Elizabeth Hepburn added, leading the way, "I never slept with anyone named Fifth, so what'd be the point of going there?"

I would have fallen in love with the Jimmy Choo's on Madison even if it weren't for the shoes, because walking into that cool air-conditioning after the August heat of the New York streets was like walking into a peppermint breath of…

Okay, really, it was the shoes.

There they were, at last, in all of their architectural-marvel glory.

And I'll admit it: I was like a kid in a candy store or a chick in a Choo store.

"Ah," said Elizabeth Hepburn, holding up the Momo Flat, its color matching her outfit, its latticed star cutouts lending elegance to an otherwise ordinary flat.

"Ooh," Elizabeth Hepburn said, asking the salesgirl to get her a pair of Fayres to try on. They were gold evening sandals with a midsize curved heel that had ivory-colored oval stones set in the toe and ankle straps. "At the Academy Awards next year," she said, admiring her feet in them, "I'll finally outshine that Lauren Bacall. Who cares if I trip on the red carpet?"

Having thought she wanted the Parson Flat most, the shoe Hillary really fell in love with was the Pilar Flat.

"Where will you wear it?" I asked. "If you try wearing it to work, your clients will think you're too out-of-touch wealthy to understand their problems."

The Pilar Flat was a metallic aqua, with a spaghetti X-strap across the front and about a yard of strap wrapped a gazillion times around the ankle. It looked exactly like the sort of sandal shoe Cleopatra would have worn if she had a passion for aqua. Look out, Marc Antony!

"Who cares?" Hillary said, transfixed by the sight of her own feet. "I'll wear them while watching Jon Stewart if I have to. I'll *make* places to wear them."

But then her attention was drawn back to the Parson Flat. It was a gold leather traditional thong sandal with a big red jewel at the center, surrounded by green stones with more jewels suspended from gold threads.

"It really is more me," Hillary said.

And, really, Cleopatra would have gladly worn that shoe, too.

Elizabeth Hepburn and Hillary were so busy staring at their own feet, they almost forgot…

"Hey," they both said at the same time, "I thought we came here for *you*."

This had, of course, been the original plan. But now that we were here, I felt dwarfed into insignificance by the magical footwear around me. Sure, Elizabeth Hepburn and Hillary would be able to find places to wear their purchases, but what would I do with any of these shoes—start wearing Stella's penguin suits with these on my feet as I wielded my golden squeegee? It was just too sad a picture and I said as much.

"Oh, come on," Hillary said, "you took the day off from work to come here."

"You've come this far," Elizabeth Hepburn said. "How can you stop now?"

"Here," Hillary said, holding up a shoe. It was a green high-heeled evening sandal with a V of diamond-shaped gold and crystal jewels cascading down from the twin chain strap: the Asha.

And yet, suddenly, I felt as though I could resist the Asha. After all, how many clothes did I own that would match with that green? It was way too impractical.

I was just about to tell them that they should buy their shoes and enjoy them with my blessing, but that I was going to pass, when I saw the salesgirl return a previously unseen floor model to the display.

The shoe she placed down, as if it were *just another shoe,* was another high-heeled sandal, only this one was copper-colored, more pink than bronze, with diamond-shaped sapphire-colored stones encrusted with crystal stones across the toe strap and more sapphire and crystal bejeweling the intricate mesh of chain around the ankle with three straps of chain anchoring it to more copper leather at the back.

It was the Ghost.

And while I might have even resisted the draw of that most perfect of all shoes, sapphires had been my late mother's favorite stone. If nothing else than to do it in her honor, I had to at least try on that shoe.

"May I?" I tentatively asked the salesgirl.

She must have been a true professional, not like these rude people you sometimes read about in books, because she didn't even flinch as she watched me remove my scuffed Nikes and workout socks, sliding the desired shoes on my feet and patiently helping me figure out the straps.

"Do you have a job where you stand on your feet all day?" the salesgirl asked with a vaguely European accent.

"How could you tell?" I asked. "Are my feet that awful-looking?"

"On the contrary," she said. "I think you have the most beautiful feet I've ever seen in here. They are ideally suited to this shoe."

It's odd to think of a person's life as being transformed

by a shoe, but I swear I felt an electric shock, a magical shock, as the salesgirl slipped the Ghosts on my feet, as she strapped them on, as she stepped back so that she, along with everyone else, could appreciate the effect. And, oh, was there an effect. I swear, it was as though pixie dust was swirling all around my feet, spreading upward around my whole body.

And it wasn't just that the shoe was achingly beautiful, although it was certainly that; it was that I, for once, felt beautiful. With those shoes on, I could do anything, leap tall buildings with a single bound, balance the national budget, find my prince, you name it. I could be normal and special at the same time. I could be like other women, and then some.

It was my Cinderella moment.

I had to have that shoe.

"How much?" I blurted out.

"Yes," Elizabeth Hepburn piped up. "How much for all of these? It looks like you'll be making at least three sales today."

The salesgirl very coolly named prices for the Fayre that Elizabeth Hepburn had loved so much, the Parson Flat that Hillary coveted, my own beloved Ghost.

"Huh?" was all I could say, as the sticker shock of fourteen hundred dollars before tax sank in. Really, the tax probably came to more than I'd ever spent on a single pair of shoes before.

I suppose I must have realized in advance that the shoes

would be expensive, but it had never occurred to me that for a few straps of leather and some fake jewels…

Elizabeth Hepburn and Hillary already had their credit cards out.

"Sure, it's a lot of money—" Elizabeth Hepburn shrugged "—but I've got it. What else am I going to spend it on?"

"I'll never find shoes that are more perfect for me," Hillary agreed.

Easy to say, since the shoes they coveted cost less than mine. Hell, the ones Hillary wanted rang in at a measly six hundred and thirty dollars in comparison.

Reluctantly, I undid the straps and gave up the Ghost, handing them back to the salesgirl, who looked shocked.

"But you must buy these shoes," she said, trying to hand them back to me.

"But I can't buy those shoes," I said, taking a defensive step back, hands up as though to ward off a vampire.

"Why ever not?" Elizabeth Hepburn asked. "Don't you have a credit card?"

"Oh, she has a credit card," Hillary said. Apparently, I was back to being "she" again. "But she never lets herself use it. I guess she must realize, with her obsessive nature, she'd charge herself into bankruptcy if she ever got started."

"So what are you going to do," Elizabeth Hepburn asked, "come back another day with cash? But what if they're sold out?"

"You don't happen to have layaway, do you?" Hillary turned to the salesgirl who sadly shook her head.

"I don't have that kind of money saved anyway," I said.

"How is that possible?" Elizabeth Hepburn asked.

"Hey, you met me when I was washing your windows, remember?" I said. "Hand-to-mouth is my way of life."

Elizabeth Hepburn didn't even need to think about that for a second.

"Oh, hell, Delilah," she said, sympathy crinkling her blue eyes, "I'll buy you the shoes."

"No," I said.

"Why 'no'? I already said, I have all this money. What else am I going to use it for—monthly window washing? Leave it all to my housekeeper, Lottie, who awaits her inheritance upon my death like John Carradine playing Dracula waiting for an unbitten neck?"

"No," I said, crossing my arms in front of my chest. "I can't accept charity. I won't. If I want the shoes badly enough, and I do, I'll find a way to earn the money on my own."

"But what if they're not here in your size when you get back?"

"I'll just have to take that chance."

She must have seen that the window washer meant business because she stopped arguing.

And then she put her Jimmy Choos back.

And so did Hillary.

"Wait a second," I protested. "Just because I can't afford mine, doesn't mean you have to put—"

"Oh, yes, we do," Elizabeth Hepburn spoke with her own brand of firmness. "If you can't get what you came for, none of us can. One for all and all for one and all that other crap Errol Flynn used to say to me."

"Exactly," Hillary said.

"But what if the shoes you love aren't here in your sizes by the time I can afford to come back?" I asked.

"That's just the chance we'll have to take," Elizabeth Hepburn said.

"Exactly," Hillary said.

*Lord, what fools these mortals be.*

"But, Delilah?" Hillary added.

"Hmm?"

"Try to come up with a way to make the money quickly. I want those damn shoes."

# 5

"No."

"But, *Dad*."

"I said no, Baby. I'm pretty sure you're still smart enough to understand both sides of *no*. There's the *n* and there's the *o*. What's so difficult here?"

My dad had always called me Baby, for as long back as I could remember. It was my mother, whose own name was Lila, who'd named me.

"I'm Lila," she'd say, "you're Delilah. It's like Spanish. It means 'of Lila.'"

"There's just one problem," I'd say right back. "We're not Spanish. Okay, two problems. There's that extra *h* at the end, which your name doesn't have, so technically speaking—"

"Just eat your Cocoa Krispies." She'd always cut me off right there.

My dad always claimed he called me Baby because he couldn't stand the name Delilah. Of course, totally besotted with my mother and therefore never wanting to hurt her, despite the numerous times he'd hurt her, he only claimed that outside of my mother's hearing.

"Do you know whom she named you after, Baby?" he'd ask, as if he hadn't asked me the same question at least a hundred times. "She named you after the girl in that Tom Jones song! Your mother was a huge Tom Jones fan! I swear, if I hadn't been sitting right there beside her at his concerts, she'd have thrown up her panties right there on the stage. What, I ask you, kind of name is that to give to a baby? Delilah in the song drives her man crazy, then she cheats on him, and then she gets killed for it."

"But, *Dad,*" I tried again now.

"No, Baby. If I taught you how to play blackjack, Lila would roll over in her grave, and then where would I be?"

"Where you are right now," I could have answered, "alone."

Where my dad was right now, physically speaking, was a one-bedroom apartment in a section of Danbury just a cut above where Conchita and Rivera lived. As a professional gambler, Black Jack Sampson had enjoyed his good years (we'd once lived in a five-bedroom house even though we'd only needed two of them) and his bad years (like the last one). And, if we're being totally honest here, he was right:

my mother wouldn't approve of his teaching me how to play blackjack. But, oh, did I want those Jimmy Choos…

"Your mother might even come back to life just to kill me if I taught you how to play blackjack," he said.

He was probably right about that, too.

I studied my dad, a man whose personality was too big to be contained by his present tiny circumstances.

Black Jack Sampson had just turned seventy but had only just begun to look even close to sixty, his neatly trimmed salt-and-pepper hair and mustache, tall frame and lean body, combined with the fact that he always wore a suit even in summer, making him look more like he belonged on a riverboat in the middle of an Elvis Presley movie rather than with the polyester bus crew going off to play the slots at Atlantic City. Black Jack had met my mother, a schoolteacher who loved her work almost as much as she loved him, at a voting rights rally back in 1965—Lila was rallying while Black Jack made book on the side on whether the act would pass—and it had been love at first sight. He was thirty at the time and she was twenty-eight, but it had been twelve long infertile years before they'd been able to conceive a baby, me, hence the huge age difference between me and my parents, and there had been no more babies afterward, try as they might. True, these days having first-time parents in their forties wasn't a rarity, but, when I was little, my mother looked more like a grandmother by comparison to my friends' mothers.

Not that I'd minded.

Growing up, I thought my mother was the greatest lady

who ever lived, a belief I'd maintained until the day she'd died ten years ago. And my mother, in turn, had thought my dad was the greatest man who'd ever lived…except for his gambling.

"Blackjack killed your mother," he said.

We'd had this conversation enough times over the years for me to know he wasn't referring to himself when he said, "Blackjack killed your mother;" he was referring to the card game.

"Blackjack did not kill Mom," I said.

How I missed my mother! She was the steady parent, the one who didn't suffer obsessions that worked against her. In her absence, I'd become Daddy's Girl. But what a daddy! From my dad, I'd learned to be the kind of woman who could sit with men while they watched sporting events but nothing about what it was like to be the kind of woman men would want to do more romantic things with. I'm not complaining here, by the way, just stating.

"Blackjack did not kill Mom," I said again. "Mom died of cancer."

"Same difference," he sniffed.

"Not really."

"There was a time, when you were just a little baby, Baby, that I dreamed of you growing up to one day follow in my footsteps."

I had a mental flash of a younger version of my dad, holding baby me in his arms and crooning, *"Lullaby, and good night, when the dealer has busted…"*

"We would have made quite a team," I said. "And we still could," I added, thinking about what becoming great at blackjack could achieve for me: a pair of Jimmy Choos.

"You don't understand," he said. "I promised your mom right before she died that I'd make sure you lived a better life than we'd lived, one free of the addictions that had destroyed the two of us."

Clearly, the man didn't know his own daughter. Me, free of addictions? Some days, I thought I'd never be free of them.

"Mom was an addict, too?" I was shocked. "What was Mom addicted to?"

He studied his wing tips, his cheeks coloring a bit.

"Me," he answered. "Lila was addicted to me."

"That's not true, Dad. She wasn't addicted. She just plain loved you."

"Same difference." He straightened his shoulders. "And she'd hate it if I passed the blackjack compulsion on to you."

I thought he was making too much of this. My parents had had a happy marriage. I *knew* they'd been happy.

"C'mon, Dad," I wheedled. "Wouldn't it be great to have someone really follow in your footsteps. *'Lullabye, and good night, when the dealer has busted'*—"

"Who taught you that song?" he demanded.

"I don't know." I shrugged. "I thought I just made it up."

"It just sounded so familiar there for a second."

"But wouldn't it be great to have me follow in your footsteps?" I tried again.

"What about poker?" he said suddenly. "Everyone's playing poker these days. At least if you started to gamble at poker, your mother might get confused when she comes back to haunt me since poker's not blackjack."

I considered what he was suggesting.

Even I was aware that poker was the current "in" game and it was a game that I had some familiarity with. Back in my junior-high days, my best girlfriend and I had started a poker ring while serving an in-school suspension for getting our classmates drunk during the science fair. We'd charged a dollar a game to play and even a couple of teachers, miffed that my best girlfriend and I had taken the fall when so many others had been involved, had stopped by to play a few hands while on their coffee breaks. I think we were all vaguely aware that they could have been fired for their complicit behavior, but it was a private school—this had been one of Black Jack Sampson's better years for winning—and we were thrilled to take their money. Besides, once the weeklong in-house suspension had ended, life at school had gone back to normal and we'd folded up the gaming table with my best girlfriend and I each about fifty dollars richer. Of course, I'd never told my parents any of this because Lila would have been too mortified while Black Jack would have been too proud, thereby increasing Lila's mortification.

"Nah," I finally concluded. "Sure, poker's a trend right now, but any trend can end at any minute. Blackjack, on the other hand, is a classic. It's eternal. And, hey, I'm *Black Jack* Sampson's daughter, aren't I? I'm certainly not *Poker*

Sampson's daughter. C'mon, Dad. It'll be great. It'll be like having the son you always dreamed of."

It was a cheap shot to take, and I knew it even as I said it. Black Jack had always wanted a son; anyone could see that every time he tried to teach me how to hit a baseball only to have the bat twirl me around in such a big circle that I wound up dizzy on the lawn or every time he tried to teach me how football was played, keeping in mind the importance of covering the spread, only to have me yawn myself to sleep. But it was the one card I had to play, the only card that would get me what I wanted.

"C'mon, Dad. It'll be fun."

He ran one hand through his hair.

"You have to promise not to tell your mother about this," he warned.

I raised my right hand. "Scout's honor."

"'O, I am fortune's fool.'"

See where I got it from? Black Jack and Lila were always quoting Shakespeare at me.

He walked out to the kitchen and I heard a drawer slide open and shut. When he returned, he had a fresh deck of red-and-white Bicycle cards in his hand. He tore off the cellophane wrapper and as he did so, he looked me dead in the eye, giving me the answer I'd come there for in a single word.

"Yes."

# 6

"Those are some whack shoes, *chica*," Rivera said.

I'd been using the sheet of paper with the pictures of Jimmy Choos on it that I'd copied out of Hillary's computer as a bookmark and Rivera was studying the lovely lines of the Asha as it peeked out from the top of the latest Chick Lit book I was reading, *Still Life with Stiletto,* by Bonita Sanchez.

"Is *whack* good?" I asked. I honestly had no idea.

"*Whack* is beyond good," she said, then she reflected for a moment. "And *whack* is beyond bad." Further reflection, shrug. "*Whack* is whack."

"Ah." Well, that was illuminating. I wasn't sure if she was playing with me or not.

"*Whack* can mean bad or crazy," she elaborated. "If I say

the shoes are whack, it could mean they're really ugly or really cool. If I say some guy is whack, it could mean stay away from him or that he's doing something unbelievable, like saying 'Shaq is whack.' Get it? Shaq's so good it's unbelievable."

"Wow," I said, "a linguistic paradox." Then I remembered something from TV. "What about that pop star who says 'crack is whack'?"

"She means it's bad for you."

"Huh. And here I thought she meant 'I love crack! Give me more!'"

Rivera favored me with a rare smile before looking back at the picture of the shoes. "I think I'm going to get me a pair," she said. "How much?"

While visiting the store in Manhattan, before leaving I'd asked the salesgirl the price of a few more pairs of shoes that interested me. You know, just for fun. Then I'd committed the prices to memory.

"Unless I'm mistaken, those shoes go for one thousand and one hundred and fifty dollars a pair."

"For *real?*"

"Yup," I said. "You get both for that price."

"That's insanity!"

"Mmm-hmm," I agreed, "but look at these." I showed her the Ghost.

"Now those shoes I would pay one thousand and one hundred and fifty dollars for," she said. "Those shoes are beyond whack."

"That's nice," I said, "except those shoes will set you back one thousand and four hundred dollars."

"Insanity!" she said.

"Beyond insanity," I agreed.

"So how come you're carrying around a picture of them like they're a prayer card from church?"

"Because I really want them," I admitted, "more than I can ever remember wanting anything."

"Wanting and getting are two different things, *chica*. How do you think you'll ever be able to pay for something like that?"

"I'm working on it," I said. "As Shakespeare says, 'To do a great right, do a little wrong.'"

"Fuck Shakespeare. You think Stella is just going to give you a raise? Even if she gave you like a dollar an hour raise—and do you think Stella's going to ever part with another dollar, let alone forty of them a week?—it'd take you half a year to save that much money at that rate. By then those shoes'd be long gone."

"Hey," I said, ignoring her last sentence, "your math skills are whack."

"What I should do is whack *you*," Stella said to Rivera, surprising us. "What are you trying to say, that I'm cheap?"

"No way, boss." Rivera took a step backward, hands raised in self-defense. "You are an all-American entrepreneur and you are very, very smart."

"She's right, boss," Conchita said. She was suddenly there, too. "You're just a very smart entrepreneur. No exploitation going on here."

Stella stared at them both closely, as if trying to judge if they were each pulling a leg. She must have been satisfied with what she saw, for she turned to me next.

"If I'm not going to give you a raise—and I'm not, because you know times are tough and the economy is rocky—then where are you ever going to get the money for those Choos?"

"You know Choos?" I was surprised.

"Of course I know Choos." Stella fluffed her hair. "I'm an all-American entrepreneur, aren't I?"

The way I figured it, Conchita and Rivera were stroking her ego enough. Certainly, *I* didn't need to do that, so instead I merely told them of my plan, the one Hillary and I had devised the night before.

"I'm going to Foxwoods Casino," I said, "this Saturday night."

Conchita's eyes grew big. "You mean the one run by the Mashantucket Pequots?"

"Is there any other?" I replied.

"You're just going with your roommate?" Stella asked now.

"That's what I had planned on," I said.

"What are you planning on wearing?" Conchita demanded.

"I hadn't thought about it." I shrugged.

"Hadn't *thought* about it?" Rivera whacked me in the head, lightly, but it was still a whack. "What the hell's the matter with you?"

"I don't know," I said. "I figured I'd just wear some shorts, maybe a T-shirt. It's been so hot lately."

"What the hell's the matter with you?" she snapped, raising her hand.

"Don't hit me again!" I said, moving my arms up to protect the coconut, meaning my head.

"She's right," Conchita said, hitting me from the other side. "You can't go to a place like Foxwoods Casino, especially not on a Saturday night, looking like you're just going off to McDonald's for a Big Mac."

"If you want to be a winner, you need to dress like one," Rivera said.

"Saturday morning, we're taking you to the Nail Euphorium," Conchita said.

"How do you know about the Nail Euphorium?" I asked. It was the place Hillary always went to.

"Who do you think we are—" Conchita hands-on-hipsed me "—*you?*"

Hey, I resented that. Every time someone said that to me, I resented it.

Then they all started talking about me, as if I wasn't even there, so much talk that the sounds started swirling together until it all sounded like, "Delilah, Delilah, Delilah." That's what it all sounded like, exactly…

"Never bet more than you can afford to lose," Black Jack had told me.

"Always start with a stake you can afford," Black Jack had told me.

"Set a goal on how much you want to win," Black Jack had told me, "and if you reach it, walk away."

"When you start to lose, walk away," Black Jack had told me. "If you lose your whole stake, *definitely* walk away."

Then he'd handed me a hundred-dollar bill.

"What's this?" I'd asked.

"It's your stake," he'd said. "Whatever you do, don't lose it."

Then I distinctly heard Stella say, "Of course I'm going to go, too." Her words when they came were spoken in a huff. "You don't think I'm going to be the only one left behind, do you?"

"I don't know, boss." Rivera shrugged, awkward. "It would just be way too weird—you know?—partying with the boss."

"Wait a second," I said. "No one ever said anything about *partying*. And, anyway, what are you all talking about? You're not all coming *with* me."

"Oh, uh-huh, *yeah,* we are," Conchita said.

"When was this decided?"

"Weren't you paying any attention to us at all?" Rivera demanded.

"It was *decided,*" Stella said, "while you were busy daydreaming. But, don't worry, we've got it all figured out…*Golden Squeegee.*" Then she picked up my bucket and thrust it at me. "Now get back to work!"

"Wait just one second," I said. "You're all coming with me, with me and Hillary to Foxwoods—is that what I'm hearing?"

"Pretty much," Stella said.

"Then one other person is coming, too," I said, "Eliza-beth Hepburn."

"My *customer?*" Stella said.

I nodded firmly.

"You've been talking to my *customer?*" Stella said.

I nodded meekly.

"She won't want to go," she scorned.

"Oh, yes, she will." I nodded enthusiastically, knowing the answer instinctively. "She'll be the balls of the operation."

"The…?" Stella could barely mouth the words.

"Wait just one more second," I said. "You, me, Hillary, Conchita, Rivera, Elizabeth Hepburn—" I did the math in my head "—there'll be six of us. How will we all fit into something to get us there?" I eyed the Squeaky Qlean van, the only vehicle any of us owned that would be big enough. "I'm not going off to win my fortune in that thing."

"Thanks a lot," Stella said. "I'll have you know—"

"Don't worry about it, *chicas,*" Rivera said, putting one arm around Stella and the other around me. "Me and Conchita will work all of that stuff out. Delilah, you just be up early Saturday morning. Really, we've got all your bases covered."

Which was how I found myself, up brighter and earlier than usual on Saturday morning, surrounded by my helpful elves.

Of course, my elves were all taller than me and their help was probably going to wind up killing me, so there was that, too.

"If they just shape them so that they actually *have* some

shape, it'll be an improvement," Hillary said when we got to Nail Euphorium. "Maybe a little clear polish for gloss."

"She should get a full set of acrylics," Conchita said, "painted red."

"Who do you want her to look like, *you?*" Rivera demanded.

It was nice at least to hear someone else get asked that question for a change.

"She should get the acrylics," Rivera said, "but then she should get a French mani, pedi, too."

"She'll look like Jackie Kennedy Onassis," Conchita objected.

"And this is bad?" Rivera said. "May she wind up with a mansion and a yacht."

"Wait a second," I said, which had apparently become my new favorite thing to say. "I can't afford this. If I get a French manicure and…and…and a…*pedi*—" the word was so foreign to me "—half my stake money will be gone…and that's if I don't leave a tip!"

"I've got you covered on this one," Hillary said, waving her Amex gold card in the air.

All I had was a regular Amex card, no gold for me, and as I'd shown when we went to Manhattan, I never used the damn thing, not even to buy something I wanted as much as the Ghost. For an addictive personality like me, that way, the credit card way, madness lay.

"I already told you when we were in New York," I told her. "I won't accept charity."

"It's not charity," she said. "It's my birthday present to you."

"My birthday's not for another five months. It's in January, remember?"

"So? Just don't expect anything else on January 10."

It was the same at Now We're Styling!, the salon where Conchita and Rivera regularly got their hair done. Hillary had suggested The Queen's Coif, where she got her own hair done, but had been outvoted. Still, she paid.

"Christmas present," she said, surrendering her Amex card again.

"Christmas isn't for another four months," I pointed out.

"So?" she said. "Don't expect anything on December 25."

"She looks sooo…*not* like her," Stella said when the hairdresser was done and we were all admiring the new me in the mirror.

It was weird because my hair didn't look radically different than it usually did. It was the same short, dark hair, kind of spiky. But whatever magic the stylist had performed on it, using paste artfully as well as a razor to create tiny little jagged wisps all around my face, well, it made me look like I was *styling*.

"You'll need to get your makeup done, too, of course," Stella said. "You can't have hair like that with no makeup." Sighing, she extracted her own Amex gold card from her purse.

"What are you doing?" I asked.

"It's your early Halloween bonus," she muttered. "You can get it done here. They do makeup, too."

*"Boss has got a he-art! Boss has got a he-art!"* Conchita and Rivera singsonged.

"Ohh…shut up," Stella said.

"She still needs the right clothes," Rivera said.

"We still need to get a car big enough," Conchita said.

"I'll get the clothes," Rivera said.

"I'll get the car," Conchita said.

The clothes turned out to be items from Rivera's own closet.

"I wore these black slacks the night Flavia fell in love with me," she said, holding up a pair of black capris.

"Flavia?" I asked.

"Long gone." She shrugged. "And don't worry about the length. I've got Hollywood tape in my bag, works like a charm."

She pulled a silver lamé tank top out of her bag.

"And I wore this," she said, "the night Emmanuella fell in love with me."

"Emmanuella?" I asked.

She shrugged again. "I think she's with Flavia now. We can use the Hollywood tape to tuck up the hem of the tank, too."

As I put on the clothes, I tried not to think about the fact that I was being clothed wholly in garments that had loved and lost a lot of girl-on-girl love.

In the beginning I'd felt resistant to their efforts. Why, I felt, bother trying to turn a sow's ear into a silk purse? But, and here was the strange thing, as the day wore on, a feeling welled in me, the same Cinderella feeling I'd had when I'd slipped the Ghosts on at Jimmy Choo's in New York. Here were all these women—Hillary, Stella, Conchita, Rivera—doing everything in their power to help me achieve my moment. I was like the real Cinderella, with the Fairy God-mother and all the creatures in the house helping her get ready for the ball. I felt magical. There was still one thing missing, though…

"Who would have guessed you could look so good?" Rivera admired her own handiwork when I was done dressing, when she was done taping me. "But shoes—" she put her finger to her lips "—that's the big problem."

"That's how this all started," I pointed out. "Remember? Once I get those Jimmy Choos, I'll have great shoes."

"Right," she said, all business, "but you don't have them now." She looked in my closet. "All you've got right now are a pair of flip-flops, some winter boots and those stupid Nikes you're always wearing."

"Stupid—?"

"I know," she said, cocking an ear. Yup, the shower was still running. "While your roommate's in the shower, we'll raid *her* closet."

"Oh, no," I said. "No, no, no, no, no. I'm sure she won't like—"

"Come on." Rivera yanked on my arm.

I was right: Hillary didn't like it… At All.

"Those are my New Year's Eve shoes!" she shrieked, towel still wrapped around her head, another around her body, when she glimpsed my twinkle toes five minutes later.

"I know," I said.

They were her New Year's Eve shoes, the same shoes she'd worn every New Year's Eve for as long as I'd known her. Shaped like a simple high-heeled pump, they were covered in glittery silver, kind of like Dorothy's red slippers, only a different color and without the bow but with a big heel. Hillary claimed they were good luck and that wearing them on that one night, and only that one night, ensured her a great year ahead.

"You look great in those towels." Rivera winked at her.

"Shut up," Hillary said. "My shoes! But wait a second. Your feet are much smaller than mine."

This was true.

Extracting one foot from one shoe—really, that expensive pedi was wasted inside a closed-toe shoe—I revealed Rivera's handiwork: wadded tissue paper. Honestly, it was hard to feel like a glam winner when there was Kleenex cuddling my piggies before going to market.

"But it's such a good cause, Hillary Clinton," Rivera said sweetly, enunciating each word of my roommate's name silkily as though she were trying to sell rich cordovan leather. "And it's not like it's as bad as it could be, like if her feet were bigger than yours and there was a danger she might stretch them out. And you really do look great in those towels."

"Ohh…*what…ever,*" Hillary conceded with poor grace, going off to dry her hair.

"Where the hell did you get that thing?" I shouted down to Conchita from the balcony of the South Park condo.

A minute before, a white stretch limo had pulled into the parking lot and Conchita had emerged from the driver's seat, opening one of the passenger doors from which emerged Elizabeth Hepburn. Seeing the four of us out on the balcony, Elizabeth Hepburn did a little red-carpet curtsy.

Conchita smiled up at me, shielding her eyes against the blaze of sun going down behind us. "You don't want to know, *chica.*"

"Ready to roll?" Elizabeth Hepburn asked. "You know, John Wayne used to always say that to me. Count Basie, too, come to think of it."

"But wait a second," I said. "Don't you all need to get dressed?"

I looked at the five of them. It wasn't that they were shabbily dressed. Indeed, they all looked better than I looked most days, but they were still all relatively casual, in summer slacks, light blouses and sandals. Really, I was the only one who looked like she might be going out on a Saturday night to a casino that had nightclubs in it.

"Oh, no," Elizabeth Hepburn said softly. "This is *your* big night."

# 7

Foxwoods Casino was a fair drive from where we'd started, but when we walked into the casino en masse it felt as though no more time had passed than the length it would take for a reader to turn the page.

Maybe it was that Conchita drove like a maniac. Or maybe it was the single drink I'd allowed myself from the minibar—"Never get drunk while you're playing—" my dad's words rang in my brain "—only losers get drunk at the table"—the champagne going down like silk bubbles as I listened to the Brazilian music Conchita was blaring on the stereo.

"Hey." Hillary smiled at me lazily over the top of her own flute of champagne. "You're drinking something with alcohol in it and it's not even Jake's Fault."

For a moment, I felt a frisson of anxiety. I was starting to get hungry and I wondered if they had any Michael Angelo's Four Cheese Lasagna kicking around the casino kitchen, but then I pushed the anxious feelings away. This was a special night. I would do special things.

Whatever the case, whether the ride went so quick because of the speed of the driver or because of the buzz from the champagne, I felt great as we walked through the door.

I'd never been part of a group like that before. Much in the way of people who are serially monogamous in their romantic relationships, I'd always been serially monogamous in my friendships. My mother was so sick for so many years before she died, we'd spent so much time one-on-one, it was as if I could only relate to other women one-on-one. Back at the private junior high, there'd been the best girlfriend I got drunk with during the science fair. During high school, there'd been another best girlfriend. And, ever since then, there had been Hillary. Hillary herself had other friends she sometimes did things with, and sometimes I went along, but for whatever reason, the dynamic never worked for me, unless it was something fairly innocuous like a group going to a movie. I didn't mind her other friendships, wasn't jealous of them in any way; the group thing just wasn't for me. Oh, for years I wished I could be the kind of woman you see in the middle of a group of other women—laughing louder than anyone else, living large—I just didn't know how.

It was hard to believe then that, as we strode through the casino, for the first time in my life I had a posse.

In the entryway, just outside of the casino proper, there was a woman with balloons pinned all over her clothes—she even had on a balloon hat—who was blowing brightly colored balloons into all different shapes: flowers, animals, one even looked weirdly like Bill O'Reilly. She was handing out her creations to anyone who wanted them.

"That's kind of an odd thing to have in the entryway," I said, "don't you think?"

"Oh, I don't know," said Hillary, "it's probably one of those little extras, like free rolls of coins for the people who get bused in, that are devised to lull gamblers into forgetting how much money they're pissing away at the tables."

She must have seen my expression, because she quickly added, "Oops, sorry."

"Plus," said Stella, "they need to give people something to entertain them when they're not gambling."

"Yeah," said Conchita, "but every time one of those things pops, I'm going to be wondering about who's getting shot."

"I once dated a balloonist," said Elizabeth Hepburn.

And then, before I even knew it, my posse was splitting up.

Going up to an information desk, Stella grabbed a bunch of brochures that she distributed to the others.

"Ooh, I want to go to the Club BB King," Hillary said. "Look—" she pointed "—Hall & Oates are playing later on tonight, with Todd Rundgren."

"I used to hang with B.B. King," Elizabeth Hepburn said.

"I want to go to the Hard Rock Café," Conchita said.

"And how," Rivera said. "They've got a 'Pimp and Ho Party' going on with The Dizzy Reed Band."

For once, Elizabeth Hepburn looked perplexed. "I don't think I know anyone from the Pimp and Ho band," she said, then she brightened, "but I did used to go out with Dizzy Dean! He played ball for—"

"I'm hungry," Stella said, flat statement.

"Oh, I'm sure there are lots of great places to eat here." Hillary cheered her. "How about this, I'll go with you to get a quick bite…and then we'll both go to the Club BB King!"

"Meanwhile," said Conchita, "we'll go see Dizzy and then we'll all meet up after the shows. How does that sound?"

Rivera turned to me. "What are you going to be doing while we're all doing all of that?"

It was all I could do not to grit my teeth at my posse.

"I'm going to do what I came here to do," I said. No matter how hard I was trying, the words still came out like bullets. "I. Am. Going. To. Gamble. And, hey, why'd you all help me and pay for my makeover if you're just going to take off?"

"Hey right back at you," Hillary Clinton said, always the voice of reason. "Just because you feel the need to gamble all night, it doesn't mean the rest of us can't each have our own brand of fun. Don't worry. We'll be back in time to take you home."

"Besides," Elizabeth Hepburn added, "does the Fairy

Godmother stick around after waving her magic wand and giving Cinderella the perfect dress and coach? Never." She shuddered. "The stage would look too crowded."

And, just like that, I was alone.

I cruised the inside of the smoke-filled casino—there were designated nonsmoking areas, but I knew from the brochure that for the bulk of the action, I needed to be right where I was—for a while on my own, taking the lay of the land. After all, even if one hundred dollars seemed like a lot of spare change in my usual life, I knew that if I sat down at the wrong gaming table, that C-note could disappear quickly like so much cash right down the toilet. So I strolled around, studied the slot players, even saw one blue-haired lady hit it big on the jackpot. Maybe, I thought, I should just get two thousand nickels and play until the one-armed bandit caused my arm to fall off? Maybe that way my fortune lay?

I shook my head.

Then I watched the roulette games for a time. It was a game that could be as precise or as general as the player wanted it to be. Sure, Black 27 would be a daring bet that could pay off big, but what were the odds? Then again, how hard could it be to choose between red and black? Fifty-fifty seemed like great odds to me. At least those odds were even.

But, no, I hadn't come for that, either. Nor had I come for poker or baccarat.

I had come for one thing: blackjack.

As I meandered through the tables, though, looking for a place to start, I saw that except for the tables that had the highest minimum bids, bids I couldn't even meet to open, most of the seats were filled. Besides which, my dad had cautioned that it wasn't good enough to just find any table; you needed to find a table where, after studying the dealer for a bit, you had a strong sense you could win.

"But isn't that kind of, oh, I don't know, *unscientific?*" I'd asked him.

"Hey, if it was a science," he'd said, "anyone could win. Besides, you're too new at this to worry about something more scientific like counting cards. So you'll just have to go with your senses. Oh, and try if you can to get a seat to the far left facing the dealer. Even if you can't count cards, at least from there, the anchor seat, you can get a sense of how the cards are running as the dealer chutes them out."

And, suddenly, there he was: the dealer of my dreams! He had short red hair and freckled skin with a Vandyke beard and mustache, making him look kind of like the grown-up version of that kid from *The Partridge Family*. But that wasn't what made him the dealer of my dreams. Who cared what he looked like? He'd just busted at twenty-three, having been forced to deal himself an Eight to a King and Five. Whatever his luck had been earlier, it was taking a turn for the worse now and I was sure that meant mine would take a turn for the better.

There was just one problem: the seat on the far left was taken up and then some by a big guy in a purple shirt who reeked of cigars.

Oh, well, I sighed, taking the one vacant seat left at the table, right next to Cigar Man, if I waited for conditions to be perfect, I'd never play.

I tossed my hundred on the table as if I'd been tossing hundreds on blackjack tables all my life and felt a tingle inside as the dealer pushed twenty red chips back at me, valued at five dollars each. The table itself had a red sign on it, meaning it was a minimum five-dollar table. Red was my favorite color, despite that I hadn't cared for any of the red Jimmy Choos, and I was feeling incredibly lucky.

Let the games *really* begin.

Apparently the last game had caused the supply of cards to go so low in the six-deck chute that the dealer needed to reshuffle, a dexterous display I really enjoyed, plus it delayed my moment of truth.

"C'mon, c'mon," Cigar Man muttered.

I sniffed something unpleasant and realized that, underneath the Havana stench, Cigar Man was sweating like crazy. And when I looked over expecting to see a stack of chips in front of him at least as big as mine, I saw he had only one lonely red chip left.

Apparently, red wasn't *his* favorite color.

When the dealer finished shuffling, he offered me the deck to cut. I knew, from my conversation with my dad, that as the newest player to a table, this might happen. But now that it was actually happening, I was unsure.

"Do you want me to cut that into two piles," I nervous-laughed, "or three? It is kind of a big stack…"

"Oh, Christ," Cigar Man said, snapping his one chip back off the table as he heaved his bulk off of the seat, "I hate playing with pikers."

Well, at least with him gone, I could slip into that far-left seat, just like so…

"You can split the deck into as many piles as you'd like," said this incredible voice in my ear, a voice good enough to blow Hall & Oates *and* Todd Rundgren off the stage at the Club BB King. "And while I really don't mind your staying in my lap while I gamble, I do believe that two players gambling from one seat is kind of frowned upon around here."

"Oh!" I reddened as I raised myself from the lap of the body that was connected to that amazing voice. "Sorry!"

All I could think of that could have happened was that as I was sliding over from the left, he must have been sliding into the seat from the right and just got there before me.

I cut the deck several times without counting, only looking to the side to check out the bearer of The Voice as the dealer began to deal.

If Rivera were with me right then, I knew what she'd say. *"Chica,"* she'd say, "that guy is *whack."*

At which point Conchita would probably slap her across the head. "What are you talking about, *whack?* That guy is more than just *whack*. He's *beyond* whack." At which point, I'd need to ask them to define *whack* for me again. Then I'd need to remind them that they were both lesbians, so why were they hornying in on my game anyway?

And if my mother were here, my late mother, she'd have said the same thing she always said about my father: "He's so dreamy."

And he was, he really was, with short blond hair, blue eyes and a strong jaw that made him look as if he'd just walked out of the pages of a Fitzgerald novel, not to mention he was wearing a tux that he wore like he owned, rather than rented it.

Then Stella and Hillary would knock each other out trying to give him their phone numbers, leaving only Elizabeth Hepburn left to play the field and, given her track record, she'd probably slept with him at some point already.

But since there was only me…

"Come here often?" I asked, immediately wanting to slap myself in the head.

"Yes," he said.

The word *yes* is usually a positive thing; certainly it provides a more obvious conversational opening than a flatly dismissive *no*. But when I looked at him, I realized his *yes* just as well might have been a *no*, because his eyes were all on the cards, his gaze shifting around the table as he took in what other people had, what the dealer had, what he had.

Then I noticed something else: like Cigar Man before him, The Voice had one lone red chip on the table in front of him, which he had pushed forward as his ante. Well, at least we had that in common, since wanting to start out cautious, I had only wagered one red chip, as well.

I began wondering what else we might have in common…

"Card?"

The dealer was studying me with mild impatience, his left hand drumming on the top of the chute.

"Oh!" That was fast. It was already my turn and I hadn't even looked at my cards yet. I looked then and saw I had a Queen and a Six: Sixteen. The dealer was showing a Ten and I wouldn't know until all the players had finished, what he was hiding in the hole.

"Card?" He tapped the chute some more.

Looking around the table fast, I saw a preponderance of low cards and, remembering some of what my dad had said, instinct told me the cards might be about to run high. I didn't want to take a chance on busting with my first hand, which would be demoralizing that early in the evening, so I held out my hand flat over the card as my dad had shown me.

"Pass," I said.

The Voice was showing a combined Twelve. The only cards that could bust him were those worth ten, but he was taking his time deciding.

"Card?"

The Voice looked at my Sixteen rather than at his own cards, then he laid his hand out flat. "Pass."

The dealer at last turned over his hole card to reveal a Six, so he and I were pushing at Sixteen, but House rules said the dealer always had to pull at Sixteen, stand on anything Seventeen or higher.

I felt another tingle inside as the dealer slid the next card out of the chute and saw that my dad had been right: it was a Queen. The dealer now had Twenty-six and was busted.

The Voice beside me let out a deep breath. Then he turned to me with a winning smile.

"Wow," he said, "that's the first hand I've won all night. It must have been a stroke of luck, me sitting down at this table just in time for you to sit in my lap."

His words made me feel good because what single woman wouldn't want to be thought of as good luck by a man who looked like The Voice? Plus, his words made me want to sit in his lap again. Plus, it'd been a long time since I'd sat in any guy's lap, so I was really wanting to sit there.

"'Herein Fortune shows herself more kind than is her custom,'" I started to say, but then a new hand was before me on the table and I realized I'd better get serious and stop quoting ol' Bill. Sure, I'd felt great making the right decision and winning the last hand against the dealer, because if I'd asked the dealer to hit me instead it would have been me who busted. But let's face it, I had only won a single round, and one red five-dollar chip does not a Jimmy Choo buy.

I realized the only thing to do was to follow what my dad had told me: narrow my concentration down until it was the size of a dime, ignore the noise and the smoke and everything else that was going on around me except for what was happening right at that table, and just play. Hell, I was sure if my dad was right there, he'd tell me to ignore the beautiful sound of The Voice, as well. There would be time for that—or not—once I was finished with doing what I came there to do.

So the only thing for it was to concentrate totally on the hand that was dealt, making the best decision possible based on the cards I held and the cards I could see in front of the others.

Except there was no decision I needed to make because when I looked down, I saw the dealer had dealt me a Jack and an Ace: Twenty-one. It's the name of the game, *baby*.

My first blackjack.

"You're better than a stroke of good luck," The Voice said exultantly. "You're a talisman!"

I looked over at The Voice sitting next to me and the cards on the green table in front of him.

He had blackjack, too.

It's the other name of the game, *baby*.

For the next hour, we played side by side. We each lost a few, but mostly we won, and I quickly realized he was a more adventurous gambler. I was adhering strictly to what my dad had told me in terms of strategy: when I increased my winnings at the table by fifty percent, I increased my bets to double; but when the ten-value cards and Aces were being used up rapidly, I reduced my bet to the minimum. The Voice, on the other hand, while keeping a close eye on what I was doing, steadily increased his bets. This meant that when we won, he won bigger; but when we lost, he lost bigger, too.

When the dealers changed shifts, I took the opportunity to count my chips and was surprised to see I was up to over seven hundred dollars; I even had a fair number of green chips now, valued at twenty-five dollars, that I'd been using for my bets for the last few hands.

"Don't you realize it's bad luck to count your winnings while still at the table?" The Voice said, leaning in to whisper from the side.

"Well, but how else will I know…?" I let my voice trail off, recognizing how absurd it would be to utter the complete thought, "But how else will I know when I've won enough to buy some Jimmy Choos?" The way I figured it, at the rate I was going, in another hour I'd have enough money to buy the shoes I so desperately wanted.

There was no time for that now, though, because the new dealer was the dealer from hell.

If the last dealer had looked like Danny Bonaduce all grown up, the new one was a thin Asian woman, resembling no one so much as that villainous lawyer who used to be on *Ally McBeal*. In fact, there was something about her that rattled me so much that when she dealt my hand—a Queen and an Eight—I got so nervous I started tapping my finger on the table, using the universal sign for "hit me," and before I knew it I'd busted at Twenty-eight.

Ouch!

Then The Voice busted, too.

And we kept on busting until I was down to just over five hundred dollars.

Even though this was in no way going to get me the Ghost I wanted, and fighting the compulsion to stay right where I was every second, I pushed away from the table.

"Oh, no!" The Voice said, placing a restraining hand on my arm.

My, his hand was beautiful, like a world-class pianist's. And I'd bet my last five-dollar chip those nails weren't acrylics.

"You can't leave now!" The Voice said.

Oh, how I would have liked to stay, if only just to please him. But I had to go. I was following my dad's rules. "When you start to lose, walk away," he'd told me, making the point that in some games quitters actually stood a better chance of prospering, at which point I'd pointed out that wasn't it cheaters that didn't prosper anyway? Whatever. Sure, if I stayed, I might win some back, maybe I'd win more than some. But the cards had turned cold on me and if I stayed, I could lose everything. Then where would I be? Besides, I was still ahead by over four hundred dollars from when I started. Washing windows, it took me a few days to earn four hundred dollars.

"Sorry." With reluctance, I peeled his fingers off. He had some grip! "I really do have to stop now."

"How about just one more—?"

But the dealer from hell cut him off.

"Bet?" she commanded me, pointing one talon at the table in front of me.

"No, thanks." I forced myself to be firm. "No."

"Bet?" she commanded The Voice, shifting her finger to him.

The Voice smiled ruefully before pocketing his chips. Even though his losses had been more spectacular than mine, his wins had been that much more so, and I figured he had at least a thousand dollars in his pocket.

"Sorry," The Voice said to the dealer. "But if the lady goes, I go. After all, I can't keep winning without my talisman." Then he tossed one of his twenty-five-dollar green chips on the table as a tip for the dealer. "Perhaps another time."

Hey, it was impressive he was such a great tipper, and I liked to tip well, too, but I could have used that chip right then.

Oh, well. It was time for me to go.

I was a few tables away, when I felt that firm hand on my arm again.

"Hey," said The Voice, "what's the big hurry?"

"I don't know…I just thought…" Then I blurted out, "What's your name?" I couldn't help it. I needed to find something to call him in my mind other than The Voice.

He smiled. "Billy Charisma," he said.

"Of course. Why didn't I think of that?"

"And yours?"

"Delilah Sampson."

"Ah." He smiled again. "Your name is both strong and weak. If I stick with you long enough, will I lose all my hair?"

I'd actually heard that one before, or at least something similar.

I shrugged. "Maybe just all your chips."

"Well, that would certainly be devastating. Although, thanks to you, I had a very good night. Before you came along, the night looked to be a lousy day at the office. But after you showed up?" He twinkled his fingers in the air. "It turned magical."

I wasn't used to a man, let alone such a gorgeous man, paying such attention to me. And I knew I should have encouraged him, since who knew when, if ever, Fortune might shine so again? But I'd come there as a woman with a mission and a sort-of posse, and a woman with a mission and a sort-of posse I was still.

"That's great," I told him, feeling like Cinderella as the clock strikes midnight, "but I really need to go. I'm with some friends and I need to go find—"

But he'd already flagged down a cocktail waitress, ordered two glasses of champagne.

"Surely your friends can wait a few more minutes," he said. "We need to celebrate our success. Always have to celebrate the small successes. Pity we have to pay for the celebration, though," he said, handing enough chips to the waitress to cover the tab. "If we'd ordered them while still at the table, we'd have been comped. Eh, cheers!"

I drank.

A part of me knew it was time to find the party I'd come with, and yet I felt very much as though I'd been deer-in-the-headlightsed, like Billy Charisma was too bright a thing and I too dull to even speak.

"So, tell me, Delilah Sampson," he said, taking a sip from his own champagne, "do you have any nicknames?"

"Nicknames?" I was getting duller by the minute.

"Yes. It's just that the name Delilah brings up too many bad associations for me. You know, bad nights in Vegas, Tom Jones and all of that."

I tried to think. I'd never been much of a nickname person, not the kind of cool person to have a really cool nickname like Legs or Bright Eyes or Pepper. "The girls I work with call me *chica* sometimes."

He thought about it for a moment. "Nope," he decided. "It shouldn't be anything I need to pronounce with a Spanish accent."

"Well, my dad always calls me Baby."

What can I say in my defense? I certainly wasn't about to tell him Hillary sometimes called me Shit For Brains.

"Baby?" He tried the name out, studied the high ceiling beyond the smoke clouds, nodded. "I *like* Baby. I think then that from now on I'll call you—"

"There you are, *chica!*" It was Rivera. She spoke to me as though this gorgeous guy I was standing next to wasn't even there; which I guess, to her, he wasn't. "Boss ate some kind of bad clam when she was eating with Hillary. Either that or she choked on the prime rib and Hillary had to do the Heimlich. I forget which. Anyway, it's time to go."

"Are you sure Stella doesn't suffer from emphysema?" I asked, concerned.

"Huh?" Rivera said.

I explained how just recently I'd seen the author John Irving getting interviewed by Jon Stewart on *The Daily Show*. Irving had related an anecdote about being out to dinner with his mentor Kurt Vonnegut when Vonnegut had started choking. Irving, unwilling to let his mentor die while dining with him—talk about someone thinking everything that happened around them was about me, me, me (or them, them, them)—he immediately started performing the Heimlich. But Irving is a short man, Vonnegut a tall one, and Irving's first efforts…well, let's just say he did *not* apply the pressure to Vonnegut's stomach. So then Irving, a man with a lot of wrestling in his past, somehow got Vonnegut down on the floor on all fours, whereupon he proceeded to continue to Heimlich him. At one point, Vonnegut managed to gasp, "John, I wasn't choking on anything. I have emphysema." As punch lines go, it was a doozy.

Rivera gave me a strange look. "*Chica,* I have no idea what the fuck you're talking about, but we gotta go."

And with that, barely giving me a second to throw a goodbye wave over my shoulder to Billy Charisma, she tugged me away.

Back out in the entryway, the rest of our group was waiting for us. But they certainly weren't bored. They were standing on the edges of a huge crowd whose attention was focused on someone in the center.

In the middle of the room, replacing the Balloon Lady from earlier, was The Yo-Yo Man.

Oh my God! It was The Yo-Yo Man!

At least that's what the sandwich-board sign on the easel said: *Chris Westacott, The Yo-Yo Man.*

"Oh my God!" I shrieked at my gal pals. "It's The Yo-Yo Man!"

I'm sure they thought I was nuts, but I didn't let that stop me as I elbowed my way through the crowd. Besides, I didn't want to stick around long enough for Elizabeth Hepburn to tell me she'd once slept with someone named Duncan.

I was going to finally see the man from the commercials up close and personal! I was going to finally see the man of my dreams in the flesh!

But when I got to the front of the crowd, I saw it wasn't *The* Yo-Yo Man at all. It was merely *A* Yo-Yo Man. And not even any kind of great Yo-Yo Man. It was Furthest Guy in the commercials, the guy who was always dropping his yo-yo in the background, while the real Yo-Yo Man, *The* Yo-Yo Man, showed his stuff.

But, *hey.* Up close and personal, Furthest Guy wasn't half-bad, at least not in the looks department. He was taller than I'd have expected—he always looked so tiny and insignificant in those commercials—and his hair was no longer so short, the curly chestnut strands poking out from the bottom of the Mets cap he wore backward. This near, I could finally see his eye color as he kept those warm brown eyes focused on the twin yo-yos he was twirling simultaneously. And his body... True, he had on those oversized long shorts, the ones that I hate with the waistbands that reveal the tops of guys' underwear, on top of which was a T-shirt advertising the casino we were in; I figured the casino probably made him wear the T-shirt. As for the obnoxious long shorts, I figured it was probably part of the cool yo-yo guy persona. I mean, why else would anyone our age—and he did look to be about the same age as me—wear those stupid long shorts if they didn't have to? As for the Mets hat, I was hoping that was for real. I may not have cared about sports, but my dad was a big Mets fan and it would please him greatly once I brought this Chris Westacott home.

What was I thinking? I shook my head to clear my thoughts. Clearly the champagne, coupled with seeing a real Yo-Yo Man, was going straight to my head.

I decided to stop fantasizing and instead just watched him perform. While technically not as proficient as The Yo-Yo Man, he was still pretty darn good; certainly the crowd thought so.

He was pretty darn good, at least, until he lost control of one of his twin yo-yos and the darn thing nailed me in the eye. Then, suddenly, he was Furthest Guy again.

"Shit!" He dropped his other yo-yo and rushed over, placed his hands gently on my shoulders. "Are you okay? Do you think you're going to lose it?"

I looked at Furthest Guy out of my one good eye. Despite that he'd just popped me one, he still looked really cute. Plus, he looked so concerned…

"Don't you think you've done quite enough?" It was The Voice again and now he was pushing Furthest Guy out of the way. "Here, let me look at that."

Billy Charisma placed his fingers gently but firmly under my chin, tilting my head slightly upward. In his other hand, he'd produced a pristine white silk handkerchief, as though he'd expected all kinds of carnage.

"Oh," he said, full stop, surprised. "It's not nearly as bad as I thought it would be. No doubt you'll have a shiner by morning, but the skin isn't cut at all and I don't even see any broken blood vessels. If only this *jerk* had been more careful..." He gestured at Furthest Guy.

"I'm sorry," Furthest Guy said humbly. "I don't know what happened. I keep practicing and practicing this Double Whammy trick and it goes well enough whenever I do it at home. But every time I try to perform it in public—"

"Maybe you should only perform it at home alone then," Billy Charisma said. There was a smile on his face, but his tone was all ice.

"Are you okay?" Hillary said, busting through the crowd.

"Don't Heimlich me!" I shouted.

"Huh?"

"I think it's time we all went home," Stella said.

"Good night, Baby," Billy Charisma said softly, kissing me gently above my injury.

I opened my mouth to thank him, but before I could even get the *th* out, Conchita and Rivera were hustling me toward the exit.

We were nearly out the door when one of the others thought to ask—I'm pretty sure it was Hillary, but I was pretty out of it at that point—how I'd done at the tables.

"Fair," I said. "I've got a little over five hundred dollars in my pocket."

"A little over…and you call that just *fair?*" Hillary said, encouragingly. I was sure it was her that time. "I think that's phenomenal!"

"You know," said Elizabeth Hepburn, "back in my Louis B. Mayer days, there were whole *weeks* when I didn't make that kind of money. You hear some of these young actresses now complain they're only making fifteen million dollars a picture. Ha! I'd like to see them try to survive back when we had the studio system. Then let them talk to me about hardships."

"But it's not enough," I answered Hillary. "It's not even half of what I need for the Ghost."

"Oh." Hillary's face fell on my account. Then she brightened. "I know—you just need a good, solid plan."

"You're right," I said, suddenly brightening, as well. "I do need a plan. And I've got one."

"You do? Already?"

"Yes. Next Saturday, I'm taking the bus to Atlantic City. I'll use what I won tonight as my stake. Just think about it. Tonight, I managed to walk out with five times what I walked in with. If I can do the same next week, I'll be able to buy Ghosts for both of us!"

"Are you sure you don't have a head injury?" Stella asked. "Because I'm doing the math here and, frankly, I think you're nuts. You really think you can take five hundred dollars to New Jersey—*New Jersey!*—and come back out with twenty-five hundred?"

But I never got to reply to her skepticism, for as we approached Conchita's white limo, I heard footsteps that I'd vaguely registered behind us before, as those footsteps sped up, passing us on the left.

"Hey!" Rivera said. "Isn't that the same guy who you were talking to back in the casino? Isn't that the same guy who saved you from that stupid jerk with the flying yo-yo?"

I saw the back of that black tux walking away from me, a wisp of smoke trailing up over his head. I'd have bet all the money in my pockets it was Billy Charisma.

"Yes," I said. "That's Billy Charisma."

"Huh." Rivera put one hand on her hip, thrust that hip out. "I don't think so, *chica*."

"No, really, he is, and—"

"I don't like that guy, *chica,*" she said. "I don't trust him."

"Why do you say that?"

"Because she's jealous of anyone who's prettier than she is…like me," Conchita said. "C'mon, ladies."

Rivera's words made me feel uneasy. Why would she say something like that about Billy Charisma? She didn't even *know* Billy Charisma. And besides, no matter how uneasy her words made me, feeling the light of his attention all night had made me feel *good*. It was the first time any guy had paid that quality attention to me in I didn't want to think about how long, and I pushed away the negative feelings: the ones I'd felt when Billy had cowed Furthest Guy—after all, Furthest Guy didn't *mean* to yo-yo me—or the mixed feelings I'd had, feelings of being cared for and conde-scended to all at the same time, when he called me Baby.

As Conchita drove into the night, I heard the soft snores

of Hillary and Stella and Rivera. Elizabeth Hepburn, still wired like a kid allowed to stay up too late on New Year's Eve but losing energy fast, rested her head on my shoulder, reliving the night.

"I'm glad you had a good time," I said when she paused for breath, meaning it.

"Oh, God, yes," she said. "I had a blast! And seeing that yo-yo guy at the end? It reminded me of the time me and Duncan…"

See? I knew it would come to that.

"Elizabeth?" I said, gently cutting off her reminiscences.

"Hmm?"

Even though Conchita couldn't hear me because she was too busy driving up front, and the others were asleep, I whispered as I spoke. "I was wondering," I said, trying to tread delicately, "all these men you say you've been with in the past…some of them have been dead a really long time and some of them I'm pretty sure were, well, gay. So did you really…?" My voice trailed off. I couldn't bring myself to accuse her outright of lying.

"You caught me," she said ruefully.

Now I was sorry I'd even brought it up. The last thing I ever wanted to do was hurt her. "No, I—"

"It's all right," she said. "But I did sleep with at least half of them…and I'm not saying which."

"No, of course not. I just wanted to know why—"

"Why I exaggerate so much? Why I claim to have twice as many notches on my belt than I really do?"

In the relative darkness of the limo, I nodded.

She sighed. "Everyone wants to be cool, Delilah. Don't you know that by now?" She sighed. "Even old ladies." I felt her frail shoulders shrug against my side. "I guess I just always figured that if people thought I lived this exciting life, they'd think I was still cool and want to talk to me. When you're young in Hollywood, everyone wants a piece of you. But once you get old? All they do is trot you out once a year, so everyone can stare and say, 'You're still here? We all thought you were dead.'"

"You are so still cool," I said, putting my arm around those frail shoulders, smoothing her hair with my hand. "You have led an exciting life. Why, you're *the* one and only Elizabeth Hepburn!"

"I am that," she said. "And," she added, with a twinkle in her voice, "I've slept with at least half the men I've said I had."

"That, too," I agreed.

"You won't tell anyone," she said, "will you? That I exaggerate my CV a bit?"

"Never," I vowed.

"Thank you, dear." She yawned. "And thank you for everything else."

"What? I haven't done anything."

"Are you kidding me? The trip to Manhattan, tonight at Foxwoods—thanks to you, I've had the time of my life, and at a time when I thought I was all finished having the time of my life."

A few minutes later, she was snoring softly with the others and I was back to confronting the paradox that was my feelings about Billy Charisma. Was he good whack or bad whack?

Oh, well. I sighed as I fell asleep in the back of the limo, none of it mattered anyway since I was sure I'd never see either of them again, neither Billy Charisma *nor* Furthest Guy.

But I did see them both. Oh, did I ever. Just as soon as my eyes closed completely and REM kicked in—not the rock band; I'm talking about the sleep thing here—I dreamt of both of them together. I don't mean they were together, which would be really strange, but rather, they were both there and they were each taking turns dancing with me. Billy Charisma was a great dancer, as you'd expect, but the big surprise was Furthest Guy: with a girl in his arms—me— he was just as good a dancer.

Maybe even better.

# 8

"What's this?"

We were sitting out on our balcony the following day, enjoying the late-summer sun while drinking some recuperative Bloody Marys, and I'd just handed Hillary three hundred dollars in cash.

"Are you sure you can stand to drink something other than Diet Pepsi Lime or Jake's Fault Shiraz?" Hillary had said when I'd suggested the Bloody Marys. Then she'd put her hand to my forehead. "You don't feel feverish," she'd said.

"Cut it out," I'd said, brushing her hand away. And, hey, hadn't I just drunk champagne the night before? "I've been doing so many things lately that I wouldn't normally do, what's one more?"

In truth, all of the "doing so many things lately that I

wouldn't normally do" was making me feel edgy in the extreme, like I'd gone ice skating on a lake that was about to melt through. But if doing things like going to Foxwoods the night before and the prospective trip to Atlantic City was to become a part of my new reality, I was going to have to break from my old "I only eat the same foods at each meal" mode. Either that, or become the crazy lady on the bus carrying her own purple lunch bag with her to the casinos.

"It's for you," I said now, referring to the three hundred dollars.

"I don't get it," Hillary said.

She might not get it, but I certainly did. For years now, she'd been a great friend to me. Not only was she undyingly supportive—wasn't that her the night before telling me I'd done great and encouraging me to do even better in the future?—but she was also the codependent who was always letting me be just as weird as I needed to be…except for when she was making fun of me for it, that is. Despite the latter, Hillary deserved some kind of reward for being the greatest friend I'd ever had and I was determined to give it to her.

"At first, I thought maybe you could get the Pippa with it. It's a metallic flat thong that retails for three hundred and thirty dollars—I found that out when I looked online last night."

"Wait a second," she said. "You were in my room after we got home last night, surfing on my computer, *while I was sleeping?*"

"Yes, and it's getting kind of messy in there. I think you should clean—"

"You were in my room—"

"Hey," I said, "what can I say? I couldn't sleep. So I started planning for my Choo shoes future. But then I started thinking about you."

"And you thought I should have the Pippas?"

"Well, yes, until I realized they were a little more than I can budget right now, so I think you should get the Momo Flats."

"Why does that name sound familiar?"

"Because Elizabeth Hepburn flirted with them briefly when we went to New York, before rejecting them for the Fayres as being the shoe that will finally knock out Bacall at the Oscars. You remember the Momos, don't you? They were a metallic laser-cut shoe. The label underneath said they were available in blood-orange, bronze, charcoal, chocolate, gold, purple and silver."

"How do you remember all that detail?"

"I looked under all the shoes and committed the information to memory. It was important to me, like knowing that 'I am almost out at heels' comes from *The Merry Wives of Windsor*, not the Jimmy Choo catalog. But that's neither here nor there, because here's the best part."

"I can't wait."

"I really don't think those colors I listed for the Momo Flats would be the most exciting for you, but the display model was in that blue-green color we all liked the best. I think you should get those with the money. They're only two hundred and ninety-five dollars. I *want* you to get those with the money."

"You're paying for it all?"

"Well, no. I can't pay the taxes. You'll need to pay the taxes yourself."

"But this is supposed to be part of your stake money for Atlantic City." She tried to hand the money back to me. "I can't take this!"

I shoved the money back at her. "But you *have* to take it!" I said.

"But I'll feel lousy if you don't achieve your dream on account of me!"

"But I'll feel lousier if you don't let me do this for you!"

"But why, why, *why,* Delilah, is this so important to you?"

I cupped my hand behind my ear. "Did someone let Tom Jones in?" I asked.

*"What?"* She was exasperated.

"Never mind." I brushed it off. There was no point in letting her in on just how much weirder I was getting, meaning that ever since we'd set foot into the casino the night before, I'd been hearing an undernote of Tom Jones singing all the time. Really. She'd been psychoanalyzing me for years for free. I certainly didn't want her to start medicating me.

Instead, I speechified for a bit.

"Ever since our first day at college, you've taken care of me. You cheered for me the two times I actually got

boyfriends, even though their nicknames were The Weasel
and The Rat, respectively, and mourned with me the two
times I lost them. You cheered for me when I aced my
Shakespeare class, held my hair whenever I vomited after too
many Singapore Slings, cried with me and helped me carry
my things to the car after I flunked out. Then, as soon as you
graduated yourself, you found us an apartment I could
actually afford half the rent on—I know if you were just
looking for yourself, you could have gone higher, lived
somewhere grander than South Park—so that I could finally
move out of my dad's place. And since then, you've been
just as supportive as ever."

"But I tease you," she interrupted, "sometimes mercilessly."

"But I deserve it," I countered. "If it weren't for you, I'd
never stop and think about the bigger picture or the fact that
at age twenty-eight all I've got to show for myself is the
Golden Squeegee Award."

"But you worked so hard for that."

"See?" I pointed the celery stalk from my Bloody Mary
at her accusingly. "You're doing it again."

"Ohh, don't be so pointing-things-outish. In a minute,
I'll be giving you a hard time again."

"True," I conceded. "But I need someone to give me a
hard time. My dad never does it, my mom didn't live long
enough to do it now."

We bowed our heads for a moment of silence over the
dregs of our Bloody Marys in honor of Lila Sampson, may
she rest in peace.

"You do everything for me," I said, breaking the moment first, "but I never get to do anything for you, Hillary. Let me do this one thing."

"But if I wanted the shoes that desperately, I could afford them myself."

"But you already said you wouldn't buy them until I could afford mine. Besides, if you bought them for yourself, then I'd be denied the chance to do something for you for once. Don't deny me that."

"Ohh…all *right*. You can buy me the damn shoes."

"Yea!"

What an odd exchange: you'd think I'd talked her into doing something distasteful; you'd think I'd just won something other than the right to spend most of my stake on someone else.

But Hillary, at least, hadn't forgotten about the need for that stake.

"Those shoes really are going to look great on me," she said, "but what about your stake for Atlantic City?"

"Oh—" I pooh-poohed her concerns "—it'll be fine. Don't forget, at Foxwoods I started out with one hundred dollars and came away with five times that much. I'll be going to Atlantic City with twice that stake, so I'll probably turn that two hundred dollars into a thousand before I get home. I still won't be able to afford the Ghost, but I'll be damn close. I'll just make up the rest some other way."

"Gee, your math skills are great, Rumpelstiltskin, but don't you think you're getting a bit ahead of yourself here?"

Apparently, we were back to giving me a hard time again.

"Hmm?" I prompted, not sure I wanted to know.

"I just mean, what makes you think you can keep spinning straw into gold? What makes you so sure you'll go on winning, that you'll never lose?"

"Well, for one thing," I said, feeling huffy, "since I'm taking money and turning it into bigger money, your straw-into-gold analogy sucks because what I'm doing is something more akin to turning a little bit of gold into a lot of gold. And for another thing—"

"Stop." She stopped my madly waving celery stalk with her hand. "I just wanted you to entertain the notion that there's no sure thing about what you're doing. If gambling always equaled winning, everyone would do it. I just wanted you to be aware that you could conceivably lose, that there are always consequences."

"Of course," I said, calm once more, leaving my celery stalk at peace. "I understand that."

But, secretly, inside I was thinking: *No way was I going to lose, not ever. I was Black Jack Sampson's daughter and sole heir, wasn't I?*

True, Black Jack Sampson had lost as many fortunes as he'd won, but it was going to be different for me.

I was *not* going to lose.

# 9

"Of course you're going to lose."

"Gee, thanks, Dad."

I was at my dad's apartment for Monday night dinner, meaning I'd need to leave before *Monday Night Football* started or risk offending him with my lack of knowledge. Just because my dad had trained me to sit through sporting events, it didn't mean I understood them.

"Oh, now, don't get huffy," he said. "Your mother used to do that all the time, too, get huffy."

"Mom never got huffy!"

"Okay, but she had every right to get huffy and I could hear her carefully trying not to be huffy underneath her nonhuffiness which is almost the same thing."

"Huh?"

"Hey, I make sense to me. Don't worry so much if I don't make sense to you. Anyway—" he stirred the pasta in the pot "—all I'm saying is that if you're going to gamble, you have to expect to lose occasionally, too, maybe lose big."

"Whatever."

Ever since I'd moved out, Monday night dinner had been an on-again, off-again tradition with us. When my dad was in a good mood about his prospects for the future because he'd recently won big, it was on. When he lost or was depressed about the future, it was off.

At the time of my mother's death, my dad knew how to cook exactly two things: he could boil water for instant coffee ("instant tastes like liquid dirt, Baby, but what are you gonna do?") and s'mores ("they have all your major food groups").

"Your mother did everything for me," he'd said at the time. "She even ironed my underwear. How will I ever survive without her?"

"For one thing, you'll start wearing unironed underwear like normal people," I'd said. "But you're a grown man. Don't you think it's time you learned how to use the microwave?"

"*Feh,*" he'd said. Whenever Jackie Mason played any of the casinos my dad was working, he'd always take time out to catch the show and some of the Borscht Belt lingo had worn off on him. He'd never pass Conchita and Rivera's test of Portuguese-Spanish, but he could say *gesundheit* or *schmuck* with the best of them. "*Feh.* I hate all that modern-technology *mishegas*. I'll learn how to cook for myself. How hard can it be? Your mother always said if a person could read, a person could cook. I'm pretty sure I can read."

But his earliest efforts gave the lie to that.

"Is pasta supposed to look like that?" he'd asked in dismay, showing me the contents of the pot—it was a cream-colored sodden mess without a complete noodle in sight.

"You bought gluten pasta," I'd said, studying the box. "I think that maybe you weren't supposed to cook it that long?"

"Shit," he'd said. "I didn't know pasta could melt." Then he'd tossed it over the fence of the family home—he'd still lived there right after Mom's death—into Mr. Finnigan's yard.

"Brownie'll eat it," he'd said, referring to Mr. Finnigan's gray-and-white schnauzer. "That mutt'll eat anything."

"I hope that stuff doesn't kill him."

"I should be so lucky."

Then there was the time, that very same first year after Mom's death, when he'd tried to make my birthday cake.

"I wanted it to be so special for you," he'd said.

"I don't think an angel cake is supposed to be charcoal-broiled, Dad."

"I wanted it to be so special for you," he'd said again.

"Maybe we can just scrape some of the black stuff off the outside and dunk the inside into the leftover pink frosting."

And that's exactly what we did.

But as time went on, my dad got better at it.

"I found some of your mother's old recipe cards! I can read! I can cook!"

If not exactly a Julia Child or Emeril Lagasse, he could now do a lot more in a kitchen than I could, which may not be saying a lot but it was enough.

And he knew my habits.

"I've got the lasagna you like as backup!" he said, opening the freezer to reveal my beloved Michael Angelo's Four Cheese. In the past year, he'd even broken down and learned how to use the microwave.

"Are you making one of Mom's recipes or your own version?" I asked.

"Your mom's."

"Then I'll have what you're having."

Despite my devotion to all things frozen, I was always okay with eating the foods I'd grown up with.

What was okay to eat, what wasn't okay to eat—Hillary often said most people saw their lives in terms of choices. But not me. I saw my life in terms of a series of compulsive obsessions that were like touchstones for me—things I *had* to do, foods I *had* to eat in order to stay sane. I didn't want to be like that. How I would have liked to learn how to be one of those people who saw their lives in terms of choices. How I would have liked to be like everyone else.

I set the table and Dad got a bottle of Jake's Fault Shiraz out of the fridge.

"Do I know my girl or do I know my girl?" Dad asked.

"You know your girl," I admitted.

"Good." He sat down, put a real linen napkin in his lap. ("It's important, no matter how Fortune is going," he'd often tell me, "to eat like a man of consequence. And the hotels never even miss the napkins.") "Then you'll understand when I say I know you well enough to know what's going through that head of yours. You've convinced yourself that you can't be beat, that you're somehow smarter than the old man."

"How…" I stopped myself before finishing the thought, which would have sounded something like, *How did you know that?*

"Hey," he said. "Before I was old, I was young once. And I know how you think because it's the way I used to think, 'I'm invincible. No one can touch me.' It's my duty to tell you this because, as Hamlet says, 'I must be cruel, only to be kind.'"

"Yeah, well, 'neither a borrower nor a lender be,' right back at you. But, anyway, I've never thought that about myself, Dad. I've always thought, 'I suck. Just about anyone could destroy me.'"

"Stop swearing. Salad?"

"Are you kidding? There are green things in there."

"Sorry, my mistake. Next time, I'll try to make the salad without vegetables. As I was saying—"

"I know what you're saying," I said. "You're saying I'm like you. But I'm not. I never have been."

"Oh, no? Then how come you're all of a sudden so cocky about gambling? Sure, you made a little money in Foxwoods. Hell, you did great. But that doesn't mean you're ready for the big time."

"I'm not looking for the big time. I'm just looking for a little…more."

"Oh, right, 'more'—I know all about 'more.' 'More' is what everyone wants after getting just a little taste. 'More' is dangerous."

I put my fork down. "Does that mean you're not going to help me any *more?*"

"Who ever said that? I'm just trying to do what a father is supposed to do—protect his little girl from harm. Now clear the plates while I get the cards. I'm going to teach you how to win with the correct strategy."


An hour later, with *Monday Night Football* ready to start any minute, I knew what to do if the dealer dealt me two Eights and was showing a Ten for his own upcard.

"Always split Eights," Black Jack said, "no matter what the dealer is showing."

"What if I pull another Eight?"

"Split 'em again."

"But won't all the other players think I'm crazy?"

"Who cares what the other players think? You're not playing against them. You're playing against the House and you should never care what the House thinks, either. The only thing that matters, is how the cards are running and how you play the hand you're dealt. Split the three Eights. I'm telling you, you can't go wrong."

For practice, he dealt a hand that included four imaginary players, stacking the deck so I wound up with two Eights.

My hand hesitated over the cards.

"Split 'em," Black Jack commanded.

I did what he said, in effect doubling my bet since I now had to match the bet on the second Eight so that the bets were equal.

"Don't look so white," Black Jack said. "Those hundreds you're playing with are just Monopoly money."

Black Jack dealt me my third Eight.

"Split 'em again," he commanded my hesitant fingers.

Great. Now I had three hundred dollars' worth of funny money on the line. Should I be sweating?

Black Jack dealt cards to the imaginary players. Two busted, one stood on a soft Seventeen, one on a hard Sixteen.

The dealer—my dad—turned over his hole card to reveal a Five: Fifteen. Then he dealt himself a Two and had to stand on Seventeen. The other players at the table, even if they were imaginary, had all either busted, lost or pushed with the dealer.

I was the only winner.

My original one-hundred-dollar stake? It was now worth a cool six hundred. Of course, I'd had to nerve-rackingly risk another two hundred to get myself there, but still.

"Does that feel good or what?" Black Jack asked.

"It feels…*great!*" I had to admit. I was still tingling. Then I thought about it too much and I deflated a bit. "But that'd never happen in real life," I said.

"Are you kidding? Stuff like that happens in casinos all the time. Believe me, it'll happen to you. In fact, you can bet on it."

He seemed so sure of himself, but it was impossible for me to believe I'd ever get dealt a classic textbook case like that.

"It's almost time for the kickoff," he said, grabbing the remote control. "I think Jerry Rice might retire this year, but who knows."

"Dad, what you were saying before…"

"Which part?" He was already clicking through the channels.

"About thinking you were invincible when you were younger. Does that mean you no longer believe that? Does that mean you think you can be beat?"

Of course, the evidence that he could be beat was right there in the shabbiness of our surroundings. My dad could be beat, had been beat.

"God, no," he said, clearly offended. Then his expression softened. "If I believed that, ever really believed that, I'd have to quit, wouldn't I?"

I surprised my dad, and myself, by staying through the first half.

"You're still here?" he said, surprised, as the cheerleaders took the field for the half-game show.

"Didn't you notice me exchanging your empty wineglass for a beer sometime around when that guy tried to kick the ball through those post thingies?"

He looked at the beer, now empty, in his hand. "Huh." He got up out of his chair, went to the fridge to get another. "So, what do you think of the game?"

"I think I still don't understand it. Or why anyone would do it. Or why anyone would watch it."

"Just like your mother." He held the bottle of Jake's Fault out. "Another?"

I shook my head. "I still have to drive."

He popped the top on his beer.

"So," he said, "Atlantic City, huh?"

I swung my arms back and forth. "Yup."

"You know, there are only two real meccas for true gamblers—Atlantic City and—" he paused for the kind of respectful moment of silence normally reserved only for those times when he mentioned my mother's passing "—Vegas."

"What about all those casinos that have sprung up on riverboats and tribal land all over the country?"

"Pale imitators. Just looking for a way to bump their economies. They might as well stick to Lotto."

"What about Foxwoods?"

"Bite your tongue."

"But you go there."

"Only because it's in Connecticut. If I had to cross state lines to get there, I wouldn't bother."

I felt curiously miffed on Foxwoods's behalf. It had certainly seemed nice enough to me. They had Billy Charisma there and Furthest Guy. I'd won decent money there.

In defense of casinos everywhere, then, I tried one last time.

"What about *Monte Carlo?*" I asked, rather belligerently, I must admit. "Doesn't *Monte Carlo* rate?"

"Well," he said, getting his own belligerent jones on, "if you want to go all foreign on me…"

"Go…foreign…*what?*"

"It's just that if you have to hop on a plane—"

"But don't you have to hop on a plane for Vegas?"

"—and go to some foreign country where people wear crowns, then you might as well be in a James Bond movie and who wants to be in a James Bond movie?"

"Roger Moore? Sean Connery? Timothy Dalton? Pierce Brosnan? That new guy?"

"You remember Dalton?" He swigged from his beer. "I'm impressed."

"What does this have to do with anything?"

"I guess it's just my way of saying I'm proud of you, Baby. One night at Foxwoods and you're off to Atlantic City. You don't mess around. Next thing you know, you'll be cleaning up in Vegas."

# 10

"All I'm saying," Conchita said, "is that Atlantic City is no Vegas."

"Atlantic City ain't even no Foxwoods," said Rivera.

What? Did everyone in my life have an opinion on the hierarchical ranking of casinos?

"Does this mean you're not coming?" I sort of whined.

It was now Thursday. We were on our way to the first job of the day and all week long, I'd been putting off asking them about the upcoming weekend. Maybe I'd sensed they wouldn't be as enthusiastic as they'd been the first time.

"Look, *chica,*" Rivera said, "Foxwoods was a lot of fun. I'm not saying no different. But spending a whole day on a bus driving to *New Jersey*…"

"What about the limo from last time?" I asked. I'd kind

of envisioned us hitting the boardwalk in style, kind of like the Rat Pack, only with prettier hair. My dad always had stories about Sinatra and Company in Atlantic City.

"Remember when I told you, you don't want to know where I got the limo from?" Conchita asked.

I nodded.

"Well, you still don't and it was a one-off so we can't go there no more."

"What about you?" I turned to Stella.

"Don't look at me," she said. "If it's not good enough for The Girls From Brazil, I'm taking a pass on this one."

"Great." I sulked. "One minute I've got a posse. The next minute I've got *bupkes*."

"You thought we were your posse?" Rivera could barely contain her laughter.

"What about your best friend and, might I add, very pretty roommate, Hillary?" Conchita asked. "Isn't she going?"

"Oh, she's going all right."

"Well, then," Conchita said, "I don't think she'd like to be compared to bupkes."

"Do you even know what *bupkes* is?"

"Stop with the language squabbles," Stella said. "I need to keep my eyes on the road." She turned to me. "If you need a posse so bad, why don't you call Elizabeth Hepburn again?"

"I guess," I muttered. "I'll give her a try on my lunch hour." I'd actually been planning on inviting her, anyway. I'd just been so busy lately with things like practicing blackjack with Black Jack as well as other stuff like, you know, dreaming about Billy Charisma.

I'd also been busy with Sudoku, the nine-by-nine Japanese form of crossword puzzle that uses numbers instead of letters, which was, I might add, ruining my life. Degree of difficulty ranged from "easy" to "fiendish."

I blamed Hillary for this newfound addiction, an addiction that had me working the puzzles at breakfast, in the bathroom, in the van on the way to work; it was even getting in the way of my reading. I blamed Hillary because it was Hillary who had, oh so innocently, opened up her copy of the *New York Post* one day and, oh so innocently, observed, "Oh, look! In addition to the jumble puzzle, they now daily carry these little Japanese number puzzles. It says here that Sudoku is 'the Official Utterly Addictive Number-Placing Puzzle.'"

Hadn't she realized what was inevitable even as she said that? She might as well have found a heroin addict and donated a truckload of syringes and a lifetime supply. Those innocent-looking yet evil numbers were now raising my blood pressure on a daily basis.

"Should that be a one in the center of the third grid or a nine?" I muttered. "Crap, I should probably do this in pencil."

"Put the puzzle away," Stella said. "You can have your little nervous breakdown on your lunch break. It's almost time to go to work."

We pulled up into the driveway of the first job of the day, but I was still in mutter mode.

"It was just so much nicer when we were a group."

So what if we hadn't really hung out as a group—to me it'd felt like we were one.

As Conchita got our equipment out of the back of the van, Rivera stood off to one side, arms folded.

"I just got a bad feeling about this place," she said.

"What are you talking about?" Stella said. "We've never even been here before."

"That's what I mean," Rivera said. "How often do we have to tell you, boss? Read my lips. No. New. Jobs."

"You two are crazy," Stella said. "How do you expect me to make enough money to pay you if we don't take on new customers occasionally? Sure, our base is strong—" there were times when Stella sounded more like a candidate for the presidency of the United States than like the proprietor of Squeaky Qlean "—but if we don't keep adding new constituents, we'll just crumble."

"Maybe." Rivera sulked. "But I don't like this new constituent. I'm telling you, boss, I've got a bad feeling about this one."

Rivera's prophetic bad feeling proved true in record time.

Not five minutes into the job, Mrs. Josephine Cornwall, owner of the McMansion we were doing in Weston, was trailing my every move.

One problem with being the Inside Girl is that all of the wackos follow you around. After all, they're not about to get up on a ladder with wheels to trail the Outside Girls. The Outside Girls typically only had to listen to complaints when the job was done.

"I think you missed a spot on this window," Mrs. Cornwall said.

"Aren't you going to clean out the tracks and the window wells better?" Mrs. Cornwall said. "Stella said you would clean those things."

I went back to the first window and cleaned a spot that wasn't there. I recleaned tracks and window wells that were already as clean as they would ever get.

"I think you missed a spot on this window," Mrs. Cornwall said.

She was talking about the first window again.

"Have you ever tried Clorox for the tracks and window wells?" Mrs. Cornwall said. "Here, let me go get you a bottle of Clorox."

If I used Clorox on every track and window well, I'd wind up with the skin peeling off my fingers, plus I'd die of asphyxiation. But she was the paying customer…

"Here, I brought you a new toothbrush. You can clean out the cracks with that."

While I got busy with the toothbrush, Mrs. Cornwall got busy persecuting the Outside Girls. But, instead of using the ladder on wheels I'd always envisioned—you know, like the kind they have in bookstores and fancy private libraries—she just opened the next window over from me and screeched.

*"I think you missed a spot on the window!"* Mrs. Cornwall screeched at Rivera.

*"I think you missed a spot on the window!"* Mrs. Cornwall screeched at Conchita.

*"I think you missed a spot on the window!"* Mrs. Cornwall screeched at Stella.

It's never a good idea to screech at Stella.

Then Mrs. Cornwall started in on me again.

*"I think you—"*

God, she didn't have to screech; I was standing right there. And, anyway, as I said, it's never a good idea to screech at Stella.

"That's *it!*" Even from the inside, Stella's words were louder than Mrs. Cornwall's as she threw down her squeegee from the extension ladder and started to descend. But by the time Stella was in the front door, she had mastered her temper and her voice was calm as she called up the stairs to me, "C'mon, Delilah, we're moving it out."

I dropped my own squeegee in my bucket, gathered up my paper towels.

"What's going on?" Mrs. Cornwall asked, perplexed.

"We're leaving," I said, passing her on my way out the bedroom door.

"But why?" she asked, following me down the circular grand staircase.

Well, I couldn't very well tell her it was because she was a colossal neurotic bitch, could I?

"I'm not sure," I said, going out through the main door. "You'll have to talk to Stella about that."

At the van, Rivera and Conchita were already packing away the equipment. I tossed my bucket in behind theirs as Stella strapped the extension ladder down on the roof.

"Where are you going?" Mrs. Cornwall wanted to know.

"I'm afraid we have to go now," Stella said and I could tell that suddenly there was no anger left in her at all. "Thank you for the opportunity to do your windows, but we're leaving."

"But how can you leave me like this? You didn't finish the job!"

"You have forty windows on your house, Mrs. Cornwall. It just took us two hours to clean four windows. That's about eight times slower than our usual rate."

"You usually clean at a rate of sixteen windows an hour?" Mrs. Cornwall was stunned. "But what human being can clean that fast?"

Stella nodded at me and I saluted with two fingers proudly. I was, after all, The Golden Squeegee.

"If we continue on like this," Stella explained with the painstaking care Hillary might use when talking to one of her more unstable clients, "it will take my crew two and a half days to complete a job that shouldn't even take a full morning. I'm sorry, but I just can't have that."

"But how can you leave me like this? You didn't finish the job!"

"But you're ahead of where you were when we got here. Just look," Stella said, pointing to the four windows on the top floor. They sparkled like a South African diamond mine magically turned inside out to let in the sun. "You've got four windows that are cleaner than any four windows in the world…and you got them for free!"

"But how can you—?"

At last, Stella just had to drive away, with Mrs. Cornwall still shouting after us from the driveway. I was scared to turn around in my seat, scared I'd see her chasing after us, shouting like that boy at the end of *Shane*.

"Window washers! Come baaack!"

"Some customers are just crazier than others," Conchita said.

"What makes someone get like that?" Rivera said.

"The nice thing about being the boss," Stella said, "is that I can just decide to bag the money if the job isn't worth it."

"It must be great having that kind of authority." I sucked up. "Maybe we could bag—"

"We're not bagging Mr. Johnson as a client," Stella cut me off. How did she know I was going to suggest that? I guess she, like everyone, knew how much I hated doing Mr. Johnson's house. The rest of the crew called him Mr. Clean, but they said it kindly. That's because they never had to be Inside Girl for Mr. Clean.

"I just hope I never get as crazy as Mrs. Cornwall or Mr. Johnson," I said.

"Ha!" Stella laughed. "You already are."

During the unanticipated downtime between the job we had walked out on and the next job, I pushed my Sudoku puzzle aside just long enough to give Elizabeth Hepburn a ring.

"Let me see if she can come to the phone," Lottie said.

I knew from what Elizabeth Hepburn had said previously that Lottie was her housekeeper. She didn't sound as awful as her boss had said, maybe a little bit abrupt. Could she really be rubbing her hands together in anticipation of her boss's death?

"Delilah!" Elizabeth Hepburn said. Despite the enthusiasm of her greeting, her voice sounded weak, thinner than I remembered. "I told Lottie I wasn't in to anyone this week, but that if you called, I'd want to talk to you."

Why wouldn't she be in to anyone but me? I knew she was lonely a lot of the time. Surely, if Lauren Bacall decided to give her a ring…

"I'm calling about the trip to Atlantic City this weekend," I said. "I figured we should coordinate what time—"

"I was just telling Lottie this morning that I was sure you'd call about that today. I knew you wouldn't forget about me."

"Of course not."

"But I'm afraid I've got some bad news."

"Bad news?"

"My heart's been going pitter-patter lately and it's not the good kind of pitter-patter, like I used to get with Danny Kaye. My physician says I should just take it easy for a few days while he monitors the situation."

"That doesn't sound good. Do you want me to come over?" Stella would probably kill me, or at least fire me, if I asked her to drop me off on the way to the next job, but so what? "Can I bring you anything?"

"Oh, no, dear, you're very sweet. But I've got everything I need right here. Lottie takes very good care of me. Well, sort of. There's just one thing I need for you to do for me?"

"What's that?"

"Win this weekend!"

"I can do that!" I tried to match her enthusiasm.

"Oh, and maybe just one other thing."

"Yes."

"Kiss Frank for me."

"Frank?"

"Sinatra. You are going to Atlantic City, aren't you?"

But wasn't Frank…

Then I remembered my promise to her that night in the limo after Foxwoods, my promise to keep her secret, implicit in which was my promise to go along with the game.

"Of course," I said brightly. "As soon as I see Ol' Blue Eyes, I'll pucker right up."

# 11

The bus to Atlantic City was like, well, a bus to Atlantic City.

"Don't scuff the Choos on the metal steps!" Hillary admonished as she boarded behind me. Great. Most people had a backseat driver. Me, I had a backseat boarder. Her admonition, the third of its kind in as many minutes, made me regret her largesse.

Earlier in the week, after I'd given her the money for the Momo Flats, she'd immediately phoned the Manhattan store, ordered the shoes and had them express mailed. When the package had arrived, I'd thought she'd want to try them on right away (that's what I would have done) and that she would have then modeled them for me with pride right away (that's what I would have done). But, being the annoyingly atypical human being she could sometimes be, instead she'd merely snatched the package from the UPS man and scurried off with it to her room, slamming the door behind her. What was she going to do in there all alone with them, some kind of satanic rite?

"Aren't you going to model them for me?" I'd asked.

"No."

"Did you try them on yet?" I'd asked. I'd been dying to know, if only vicariously, what it felt like to walk in one's very own Jimmy Choos.

"No."

"But aren't you going to—"

"No! I'm saving them for our trip to Atlantic City on Saturday. It's bad luck to try new shoes on before the special occasion you plan to wear them for."

"Huh?" This was a new superstition on me.

"Oh, just eat your lasagna and go do your Sudoku."

But then Saturday came and Hillary brought the box of Choos right into the kitchen, trying them on with no more ceremony than if they were from Payless.

"Huh," she said, after trying to force her foot into Choos that were clearly too small for her feet. She picked up the box, studied the label. "The store sent me the wrong size."

"This is the first time you've even looked at them?" I was shocked. The woman had nerves of steel.

"I thought I already told you, it's bad luck—"

"I know what you said about trying them on. But

you didn't even *look* at them? What kind of insane person are you?"

"I'm the kind of insane person that makes you lucky I'm insane, that's the kind of insane person I am. Look." She held the box out to me, pointed to the label. "It says size six. *You're* a size six. They sent me *your* size by mistake."

It was true. Everyone knew that about us. I was a six; Hillary was a nine. Even with a crowbar, she'd never get her feet into those Choos, not without ripping the seams.

"But that's awful!" I said. Then I sighed. "Oh, well. I guess there's nothing for it. You'll just have to exchange them. Still, you'd think a store as expensive as that wouldn't dyslexically mistake a six for a—"

"I can't do that," she said hurriedly.

"Why ever not?"

"Because it's bad luck to exchange shoes once you've had them express mailed."

*"Huh?"*

"So I guess you'll just have to wear them today instead."

Suddenly, I smelled something, and it was dirty feet.

"You did it on purpose!" I said.

"What?" Her eyes were all innocence, so innocent it set me thinking her eyes doth protest too much.

"You deliberately ordered the Choos in the wrong size!" Then my own eyes filled with tears. "This is all just so… so…so…so *Gift of the Magi!*"

"What are you talking about? This is not a thing like *The Gift of the Magi*."

"Yes, it is! I give you the money I won at Foxwoods, you use it to buy Choos that could never fit you so I could have them instead. It's exactly like *The Gift*—"

"Delilah?"

"Huh?" I spoke through my tears.

"Just take the damn Choos. Wear them in good health."

But now as we settled into our seats on the bus and she extolled, "Don't scuff the Choos on the metal footrest!" I wished she hadn't been quite so generous with my gift.

She'd taken the window seat, claiming she got carsick on buses. I'd have tried the same ruse, but she beat me to it.

"You'd think," she said, "that since you're the one wearing the Choos, you'd have thought to dress in a more present-able fashion."

"What's wrong with how I'm dressed?"

She looked at my old jeans, my pink-and-green striped oxford shirt with the sleeves rolled up.

"Everything?" she suggested. "I just think if you're going to wear the Choos—"

"Do you want them back?" I asked. "After all, your own outfit—" she was wearing a blue-green sleeveless linen dress that was a perfect match for the Choos in question "—more befits their…*grandness.*"

There was a part of me that couldn't believe we were talking this way about a pair of shoes, even if they were Choos.

"Oh, no. No, no, no," she demurred. "They're yours to keep, my gift to you."

Some gift. I mean, I did pay for them.

As the bus driver pulled onto the highway, Hillary extracted a book from her matching blue-green mesh carryall bag.

"What's that?" I asked.

"A guide to Atlantic City. Hmm…" She wet the tip of one manicured finger with her tongue, turned the page. "Now, let's see here… It says the first boardwalk opened on June 26, 1870, and was one mile long. Did you know it was designed by Jacob Keim and Alexander Boardman to keep the sand out of the tourist shoes? Did you know today the boardwalk extends just over four miles long?" She pondered. "Do you think it's possible that board*walk* was named for Board*man?*"

I leaned closer, tapped her on the shoulder.

"Hillary?"

"Hmm?"

"I don't want a history lesson," I whispered in her ear before practically screeching, *"I'm just going there to gamble!"*

"So-*rry.*" In a huff, she reached into her carryall—how much stuff did she have crammed in that thing?—and extracted her iPod, covered her ears with it and proceeded to ignore me. Hillary was nothing if not technologically advanced, having at least one each of everything Apple or any of those other places ever produced. Me, I was a confirmed tech-not and when she'd asked me how I could live without my own iPod I'd merely replied, "By the time I can figure out how to program it, it will be rendered obsolete by some new and improved gadget. Besides, I'd probably strangle myself on the wires."

But as I sat there beside her, the sound of the bus's exhaust and the overflow of whatever she was listening to were the only things disturbing my silent solitude—it was maddening not being able to figure out what song she was hearing clearly—I decided to switch seats. Despite her music and the no-doubt gripping guide to Atlantic City before her, she had fallen asleep and was snoring. Hillary could be a loud snorer.

Toward the back of the bus, I found a pair of unclaimed seats on the other side of the aisle and slid in beside the window. At least I had a view now. Watching the green road signs and trees zip past me, I thought about *Funny Girl*.

Okay, maybe that was an odd thing to be thinking about, but I'd been thinking about my parents' relationship a lot lately and thinking about them as a couple always made me think about the 1968 movie starring Barbra Streisand as Fanny Brice and Omar Sharif as Nick "Nicky" Arnstein. The movie, about a talented girl with a big schnoz who talks her way into the Ziegfield Follies only to wind up falling head over tap shoes for a suave gambler, had long been a favorite of my family's, at least of my mom and me; Dad had hated it. He said the character of Nick Arnstein was a "complete Hollywood fabrication" and that "no real-life gamblers would ever behave that way," even though Nick Arnstein had in fact been a real-life gambler. So we could only watch it when he was out of the house, huddled together under a comforter on the couch, popcorn and cocoa at the ready as Streisand sang big number after big number.

"But why does she have to leave him in the end?" I'd always sob.

"Because he's a gambler and a criminal," she'd say, arm around my shoulders.

"But he's her man! She loves him so!" I'd memorized the lines from all of Streisand's songs from the show so I knew this just as much as I knew that people needed people, that they were the luckiest people in the world, and no one was ever going to rain on my damn parade.

"I know, dear, but he's still a gambler and a criminal."

I'd look up at her, tears staining my cheeks. "Would you ever leave Dad like that?"

"Of course not." She'd always seemed offended that I'd even suggested such a thing. "Your dad's not a criminal."

I'd had my doubts. If Fanny could leave Nicky, what else could go wrong in the world? But as the years went on and my mother never left, we watched the movie less and less often and my obsessive nature turned to other things. Still…

*"Nicky Arnstein, Nicky Arnstein,"* I whispered-sang, face pressed against the window of the moving bus, just as Fanny Brice had done at the stage door after meeting him for the first time, except she hadn't been on a bus. What can I say? I was alone on a bus and the romantic allure of those old Streisand songs never paled. *"Nicky—"*

"Heh. Another one."

"Excuse me?" I looked up to see an elderly man with brown polyester slacks practically belted up to his chest and thick glasses making his eyes look magnified to a frightening degree.

"There's always one on every bus," he said, "young chicks obsessed with Nicky Arnstein. Is this seat taken?"

Before I could answer, he was sitting next to me.

"My wife kicked me out," he said.

"Oh, I'm so sorry," I said automatically. What else do you say to a total stranger's problems? Do you ask if maybe his wife kicked him out because he calls women *chicks?* I tried again. "Have you two been together very long?"

"For about three hours and a half."

"Oh. Well. That's not very long." How devastated could he be? He certainly didn't look devastated.

"Since we got up this morning." He must have seen my stunned look, because he added, "What? You thought she kicked me out of the marriage?"

"Well…"

"What a crazy assumption! Betty would never do that. She just kicked me out of my seat."

"Oh."

He craned his neck over the seat in front of us, searching. "Oh, look," he said, "I think Betty's getting jealous."

I craned my own neck and saw, several rows forward, a blue-haired lady with glasses on a chain around her neck glaring at me. Shit. I didn't want to get in bad with Betty. Still, if she kicked him out…

"What did she kick you out for?" I asked, settling back into my seat.

"A book."

"A book?"

"What are you, an echo? A book!"

"Must have been some book." What was he reading while sitting next to Betty—porn?

Thinking I should get away from this pervert, I craned my neck again, this time in search of Hillary to see if she was still snoring. But when I found the back of her blond head, I saw it bobbing in enthusiastic conversation and after briefly thinking that must be some great song she was listening to, further realized that she wasn't talking to herself, either. Some other blond had snagged my seat.

"Stop worrying about Betty," my companion said, tugging me back into my seat. "She doesn't even carry a gun in her bag anymore."

Gun?

"Here's the book." He pulled out a skinny paperback.

"'*Blackjack Winning Basics,*'" I read the title, "by Tony Casino. Betty kicked you out for reading *Blackjack Winning Basics* while on a bus trip to Atlantic City? What did she think you two were going to do there, get sand in your tourist shoes?"

He studied me. "You're kind of an odd chick, aren't you?" Not waiting for my answer, he adjusted his glasses and opened the book. Assuming he was going to mind his own business from now on, either because he thought I was so odd or because it was what any normal seatmate might do, I went back to gazing out the window, only to have my reverie intruded upon by…

"In the *event* that the *dealer's* upcard is *a* Two—"

"What are you doing?" I asked.

"I'm reading my book."

"But aren't you going to read it to yourself?"

"I have to read aloud. It's the only way I can concentrate." He went back to his book. "If the *player* has a *soft* Eighteen, meaning *an* Ace and *a* Seven—"

"But why are you reading it aloud like that?"

"Like what?"

"You hit *every* third word *with* emphasis. It's…*annoying.*"

"Now you know why Betty kicked me out." He shut the book. "She says it makes her crazy, but it's the only way I can read. If I told you that in the first place, you probably never would have believed me."

"Do you and Betty, uh, go to Atlantic City often?" I was back to making small talk again, anything to avoid having him read out loud anymore, since Betty was right: it *was* annoying.

"Since retiring, only every weekend," he said.

"And she kicks you out every weekend?"

"Pretty much. But at least she doesn't carry a gun anymore. The time I lost the thirty thousand dollars, she nearly shot me."

"You lost thirty thousand dollars?"

"Did you hear me say she nearly shot me?"

Of course I heard it. Hey, I'd have nearly shot him, too. Of course, back in the day, Black Jack Sampson had probably lost that much on a single jaunt. Maybe. Possibly. I'd never really given it much thought, until now, how much my dad might have lost in a single go, how much my mother put up with.

"Betty pulled her gun on me and I was sure I was a goner when she cocked the trigger."

"So what did you do? How did you get out of it?"

"I pointed out the obvious. I said, 'Betty, I *won* thirty thousand *dollars* the week *before!*'"

"You mean you won thirty thousand dollars one week and then turned around and lost it the week after?"

"Pretty much."

It was a lot to digest. I couldn't imagine winning that much, losing that much. If it were me, I'd have used the money for a round-the-world cruise or the down payment on a house. Of course, then Hillary would have to help me out with the mortgage.

"You're a professional gambler," I said finally.

"Pretty much."

"But then what are you doing reading *Blackjack Winning Basics?*"

"Didn't you see? It's written by Tony Casino. And even an expert like me needs to bone up now and then."

When I debarked, Hillary was waiting for me, a handsome man at her side. He was well over six feet tall, his Adonis hair curling over the collar of his shirt. If Hillary's life were a romance novel, he'd be on the cover and her bodice would be ripped.

"This is Biff Williams," she said, introducing us.

*Biff?*

"After you deserted me," Hillary said, "he asked if he could sit with me."

"We have a lot in common," Biff said, looking at her with more fondness than a mere hour of knowing a person should bestow. Then he offered her his arm. As casual as if she did it every day, Hillary took it.

"We both work in jobs where we have patients," Hillary said. God, could she simper any more?

"We both want to see Scotland someday," Biff said. What was with all this "we" crap all of a sudden?

"We both have Warren Zevon on our iPods," Hillary said.

"But we'd never plug in while talking to each other," Biff said. "Oh, and neither of us likes to gamble."

"We sure don't," Hillary said.

"We don't?" I said, stunned. "Then what are *we* doing here?"

"I just like bus trips," Biff said.

"Me, too," said Hillary.

"We thought we'd just stroll along the boardwalk," Biff said, "enjoy the sights, grab some lunch together."

"We thought we'd go to Ripley's Believe It or Not! Museum," Hillary said.

"We thought we'd go to the Absecon Lighthouse," Biff

said. Apparently, since they weren't listening to their iPods together, *we'd* been reading the same guidebook.

"We thought we'd go to the New Jersey Korean War Memorial," Hillary said.

"Definitely," Biff said.

"Grab some dinner together, too," Hillary said. "We'll meet you back here at the bus when it's time to go."

As I watched them walk off, they looked so good together, so *right*. Damn! Where was Betty and her gun?

Hillary had hit the jackpot. Without even having a pair of Jimmy Choos on her feet, she'd hit the jackpot.

# 12

When Hillary had previously expressed concern that the cost of the bus trip would eat into my two-hundred-dollar Atlantic City stake— "Really, Delilah, I could just drive us," she'd said. To which I now thought, "Ha! And miss the chance to meet Mr. Wonderful Biff?" —I'd told her what my dad always said, that places like Foxwoods and Atlantic City and Vegas *paid* you to gamble. Even as I'd said it, I doubted the veracity. How could that be? But as I took my first stroll along the boardwalk—not all four miles of it, but enough—my pockets fat with the complimentary coin rolls and food chits the bus driver had handed out on behalf of the casinos, I realized that once again Black Jack was right.

A part of me felt as though my gal pal had ditched me. What did Mr. Wonderful Biff have that I didn't have? Oh, yeah, right: muscles, a good-paying job, a penis. Plus, he wasn't neurotically obsessed with the acquisition of expensive shoes. But then a part of me recognized my ditched feeling for what it was. I was jealous, jealous that someone else was with Hillary, jealous that Hillary had someone else to share the glorious day with.

The day was indeed one of those gorgeous ones that lately had become typical of September, with a clear sky, temperatures in the low eighties and zero humidity, boats speckling the seascape of the ocean the city was named for, a strong sun shining overhead. In fact, it was too gorgeous a day to spend holed up in some smoky casino. I mean, I already had a pair of Jimmy Choos; Hillary had given me the ones I'd bought her. So what if they were the Momo Flats and not the Ghost, they were still Jimmy Choos. Hadn't that been my original goal? There was just one problem. How could a girl, a girl like me who had never been known to eat just one potato chip or confine myself to just one anything, ever stop at just one pair? Still, I tried to resist the pull of temptation. Maybe I should do something else with my hours there? Maybe I should visit one of the video arcades? Maybe I should visit one of the XXX girlie shows? Maybe I should get my cards read, my palm read, my fortune told? Maybe I should *pawn* something?

Oh, hell.

I ducked into the very next casino.

But as I made my way through Caesars Palace, I found it too intimidating—all those Roman columns, all those togas—and I ran right back out again. It was just too formally and obviously a gambling place, when compared with the relative casualness of Foxwoods, and I just wasn't ready for it. Besides, my dad had advised against jumping into the first casino and sitting down at the first table I came across. I wasn't supposed to jump at all. I was supposed to *feel* my way into it.

So I jumped into the curiously shaped Borgata, its two thousand-plus rooms making it way too big, and back out again. I jumped into the Sands, its puny five hundred rooms making it way too small. Then I jumped into the Showboat Casino Hotel and actually stayed for more than a minute. With its faux riverboat facade, it was just right, the whole instantly making me sad about New Orleans and glad about the Young Elvis. I was sure that when night came, with its red-painted exterior all trimmed with lights, the place would look just like somewhere on the Mississippi that Mark Twain might hang out in.

This would be the perfect place for me to gamble, a place that felt somehow both racy and literary at the same time. I could probably spend the whole day there. I'd just walk my way through the lobby, make my way toward the casino…

"Has your eye recovered yet?" a vaguely familiar voice asked as I felt a gentle hand rest on my arm.

I spun around to see Furthest Guy. Gosh, he was cute.

"Furthest Guy!" I blurted without thinking.

"Huh?"

"Oops, sorry, I mean Chris. Your name is Chris, right?"

"How did you know?"

"Um, your sign. When you were appearing at Foxwoods? You had a sandwich-board sign set up on an easel there."

But he didn't seem concerned with that anymore.

"I've been worrying about you ever since that night," Chris said. "You took quite a shot in the eye with that yo-yo, but then you disappeared so quickly afterward."

"See?" I said, tilting my face so he could see my profile. "It's fine now. By the next day, there was hardly any mark there at all."

"I was still worried," he said. "I've had a few accidents while performing before, but I've never actually injured a spectator."

"Well, there's always a first time for everything," I said brightly, tritely, regretting the words just as soon as I'd foolishly uttered them. "Hey, what are you doing here?" I thought to change the subject. "Are you in town to do some gambling?"

"I'm working," he said, holding up his other hand, the one that hadn't been on my arm. In it, resting there innocently as if it would never slam some unsuspecting spectator in the eye, was a yo-yo at peace. "I'll be performing here in a little while."

"Wow, that's so cool!" I said. "I can't believe you play with yo-yos for a living! I mean, I know I saw you doing it at Foxwoods, but I figured it was just a hobby or a little side thing."

I didn't mean to sound condescending, I swear, I'd just

never met a professional yo-yoist before. Still, I could see where my words could give offense. But if he saw it that way, he didn't let on, although he did look dismayed.

"I guess what I said was misleading," he said, "when I said I was working here. I actually have a different day job."

I couldn't stop myself from thinking that was a good thing because the way he had trouble controlling his yo-yos, cool as it might be to become friends with a professional yo-yoist, I was tempted to counsel him not to quit his day job.

"I'm on my vacation right now."

He played casinos on his vacation?

"I started my vacation last weekend with that performance at Foxwoods. I've played a different place every night since then."

"All casinos?" I asked.

"Oh, no. I've done a few conventions, too. The Shriners thought I was great. Or at least they did until I walked the dog right into some guy's lap."

"I thought you said you'd never hit a spectator before?"

"I haven't. Didn't you just hear me say the dog walked?"

"Ah."

"Anyway, the Showboat is my last gig for this trip. But, hey, I've been practicing that move I hit you with the other day. Want to see it?"

"Um, no, thanks. I don't want to get hit again."

"I didn't mean I've been practicing hitting people. I meant I've been practicing how to do the trick *without* losing control, *without* hitting anybody."

Before I could stop him, he'd taken several steps away from me. Somehow, instinctively, the passing crowd knew to grant him a wide berth as he began to spin his yo-yos.

He was poetry in motion. The yo-yos twirled and zinged away from him at his command and, when he wanted them to, they came back home.

I wasn't the only one who clapped, but I'm sure I was, no doubt, the only one who jumped up and down like a cheerleader on methamphetamines when she did so.

"Omigod, Chris! That was wonderful!"

Only the fact that I didn't really know him prevented me from throwing my arms around his neck in a solidarity hug.

"Thanks." He blushed a bit. "Like I said, I've been practicing."

"How much do you practice?"

"When I'm not working my day job? Eight hours a day."

"Eight…?"

God, talk about your obsessions.

"And when you are working your day job?"

"Six, still sometimes eight."

"Wow." I was impressed, although it was hard to say with what, either his sheer determination or his sheer folly.

"Ever since that night at Foxwoods, I've been working nearly every minute on that move. I just never wanted to hit anyone in the eye like I hit you again."

"That's, um, very conscientious of you. But don't you ever take breaks?"

"Oh, I'll take more breaks, once I master all the moves.

But see this." He demonstrated some kind of move. I had no idea what I was supposed to be seeing, all I knew was that the string somehow got wound up all around his forearm and that whatever I was supposed to be seeing, it sure as hell wasn't that.

"I'll get the hang of it one day," he said.

"Has your eye recovered yet?" a vaguely familiar voice asked as I felt a gentle hand rest on my arm.

Chris had spoken the exact same words just a short time ago, but his lips weren't moving, so unless he was a better ventriloquist than he was a yo-yoist, that wasn't him talking. Besides, the voice was all wrong. This time, the voice came from The Voice.

"Billy! What are you doing here?"

Even though it was still just late morning, he had on a tuxedo. I guess some people take their gambling very seriously.

I wouldn't have thought Billy Charisma capable of blushing, but blush he did.

"I overheard you and your friends last week," he said to me. "Outside in the parking lot at Foxwoods. I know I shouldn't have been eavesdropping, but I couldn't help but hear you say you were coming here."

"But I never said I was coming to the Showboat. I merely said I was coming to Atlantic City."

"I know," he said, "which is why I've spent all morning going into every hotel on the boardwalk in the hopes of finding you."

"Into every…? But isn't that a little excessive?" The word *stalkerish* came to mind, but *excessive* would have to do.

"I had to find you again," he said. "I haven't had a night like we shared in Foxwoods in such a long time, but I didn't know how else to find you and I just had to."

It still sounded excessive, but it also sounded kind of nice. I guessed he was right. That time we'd spent together had been pretty special.

"Ahem." Chris cleared his throat.

"Ahem." Chris cleared his throat again.

"Oh," Billy said, "you again." Then he insinuated his body so that he was standing between us, with his back to Chris. He put his hands on my shoulders. "You're such good luck for me, Baby. Come on." He took my hand, pulled me toward the entrance, now the exit. "Come with me to Caesars Palace."

"Aren't you going to stick around and see me perform?" I heard Chris shout after us.

"Sorry, pal," Billy answered for me. I'd never been with a man who answered for me before and it felt oddly exhilarating. "She's with me."

Still…

"You never said what your day job is," I shouted over my shoulder.

"You never said what your name is," Chris shouted back.

"It's Delilah," I shouted, "Delilah Sampson."

"That's a beautiful name," Chris shouted.

And then I was out the door, into the sunlight, on the boardwalk and on my way to Caesars Palace.

★ ★ ★

"Stop! Stop! Stop!"

I tried to get Billy to stop pulling me.

We'd just entered Caesars and were rapidly moving through the Temple Lobby, a dramatic four-story atrium designed in the likeness of the Forum of ancient Rome, and I realized that if I didn't get Billy to stop pulling on my arm right then, he'd pull me right into the casino part of the resort. Of course, being in a casino had been the whole point of my trip, but it wasn't supposed to go down like this.

On my third "Stop!" he turned around.

"Is something the matter?" he asked.

"A lot!" I said, trying to catch my breath. He hadn't been running, only walking at a brisk pace, but his legs were about a foot longer than mine and I'd had to scamper like a puppy to keep up.

Once upon a time, I'd been a runner, an obsessive runner sometimes going for two hours at a shot, but Hillary had put a stop to that by doing an intervention when I dropped down to eighty-seven pounds. In the dressing room of a petite store, where the salesgirl had told me I could get size double or triple 0 in the city since the size 0 jeans I had on were sliding off my hips, Hillary had used a three-way mirror to show me that it was possible to visibly count the vertebra in my spine. Even I conceded it was gross and then Hillary put me on notice. "Like countries that aren't allowed to have a standing army once they've done something too destructive, you can never run again."

"I'm pretty sure," I'd pointed out, "that all those countries are allowed to have standing armies again. And, anyway, what exactly would a non-standing army be?"

"I don't care," she'd said, "you're cut off." And I'd listened.

I'd listened so well that after my brief sprint behind Billy down the boardwalk, I was still out of breath.

"Are you asthmatic?" he asked, concerned.

"No," I gasped.

"Do you get any regular exercise, then?"

"I'm not allowed," I gasped. "I've been cut off."

The thought occurred to me that Hillary would probably kill me if she knew I'd been running in the Momo Flats.

"Well," he said, "why don't you just catch your breath and tell me what seems to be the matter?"

"It's just that I don't even *know* you," I said, suddenly finding plenty of breath with which to rant at him. "I share a gaming table with you at Foxwoods, you call me your talisman—"

"You are my talisman, Baby."

"—then you show up here out of the blue, tell me you've been looking for me all over the boardwalk, you drag me away from a nice conversation I was having with Furthest Guy—"

His eyebrows shot up. "Furthest Guy?"

"—then you pull me like…like…like…like some kind of *pull toy* all the way over here—"

"I did not pull you like some kind of pull toy. I pulled you like a woman I want to spend time with."

"—and now you're going to pull me straight into the casino without any kind of conversation first—"

"Is that what this is all about? Not enough foreplay?"

"It's just that I don't even *know* you," I said, at last deflated.

"Easiest problem in the world to fix," he said, smiling as he took my hand. "Why didn't you say something earlier?"

*Because I never got the chance* was the thought that sprang readily to mind, a thought I didn't have the courage to voice.

I'd never had much courage around men; never had much courage around anyone, really, but particularly not around men. As previously documented, at the age of twenty-eight I'd had only two serious boyfriends in my life, both of those in college. I even had to go to my senior prom with my best girlfriend from high school. Of the two, Julian Preston, whom Hillary now referred to as "The Rat," was the one I'd come closest to marrying, a paralegal who broke up with me on the one-year anniversary of our engagement in order to become engaged to the woman he'd been cheating on me with for the previous six months. The other, Bart James, Hillary called "The Weasel," because he broke up with me six months into the relationship, claiming to be in love on the one hand while telling me on the other that he just couldn't keep seeing a girl his best friend couldn't stand. Sure, since The Rat and The Weasel, I'd been on the odd date— and, believe me, they were all odd—and had the occasional one-night stand (also odd), but guys and I had just somehow never worked together in a romantic way. I'd long since faced the fact that I was an awkward person, doomed to go on having awkward relationships in those few relationships I had.

Do I sound pathetic here? Of course I do. Do I sound like a loser? Of course I do. But I can't be the only woman in the world who knows what it's like to be incredibly unlucky in love, even if my lack of luck might seem deserved to some. Would I have given almost anything to be different, to be a winner for once? You have no idea. But nature had conspired with nurture to make me who I was. If I was ever going to change, it was not going to happen right that second—much as I may have wanted to.

"You're just such a whirlwind," I said now.

"Well," he said, smiling gently, "I hope that at least I am more whirl than wind."

"The jury's still out," I said, proving the point about my own social awkwardness. I always said the wrong things.

"I know what we should do then," he said. *"Lunch!"*

He said it like he was calling an entire barracks to the mess tent, to which I replied, "Um, okay."

He put his finger to his chin, tapped. "But where to go? Where would be the perfect place to take you? Hmm…"

Then he proceeded to reel off all the eating options at Caesars. "I'd love to take you to Bacchanal, where you can relive the mythical experience named for the god of wine and revelry while indulging your palate and your imagination." He sighed. "But, alas, it's not open until dinnertime. Nero's Grill is great for steak and lobster, but, again, not open until evening. Primavera? We could enjoy the spring of old Italy with hand-painted murals of Venice accenting our warm and inviting dining experience. Service is formal. But, alas—"

"Don't tell me. Dinner only."

"Alas, you are right. La Piazza? Too buffet-ish. Café Roma? The ocean view is nice, but too many people go there. Gladiator Pizzeria? I like the four big-screen TVs from which you can keep an eye on the sports action, but I've never liked it that they put *pizzeria* right in the name— too common."

"Um, you sure know a lot about every restaurant in here." A part of me was beginning to think that, in his own way, Billy Charisma was just as weird as I was. Come to that, so was Chris Westacott, aka Furthest Guy. Maybe everyone in the world was weird and it was simply that some of us were more noticeable than others.

"Well, I have been here before, maybe once or twice. I know!" He snapped his fingers. "I'll take you to the Venice Bar. It'll be perfect!"

I wasn't sure that having *bar* in the title made a restaurant necessarily classier than one with *pizzeria* in the title, but I was hungry and I was game.

"Okay."

He led me up to the third floor, above the Appian Way Shopping Promenade and I was feeling very Venetian already. Maybe if I won enough at the tables later, I'd get my Jimmy Choos right here. After all, these big casinos always had plenty of ways for winners to spend their winnings, so they probably had all the most expensive shoes for sale, too, right?

"This is…*nice,*" I said, once we'd been seated in the

Venice Bar. And it was nice enough, if nowhere close to spectacular.

The waitress took our drink orders, club soda with a lime twist for him. "I never drink when I'm about to gamble," he said.

"Do you by any chance have Diet Pepsi Lime?" I asked impulsively. I was feeling the need for the comfort of familiarity, plus Billy asking for his twist had put me in mind of limes.

She gave me a strange look. "I can have the bartender squeeze a lime into a glass of diet cola. Would that do?"

"It's worth a shot," I said with a smile.

As she departed, she gave us menus and I glanced over the selections: hot and cold sandwiches, cold seafood appetizers, pizza any way you wanted it.

"Wow," I said. "You can get mostly pizza in the bar that's advantage is that it doesn't have *pizzeria* in the title."

"Are you disappointed?" he quickly asked.

"No, no. I like pizza." As I took a sip from the diet cola with lime squeezed in that the waitress had just set down— not bad—I thought it would be just perfect if they had an Amy's Cheese Pizza Pocket. But what were the odds?

"I'll have the spinach, radicchio and fresh goat cheese pizza," Billy said, surrendering his menu.

"And for you?" the waitress turned to me.

I really wanted to order something equally adventurous so I could impress the impressive man I was sitting with, but old habits die harder than Bruce Willis.

"You don't by any chance have...?"

"What? I'm sure the chef would be glad to accommodate any—" and here she glanced pointedly at my drink "—peculiar dietary needs."

But there was no way I was going to finish out my original sentence, which would have insanely run, "You don't by any chance have any Amy's Cheese Pizza Pockets back in that kitchen, do you?"

I took it as a sign of hope for me that I recognized how ridiculous that would be. So instead, I said, "I'll just have a cheese pizza."

The waitress looked surprised. "You don't want anything special on it? No lime?"

"No, that's okay," I said, "but could you roll it so it looks like a pocket?"

"You mean like a calzone?"

"No, I mean like a pocket, but that's okay."

"You know exactly what you want," Billy said as soon as she'd departed.

"In food, anyway." I shrugged.

"How about in men?"

"How about you tell me a little bit about yourself?" I asked, hoping to avoid his question. I mean, all the guys I'd ever slept with, dated or nearly married could only be referred to as *guys*. Certainly there was nothing about them that would make a person refer to them as something as mature-sounding as *men*. "Where do you live? Where did you grow up? Do you have any brothers and sisters? Pets?

Do you work for someone else or yourself? What kind of work do you do? Do you always wear a tux?"

He laughed out loud.

"I live in a comfortable cottage on a much larger estate in Westchester County."

Hey, that wasn't far from me! But a "cottage on a much larger estate"—maybe he was the handyman?

"I was born in Connecticut and my father was American but my mother was British so when they divorced when I was five, I went back there to live with her."

I thought I'd noticed a slight stiltedness of speech. There was no British accent so much as a formality of cadence I'd had trouble placing. Now it made sense. Maybe he was the British handyman?

"I am an only child, although I did have an imaginary friend named Freddy the Crumpet growing up, and while I like animals well enough, I'm allergic to all sorts of pet hair, and anyway I'm away from home too much to take proper care of one."

A very busy handyman?

"I work for myself, at my own risk and for my own reward. You could say I do odd jobs."

"You're a handyman?"

"Of sorts. Oh, and I only wear a tux when I'm working."

"You're a handyman in a tux?"

"No, Baby, I'm a professional gambler. Oh, look! Our food is here and the Steelers just scored a touchdown!"

"Steelers?"

I swiveled in my seat to see what he was gazing at with so much fondness just over my shoulder, because it sure wasn't the pizza. That's when I saw for the first time one of two large-screen TVs in the room. On the screen, grown men with giant shoulder pads on were doing little happy dances in the end zone and I could have sworn that one grabbed his crotch à la Michael Jackson and Madonna for the sheer joy of the moment. I guessed that, like with the Gladiator Pizzeria, the Venice Bar was set up to be conducive to those who wanted to keep a close eye on their sports bets.

"Did you pick this place," I asked, trying to keep my tone light and teasing, despite the doubt creeping in, "so you could keep a close eye on your bet?"

"You really are the best good-luck piece I've ever stumbled across, Baby," he said, ignoring my question as he picked up a slice of pizza. "I haven't beat the spread on a football game in I can't tell you how long, but I have the strong feeling that today all that will change." He put the pizza back down, covered my hand with his, caressed my fingers. "I'm so glad you're here with me."

And, in the moment, it was enough.

"Now, eat up," he said. "We've got a whole fun day to spend together."

The "whole fun day" turned out to entail gambling, gambling and more gambling. But that was okay. It was what I had come there to do and once we were at the blackjack table, I was as comfortable as white on rice, green on a dollar bill, a bear in the woods.

Through it all, Billy stayed at my side, sitting just to my left at the tables. It went against my dad's advice to yield the anchor chair, but we were such a winning combination when configured this way. Why tamper with success?

After just an hour of play, I'd doubled my original stake and was at four hundred dollars. Billy, betting with a lot more money, had turned five hundred dollars into a thousand.

"You're good at this," he said, as the dealers changed shifts.

"So are you." I was thinking if he played like this every day, I could see why he was a professional. I said as much.

"Ah, but it's not like this every day," he said. "It's only like this today because you're here."

After two hours, my four hundred dollars, moving at a slower rate, had turned into six, while Billy was up to two thousand.

"You might consider doing this for a living," Billy suggested.

"No, thanks," I said. "I'm just doing this with a specific goal in mind. When I make enough for what I want, I'll stop."

"What is it you want?"

But I couldn't tell him. For while I had no problem sharing my goal with Hillary or Stella or Conchita and Rivera or Elizabeth Hepburn, I was certain no man could ever appreciate such a goal. He'd probably think I was the most frivolous person who ever lived. I mean, it wasn't like my one specific goal was to do something important that would somehow better the world; it was just about a material thing I wanted for myself. And, anyway, I was only half telling the truth when I said I was just doing this with a specific goal in mind. Now that I was doing it, I found the goal itself growing dimmer and dimmer, obscured by the exhilaration I felt as the dealer dealt the cards, as I saw an Ace come up in front of me followed by a Queen or when I beat the House with a soft Fifteen and the dealer busted, forced to draw a picture card to a hard Thirteen.

On that last hand, when I'd placed my palm over my cards to indicate I was standing on what I had, Billy leaned over and anxiously asked, "Are you sure?" He himself was showing a Fourteen and I knew what he was thinking: if we both passed and then the dealer drew anything from a Three to an Eight, he'd beat us both.

But I stood firm.

"I'm sure," I said, after which, tentatively, Billy placed his own palm over his cards. He was standing with me.

And then the dealer busted.

Billy threw his arms around me. "That's it!" he said into my hair. "I'm never going to another casino without you!"

That last—the hand and Billy's reaction—made me feel so exhilarated, I wanted to stay right where I was forever. Who cared if there was a beautiful day going on outside? Who cared if the sun was still shining and you could taste the salt from the sea on your tongue, it was that close? Who cared if day was turning into night?

I was playing, I was winning, I was having the time of my life.

The dealers changed shift again and Billy asked me if I wanted to change tables. I knew what he was thinking: we'd been very lucky so far, winning fairly consistently even though the dealers at the same table had changed shifts once already. How lucky could one table remain for us?

I studied the new dealer. He was older than any of the other dealers, with a paunch straining his cummerbund and a horseshoe of hair rimming his otherwise bald pate, making him look more avuncular than gangster.

"Nah," I said, feeling a little gangster myself. "I can take him."

"Don't you mean 'we'?"

"That, too."

As if to test my resolve, right away Mr. Horseshoe Hair dealt me the hand my dad had prepped me on: before me lay two Eights.

"Split," I said.

"Are you sure?" Billy asked again.

"Hey," said Mr. Horseshoe Hair. "Let the lady make her own decisions."

Mr. Horseshoe Hair was showing a Seven and I had no doubt he had some kind of Ten in his hole. There was just one problem. Feeling totally giddy with the way things had been going, I'd pushed two hundred dollars worth of chips forward just before the dealers had changed hands and had neglected to change my bet. If I split the Eights, I'd need to push another two hundred dollars in chips forward. If I won both splits, I'd have a total of eight hundred dollars, nearly enough for my Choos; if I went one for two, I'd be right where I was; if I lost both hands, I'd be knocked back to the two hundred dollars I'd walked in with all those hours before.

And what if Mr. Horseshoe Hair wasn't hiding a Ten? What if it was a low card and he kept pulling until he busted? What if—?

It was too much to think about.

"I'm sure," I said, pushing the other two hundred forward and no sooner had I done so than Mr. Horseshoe Hair was turning over my prophetic third Eight.

"Split!" I said again, excitedly.

"Where are you people from, Connecticut?" Mr. Horseshoe Hair asked. "You can't split a split in Atlantic City."

"Oh." I was deflated. "My dad never said anything about that." I felt embarrassed by my lack of knowledge and in my embarrassment, blurted, "Double down then."

"Double down?" Mr. Horseshoe Hair's eyebrows shot up to his absence of hairline.

"Double down," I insisted, pushing my last two hundred dollars forward. I was betting everything that Mr. Horseshoe Hair had a Seventeen he'd have to stand at. Since I had a Sixteen, the only way to beat him was to get anywhere from a Two to a Five. Not much of a window of opportunity, I'll grant you, but it was all I had.

He turned up a Five and the table erupted. Blackjack.

He turned his attention to my other Eight and turned over yet another Eight.

"Don't forget, Connecticut," he cautioned, "you can't split it here."

"I know that," I said surlily. Hey, my sudden riches—unless the dealer also got blackjack, mine would pay out three-to-two—had gone to my head.

"Hit me," I said defiantly.

"I don't know what you stepped in on the way here," Mr. Horseshoe Hair said as he turned over another Five for me and the table erupted again. Blackjack again.

Whatever Billy did passed in a blur as I waited to see what Mr. Horseshoe Hair was hiding in his hole, but after my own excitement it was anticlimactic when he turned over the Ten I was expecting all along.

"You don't look too excited," Mr. Horseshoe Hair said, as he stacked chips on the table in front of me to pay off my winnings. At a rate of three-to-two for both blackjacks, with six hundred dollars originally at stake—all I had in my pockets—I was now looking at fifteen hundred dollars. It was enough for my Jimmy Choos and then some. I had reached my goal.

"Oh, shit," I said, everything hitting me all at once, "I think I'm going to throw up."

"Are you sure you don't want to play a few more hands?" Billy asked. "You're on such a roll."

"No, Billy," I said. "I need to get out of here. Besides, my bus is leaving soon."

★ ★ ★

We spilled out of the casino, like a pair of dice tumbling out of an expensive leather shaker, richer than when we'd gone in.

Under the light of a perfect moon, right there on the boardwalk named by Boardman, in the excitement of the moment, Billy Charisma kissed me for the very first time. It was a knockout kiss that spoke of new beginnings, endless excitement, bright futures.

Hillary Clinton wasn't the only one who'd hit the jackpot in Atlantic City.

"Come to Vegas with me?" he invited, breaking the kiss. "I've never met anyone like you before. Come to Vegas with me, Baby."

"Yes," I said.

Then he walked me to the bus and kissed me right in front of everybody as we waited to board. I swear, it was like being back in high school, only in high school I'd never had anything happen to me like this.

I didn't even mind that Hillary sat with Biff instead of me all the way home, their blond heads huddled together, didn't mind—too much—when I completely messed up the Sudoku puzzle I'd hastily shoved in my pocket before leaving home that morning.

For once in my life, I had my very own squeeze.

# 13

Of course, saying I'd go to Vegas and actually going to Vegas were two different things.

I mean, of course I wanted to go to Vegas with Billy Charisma. What girl wouldn't want to go to Vegas with Billy Charisma?

But first I had other responsibilities.

When we got back to Danbury from Atlantic City, it was already past midnight.

"I'm going back to Biff's place," Hillary said after we'd debarked.

That was sudden, I thought. But then I realized they'd been talking for over fourteen hours and had put in more time together than I'd normally put in over the course of four dates with a new guy. Really, when you looked at it that way, it was surprising they hadn't ducked into a hotel together around dinnertime.

"But how will I…?" Not to be totally self-absorbed, but I was wondering how I was supposed to get myself home, since Hillary had driven us to the bus pickup.

"Here." She tossed me the keys to her Jeep. "Biff'll bring me home in the morning."

I was torn. A part of me had been dying to get behind the wheel of Hillary's shiny red Jeep ever since she'd gotten it. A part of me was terrified that with my lousy driving, I'd wrap it around a telephone pole and she'd hate me forever. Plus, I was too short to see over her dash.

"Just sit on this," she said, reading my mind and handing me the thick guide to Atlantic City she'd been reading on the way in.

"Thanks," I said. "Have fun."

The drive back to South Park was mostly uneventful, only because I kept the speed to twenty miles an hour, the one eventful part coming when a cop blared his horn loudly before zipping by me on the left, clearly peeved that my slowness had kept him from speeding. As I inched along, I thought about the upcoming trip to Vegas—Sin City!—with Billy Charisma. True, we hadn't set an exact date, but only a blind person wouldn't see how eager he was to do this and I was sure the nebulous plan would become a reality. It was only a matter of time.

But what would I *do* in Vegas? I wondered. After all, in Atlantic City, I'd won enough to buy the Jimmy Choo

Ghosts I so badly wanted. What need had I to do any more gambling? Of course the answer was obvious: in Las Vegas—Sin City! (I couldn't stop thinking of it that way)—I'd be exactly what Billy said I was: I'd be his talisman. I'd be exactly what he wanted me to be. Plus, I'd be able to win more money so I could buy even more Choos. Maybe I'd wind up with a whole closetful.

Once I'd unlocked the door, before I even turned on the light, in the darkness I could see the red light from the answering machine blinking like crazy. Sure, we'd been gone all day, but it was still a lot of calls. I flicked the light switch on, grabbed a pen and pad, and prepared to take down all the messages. No doubt one of Hillary's patients was in crisis mode.

The first several messages were prerecordings from telemarketers—didn't they realize how much people hated those things? They should do a telemarketing survey about it and then they'd know—and the one after those was from my dad. "How did it go? Did you win as much as you wanted to win?" Perhaps he was looking for the vicarious thrill of someone else's gambling. "I forgot to tell you, just in case it comes up: you can't split a split in Atlantic City, so if you did get those twin Eights, well, I hope you didn't embarrass yourself."

Great, now he told me, and I'd tell him all about it when I saw him on Monday night. "I'm afraid I won't be free for dinner Monday night," his voice went on. "There's a new group I've been invited to join that meets then. Who knows?

I thought maybe I should check it out." All righty then. Baby was about to get a new pair of Jimmy Choos and Daddy got a new group. I wondered what the group was?

The crisis I'd been half expecting came in the next message, only it wasn't one of Hillary's clients. Rather, it was Elizabeth Hepburn, and it came in the form of a plea from Lottie, the contents becoming increasingly grave with each new message she left, although the tone, somehow lacking in human sympathy, left something to be desired.

"Ms. Hepburn really is not feeling so good. She can't remember which day you are going away, today or Sunday, but if you're there, she'd like for you to call her."

That didn't sound good.

"Ms. Hepburn is feeling worse. I called her physician and he's on his way over. She forget she asked me to call you earlier and insisted I call you now to tell you not to worry, that she is strong as Kirk Douglas in *Spartacus,* although she can't remember if she dated him or his son."

Of course I was worried. There's nothing designed to make a person worry more than another person telling them not to worry, but I also did wonder: except for the cleft on the chin, how could she get Kirk and Michael confused? She really must not be doing too well.

"Ms. Hepburn was just taken to St. Vincent's Hospital in the ambulance, with the lights blaring and sirens screaming and everything. She didn't seem to understand what was going on, but she kept saying your name."

The next message was from another automated telemarketer and I cut it off midpitch as I turned off the machine and punched in the number for Elizabeth Hepburn's home.

It took six rings before a sleepy-sounding Lottie answered, "Ms. Elizabeth Hepburn's residence?"

"What room is she in?" I asked without preamble. "I want to go see her."

"Delilah?"

"Who else?"

"Don't you realize it's one in the morning? Why are you calling so late?"

Technically, it was early, but this was no time for technicalities.

"Your words were so desperate on the phone," I said. "Your messages were increasingly desperate."

"Did I? Were they?" I heard a yawn. "That must have been because Ms. Hepburn was so upset."

She herself didn't sound all that upset at all.

"Then you mean it's not serious?" I asked. "She's really fine?"

"Oh, it's plenty serious and she's not fine at all. In fact, she's in the ICU. But you're not a relative and I'm sure they wouldn't let you in to see her at this time of night."

For some reason, I kept wanting to scream at her. I think now I wanted to scream at her so much in order to shake her obvious complacency. Elizabeth was in trouble and she was alone. Couldn't Lottie see how awful those fraternal-twin facts were?

"Just go during regular visiting hours tomorrow," Lottie

said, loudly yawning again. "In all likelihood, she'll still be alive by then. Or not." *Click*.

Bitch.

The ICU at St. Vincent's Hospital, where I'd hightailed it first thing the next morning after choking down a quick bowl of Cocoa Krispies, was about as depressing as those places are everywhere, with its share of accident victims, like the guy whose motorcycle had taken him for a ride instead of the other way around, or those who needed their vital signs closely monitored. And then there were the families. Unkempt and unshaven, distraught and distracted, they sat by their loved ones trying to hold out hope, paced the waiting room and corridor in despair. With Elizabeth Hepburn's wealth and reputation, I would have thought for sure that despite Lottie saying she was in the ICU, she'd be in a private room rather than here with what I was sure she must view as riffraff, and that she'd be surrounded by loved ones, just like everyone else.

"I like the riffraff," Elizabeth Hepburn said of the first. "Reminds me of my days in vaudeville. Gypsy Rose Lee, Schmypsy Rose Lee. I taught that girl everything she knew about feathers and don't let anyone tell you different.

"I keep telling you," Elizabeth Hepburn said of the second, "there isn't anyone else left. Why do you think I like being with the riffraff so much? You're my best friend."

I was sure she didn't mean that to come across in quite the way I heard it, that I was riffraff, and I sure was glad to find her awake.

"Of course I'm awake," she said. "Did Lottie tell you I'd died already? Lottie is always in such a hurry for me to die already."

"What do you mean?" I found it hard to believe it was true, but then, Lottie had behaved oddly during our phone conversation.

"Lottie thinks that, with no heirs and with her the only one that takes care of me, everything I have will go to her." She chuckled weakly. "Little does she know I'm still debating between that and giving it all to Literacy Volunteers of America."

How sad it must be, to have the only person regularly taking care of you be someone you knew was eagerly awaiting your death.

"Why don't you fire her?" I asked.

"Do you have any idea how hard it is to find someone who has no life of their own and is willing to live in full-time?"

Actually, I didn't.

I looked around at the absence of cards, flowers. Sure, she'd only been there twenty-four hours, but you'd think there'd be some evidence of someone in the world showing concern for her.

"Oh, in another day or two," she said, "I'm sure there'll be flowers from my agent. Even though I haven't acted in twenty years, Simon still thinks he can talk me into doing the stage version of *On Golden Pond* when they take the show to Luxembourg. And I know Bacall would be here in a heartbeat if she weren't busy with whatever that new show is that she's doing. Really, Delilah, you're not just my best friend. You're my only friend. Now, tell me, how did your trip to Atlantic City go?"

I pulled up a seat and, acting in my role as her best friend, took her crepe hand in mine.

"Never mind that silliness," I said. "I don't even know why you're here." I looked at the machines, the monitors. "What happened?"

"Oh," she laughed weakly, "that crazy doctor. When he came to the house, he said I was having an 'episode.' I couldn't help but laugh. 'Episode?' I said. 'When it happens to you, we'll call it an episode. I'm pretty sure what I just had was a heart attack!' Big mistake on my part, acting all dramatic, because the next thing I know, he's rushing me here with the cavalry and Jimmy Stewart and everything. Never, Delilah, *never* tell a physician you just had a heart attack."

"You mean you didn't really have a heart attack?"

"Of course I had a heart attack! In fact, I've been having episodic heart attacks since I've been here. It's just that if I'm going to die of them, I'd just as soon be at home. True, I'd have to face Lottie rubbing her hands together as she awaits my demise, but at least I'd be surrounded by my own things, I could kiss my Oscars one last time. But once you start the medical machinery rolling, it's tough to get them to stop. Forget, 'First, do no harm.' It's more like, 'If we have the technology to keep you alive indefinitely, we're going to do it simply because we can.' Crap. But never mind that now. How did Atlantic City go?"

"I won," I said. "Big-time."

"Yippee!" She half rose in her bed to embrace me, but that "Yippee!" must have sapped what little strength she had, because she immediately subsided back down into the pillows, unembraced. "Does this mean you're getting the Ghosts now? Will you order them today? You can use my phone…"

It was then that I had the idea.

"I decided I really don't want the Ghost after all," I said.

"You don't want the Ghost?"

"No, they're too flashy. Who ever heard of a window washer wearing Jimmy Choos? I'd get laughed out of The Golden Squeegee Club."

"You all have a golden squeegee club?"

"Well, no," I admitted, "but we should. Of course, if we did, I'd be the only member. Anyway, the point is, I really just don't have the kind of lifestyle that would justify such a purchase."

"But with shoes like that," she interjected, "you don't wait for the occasion. You create occasions."

"Well, I just don't even see the possibility for creating such occasions happening in this lifetime, so I just figured I'd—"

"Oh, no. No, you don't."

Had she read my mind?

"You can't," she said. "You simply can't not buy a pair of Jimmy Choos."

"Oh, I'm going to buy a pair all right," I said, "just not for me. I'm going to buy a pair of the Parson Flats for you." True, they were the Choos that Hillary wanted, but Hillary already had the Momo Flats that she'd given to me after I bought them for her, so she'd had her chance. Plus, the Fayres Elizabeth Hepburn originally wanted had a slight heel that was just big enough to be impractical, should she survive her current ordeal, and the Parson Flats were the only ones I could remember the price for, thereby being sure I could afford them. "Don't you remember the Parson Flats?" I asked. "It was a gold leather traditional thong sandal with a big red jewel at the center, surrounded by green stones with more jewels suspended from gold threads."

Jimmy Choos may have been known for their simplicity and elegance, but it was definitely the snazziest of the Choos that appealed to Elizabeth, Hillary and me.

Her eyes were misting up.

"They were gorgeous," I added. "Really, once we get you back on the red carpet, I'm sure you'll knock Bacall's socks off in them."

The activity level on her heart monitor speeded up.

"Are you okay? Are you having another episode?" I asked. "Should I get a nurse?"

"Oh, no," she said, "I am having another episode, but it's a good episode. Aren't you just the sweetest thing that ever lived?"

I didn't know about all that, but I did know that the

Parson Flats would set me back six hundred and thirty dollars before tax, meaning that if I still wanted those Ghosts—and I did; I'd lied about not wanting them—I was going to need to do a lot more in Las Vegas than just be Billy Charisma's talisman. I was going to need to win, too.

And I knew something else: that if Elizabeth Hepburn could just hang on long enough for me to phone Jimmy Choo's in Manhattan and order the Parson Flats, and then waited long enough for them to be delivered, that even if she died then, she'd die with happy feet.

When I got back from the hospital, Hillary still hadn't arrived home from Biff's yet, but there was on the machine my first ever message from Billy Charisma.

"Ready to go to Vegas, Baby?" he asked.

*Was he serious?* I phoned him back at the number he'd left.

"Not just yet," I said.

"Oh?" He sounded surprised.

"I have other responsibilities," I said, thinking of Elizabeth. "Besides, I don't know you well enough to just hop on a plane with you and fly off to Sin City."

Shit! I couldn't believe I'd just said that last out loud. Why couldn't I have just said "Las Vegas" and left it at that, like a normal person?

But he graciously ignored my faux pas, choosing instead to focus on something else.

"Oh, that's right," he said, "you always need a little bit of foreplay first, don't you? Very well, then. How about if you come to my cottage for dinner next Friday? I promise not to bite."

I allowed as that dinner at his cottage would be very nice, but neglected to comment on the lack of biting.

# 14

Usually, when you are waiting for something good to happen, it seems to take forever for the big day to arrive, but that week before my date with Billy Charisma just sped by.

Life may have been fast, but work was slow. Window washing sometimes runs like that: perfectly gorgeous weeks where not too many people call for help, but then Thanksgiving hits and all of a sudden everyone wants their windows sparkling in time for the holidays, despite that the cleaning fluid sometimes freezes in the frigid temperatures if you don't put antifreeze in the mix. So we had mostly half days, which even allowed us enough time to stop off for a visit to see Elizabeth Hepburn. Having received the Parson Flats I'd had Jimmy Choo's overnight to her, she was recuperat-

178 Lauren Baratz-Logsted

ing nicely at home, her happily Choos-clad feet propped up on her 1600-thread-count Egyptian cotton sheets.

"These are the best medicine anyone ever invented," she said, admiringly twinkling at her own toes.

"That was really generous of you to buy Choos for her instead of for yourself," Stella said as we were leaving. "But did you get a load of that awful Lottie person she employs as her companion?"

I had. If Lottie had been a weapon of war, she'd have been a Sherman tank—big, mean, deadly.

"A great lady like that," Stella said, "deserves better than that in this life." Which was saying a lot coming from Stella, who similarly had something of a Sherman tank about her personality.

"Maybe someday," I said, "she'll get the better companion she deserves."

And we'd both noticed, Stella and I, that The Girls From Brazil were subdued all week long.

"What's up with that?" Stella asked when they were out of hearing range.

"I'm not sure," I said. "Usually they just get nasty with me, but never with each other as they've been doing." I shrugged. "Maybe they're just upset about the scant work schedule? Maybe they'd rather have fuller days and make more money?"

"Nah," she said. "That can't be it."

If things at work were slow and odd, meaning the strange sullenness Conchita and Rivera were exuding, my more domestic life was fast and odd.

Having blown off our fairly regular Monday-night get-together, Black Jack was not very forthcoming about his reasons why when I called him about it.

"Let's just say there may be some surprises in your future," he said.

"What surprises?" I asked.

"Just some surprising stuff," he said.

"Stuff?" Well, that was very illuminating.

"Never mind that now. How did Atlantic City go for you?" he asked.

"I won! I even got dealt the twin Eights you prophesied!"

"That's great! And did you split them like I told you to?"

"Of course. But then when I tried to split them when another Eight came up—"

"Crap, you didn't get my message in time."

"No, I did not." He could probably tell from my tone that I was still miffed at being made to look like a piker. Then I shouted, "But I won! So I'll get over it!"

"That's great, Baby. So, are you going to retire now? Did you win everything you needed to win?"

"Well, yes and no." I explained how, yes, I'd won everything I'd needed to win ("You're my little girl!"), but that, no, I wasn't going to retire yet, because I'd given a good chunk of my winnings away in aid of buying a little-old-lady fading Hollywood movie star a pair of ridiculously expensive shoes. ("Oh, right. Why didn't I ever think of that? Of course a gambler should use winnings to finance the wealthy.")

I tried to explain that, somehow, it wasn't like it sounded at all.

"Save it, Baby," he said. "I'm glad you're doing good works with your winnings. Who knows? Maybe if I were more like you, I wouldn't be where I am now. Speaking of which, are you really sure you need to go on gambling? Haven't you had enough already?"

What did he mean?

"What do you mean?" Surely, this couldn't be my dad talking. This was not the Black Jack Sampson I'd always known and loved. "Actually," I said, "I was just about to ask you if, since we couldn't get together on Monday night because you were busy, if maybe we could get together on Thursday night instead so I could practice a little bit more, maybe learn some new strategies."

I figured that with my date with Billy coming up on Friday, whatever else we might discuss, we would surely be discussing gambling and I wanted to be prepared. I also figured Dad wouldn't pass up the chance to play a few hands of his favorite game, even if it was with me.

"Sorry, Baby, no can do. I've got another meeting on Thursday night."

"What's with all these meetings all of a sudden?"

"Sorry, but it's still a surprise."

"What surprise?"

But no matter how many times I asked, he wasn't saying.

"I'll tell you when the time is right," he said, "and we're not there yet."

And then there was my roommate—best friend: the woman formerly known as Hillary Clinton who could now best be described as Hillary In Love.

"Biff is the smartest man I've ever spent time with!" Hillary had said, finally breezing in on Sunday night.

"That's wonderful," I'd said, "I'm very happy for you."

"Biff is the funniest man I've ever spent time with!" Hillary had said on Monday night after what was technically their second date.

"What more could a woman want?" I'd said.

"Biff is generous to a fault," she'd said on Tuesday, just before midnight. "Even though I make as much as he does, he wouldn't let me pay for dinner…and, afterward, he didn't even want sex! He said we should wait at least until the technical fourth date!"

Was something maybe wrong with Biff?

And then came the technical fourth date, which I wasn't privy to the recap of until Thursday morning when she burst in on me somewhere between my Cocoa and my Krispies.

"Omigod!" she said, back pressed against the door and looking like a blond-haired version of a starry-eyed Natalie Wood in just about any movie Natalie Wood had ever made. "Biff Williams has the absolute biggest—"

"I don't need to know about that!" I said, picking up my bowl and thinking to take it into my room so I could eat in peace.

"He's just so dreamy," Hillary said, following me.

"Dreamy?" I asked. "Does anyone ever really say *dreamy?*"

My mom used to say it about my dad, but that was two decades ago. Next thing, she'd be launching into "I Feel Pretty," in which case I'd be compelled to put on a poodle skirt and play Rita Moreno to her Natalie.

"Oh, but he is dreamy, Delilah, plus he's got the biggest schlong—"

"I said I don't need to hear about that," I said, holding up a defensive cereal spoon.

She appeared crestfallen. "Look, Hill," I said, "just because I don't want to hear all about Biff's schlong, it doesn't mean I'm not happy for you. Of course I'm happy for you. I'm beyond happy for you."

And I was happy for her. The fact that she was out with the same guy every night, the fact that they always spent their time at his place rather than ours meaning that for the first time since we'd moved in there I came home to an empty home every night—maybe I should get a cat? None of that bothered me. It didn't even bother me in the age-old tradition of female relationships everywhere, you know, the tradition that firmly states, "I would be so happy for you that now you have someone were it not for the fact that I have no one and now your never being here only serves to highlight my I-have-no-one-ness. Really, once I have someone, too—if I live that long—I'll be nothing but happy for your happiness. Of course, you may have broken up with Mr. Wonderful by then."

But it wasn't necessary for me to experience any of that internal unpleasantness. Because Hillary having someone in this instance made me free to sort of have my own someone, Billy Charisma, and to have him without fear of what she might have to say about him or how I conducted my budding relationship with him because, thankfully, she was otherwise occupied.

So Hillary wasn't on the scene when I was fine-tuning the plans with Billy.

"I'll pick you up at seven," he said. "You just need to give me directions."

"How about if you give me directions?" I said. "I'd rather drive myself."

Hillary wasn't there to point out how combination defensive-offensive I sounded, which was great since I was determined to do this my way. The way I figured it, if I drove myself, there'd be the twin bonuses of being able to bail on the evening if it was a washout, and keeping me from drinking too much, thereby saving me from falling into bed with him on a drunken whim, because I'd need to stay sober enough to drive myself the long way home.

Hillary wasn't on the scene to negatively critique my wardrobe selections.

Going through the scant nonwork options in my clothing collection, I'd found a basic black dress shoved in the back. And when I say basic, I do mean basic. Made of some kind of stretchy nonwrinkle fabric, it could probably be rolled into a ball for months if need be without sustaining any damage, but it was so nondescript that it would never look like much unless someone like Jackie O or Princess Di wore it, and then only because they contained that inner magic while the dress clearly did not. On my feet, I slipped on the blue-green Momo Flats, figuring the color would make a strong statement and at least my toes would feel magical. Then I borrowed a lipstick Hillary never used anymore, a red that looked too bright on me, but what the hell. I wasn't trying to impress so much at this point as I was trying to look not awful.

Hillary also wasn't on the scene to question whether or not I might be making a mistake.

"I don't think he's really right for you," she might have said, echoing something Conchita or Rivera, I forget which, had said at one point.

"There's something a little bit…*dangerous* about him," she might have added, echoing thoughts I'd been regularly having myself. Whatever Billy Charisma might have wanted from me, the mere virtue of the fact that he was totally comfortable in a tux put him out of any league I'd ever been in.

Come to think of it, I didn't even have a league.

But still, I was going over to his place for a simple dinner he was going to prepare for me. How much danger could I possibly be in?

Hillary wasn't on the scene to laugh at me as I scarfed down a half serving of Michael Angelo's Four Cheese Lasagna while standing up—insurance against the possibility that maybe Billy might serve me something odd for dinner like squid or peacock, so that at least my stomach wouldn't scream with hunger when I demurred about just not having that much of an appetite—or laugh at the fact that I did so with a paper bib tucked inelegantly into the scoop neck of my nondescript, nonawful black dress.

She really would have laughed her ass off at that one.

And Hillary wasn't on the scene to give me a gal-pal hug or a kiss, wishing me the best of luck with my evening despite her own qualms, as I sailed out the door.

If Hillary kept things up the way they were going with Biff, I really was going to need to get a cat.

Billy's cottage, were it not a small part of a much larger estate in Westchester, would have been impressive in its own right. Certainly, with its Cape Cod architecture, flower boxes in the windows, and green-and-white porch swing, it was cozier and more finished-looking than anywhere I'd ever lived.

"Baby!" he greeted me at the door.

This was the first time I'd seen him without his tux on and in khaki pants, loafers sans socks and pink oxford shirt, he looked downright...*naked*.

"Yup," I said awkwardly, climbing up the three porch steps. "Sorry I'm late."

"Are you late?" The perfect host, he glanced at his watch, as though needing to verify I was indeed late, rather than doing what I would have done if a date were an hour late, which would have been to make the date feel guilty.

"I got lost," I said, something about being there with him making me feel slightly out of breath, as though I'd run the whole way over. "Twice," I added. "But it was only my fault once. The other time, there was a detour."

"Well, you made it after all." He smiled. "That's the important thing."

He offered his arm and led me inside. A part of me felt as if he was the smoothest thing since black velvet or Cary Grant, and not in a good way; a part of me was eating up every second of the royal treatment.

This was almost better than a new pair of Jimmy Choos. Maybe this was what other women went through life feeling like? Maybe this was what it felt like to be treated like a goddess by a man whose nickname wasn't anything like "The Weasel" or "The Rat"? I tried to think, if I were to come up with a nickname for Billy, what would it be...

Well, of course it would have to be "The Gambler."

"Baby? Earth to Baby?" He gently tapped on the side of my head. "Are you in there?"

"Oops, sorry," I said, blushing. Even though I'd been with him for a few hours at Foxwoods, even though we'd spent the whole day and a good part of the night together in Atlantic City, it had been so long since I'd been on a date proper, I needed to get my proper-date sea legs back on. I was going to need to remember that being in a room with a male human being actually meant interacting with that male human being.

"So, what do you think?" he asked, gesturing around.

I thought that, just like the exterior of his home was nicer than anywhere I'd ever lived since moving out on my own, the interior was, as well.

"I know," he said ruefully before I could pronounce a verdict, "it looks like a gay interior designer did it, doesn't it?"

"Well…"

Well, *I* didn't say it, I thought, taking in the floral chintz and brocade, as well as the other fabrics I'd never be able to put a name to, not even if you held my Momo Flats–clad feet against the fire, gently roaring in the small fieldstone fireplace.

"What can I say?" he said. "That's the dad in me coming out."

"You have kids?" I blurted. Sure, if he had kids, I'd need to know at some point, but this was a rude awakening I wasn't ready for. He could have waited until after feeding me at least.

"Oh, no," he laughed. "I meant 'the dad' as in 'my dad.' He was a gay interior designer, at least he was after Mother and I moved back to England, and I guess he just rubbed off on me."

"But I thought you said…" I stumbled. "Wasn't your dad married to your mom for several years?"

"Oh, yes. And if he wasn't gay before he met her, he certainly was afterward. I never saw him again after he moved out, but as you can see, he left behind him a legacy of femininely refined taste. I've found in the past that some women are put off by all this—" he gestured "—but I've lived with it for so long, I can't imagine being without rose and vine patterns everywhere. Now what can I get you to drink? Champagne? Diet Pepsi?"

"Lime…?"

"Oh, yes," he said. "Come." He crooked his finger at me, invited me into the kitchen, opened the fridge: there were at least two rows of Diet Pepsi Lime in there.

"I remembered," he said, "your asking the waitress if she had any when we were in Atlantic City and I figured it must be a particular favorite of yours. I just wanted to make sure I didn't run out."

That was so thoughtful! See? If Hillary had been around to warn me about him earlier, I could have called her on my cell phone right now to tell her how wrong she'd been.

"So." He waited patiently. "Which would you prefer, the champagne or the Diet—"

"Oh, the champagne, please," I said. "But just one glass, maybe two. I'm driving, after all."

Expertly, he undid the foil wrapping and extracted the cork from a bottle with an orange label.

"I entertained and rejected Perrier-Jouët, Moët, Piper Heidsieck and Roederer," he said, "in favor of this very lovely Veuve Clicquot. I don't know about you, but I just love saying Veuve Clicquot."

"I don't know about you," I said, taking the flute, "but I try to avoid saying things I know I'll mispronounce."

He laughed as though I was the wittiest woman ever. I can't say I thought what I said was all that funny, but by the time I was halfway through my first glass of Veuve Clicquot, I was ready to accept his obvious assessment that I was as funny as Jon Stewart and Ellen DeGeneres combined.

"Do I smell something…*burning?*" I asked, wrinkling my nose. Or maybe it was the bubbles from the champagne.

By now we were seated on the floor, backs propped against the rose-covered couch, and I was thinking that his pink shirt looked awfully nice right next to my black dress. Maybe his pink shirt and my black dress should get closer?

"Oh, *shit*," he said, swearing uncharacteristically— really, it was as surprising as if Queen Elizabeth said "fuck" at tea—as he leapt to his feet. "And I wanted it to be a surprise."

I raced after him into the kitchen, champagne glass in hand. I wasn't sure exactly why I was racing. It just seemed like a good moment to express my solidarity for whatever was going on. Host races, guest races, he races, she races, my kingdom for a horse and then we all move on.

As he grabbed an oven mitt, I entertained the vague notion that at my own home, I didn't even know if we had an oven mitt, let alone where to find it. Then he was unceremoniously yanking open the oven door, from which tiny wisps of black smoke emerged.

"*Shit,*" he said again.

"What were those supposed to be?" I hiccupped, trying to adopt a look of grave concern as I studied the two charred rectangles on the baking tray.

"They were supposed to be homemade pizza pockets," he said in dismay. "I remembered how in Atlantic City, you asked the waitress if she could turn your pizza into a pocket somehow, so I made my own dough from scratch, made my own sauce from scratch, then I grated fresh cheeses over the whole lot and gently folded them into pockets."

He'd done all that for *me?* Omigod, he was trying to *impress* me.

"Oh, well," he sighed as he threw in the oven mitt, totally missing the look of adoration I was bestowing upon him, "I suppose there's nothing for it. You toss the salad while I call Domino's. At least we've still got the champagne to drink."

Throughout the salad, throughout the Domino's, throughout the second bottle of champagne, Billy remained charming. He even did a romantic reminiscence of the time we'd spent thus far together in casinos, which was very touching until a sore subject came up.

"And what was with that…*yo-yo guy,* the one we keep running into every time we turn around?"

My back stiffened at his insult to Chris. True, Chris wasn't the smoothest guy in the world and he did drop his yo-yos an awful lot for someone who was trying to get taken seriously as a semiprofessional at it, but still…

Then I had to laugh, though, as Billy began opening and closing his Craftsman cabinets. "Yo-Yo Man? Yoo-hoo! Yo-Yo Man? Are you stalking us, by some chance? Are you hiding in the flower box with the fresh basil? Oh, Yo-Yo Man!"

Maybe it was the Veuve Clicquot, but it was funny at the time. And, despite feeling a guilty twinge about Chris, I laughed along with Billy. Besides, what did I owe to The Yo-

Yo Man, who was really only Furthest Guy, anyway? I was with The Gambler.

"How about—" Billy's eyes flashed "—a game of cards?"

"I think I've had too much to drink," I said, suddenly realizing how drunk I was.

"Come to think of it—" I burped "—I think I'm too drunk to drive."

Billy put his arms around me, pulled me close, tilted my chin upward with one hand and looked deep into my eyes.

"Too drunk to play cards," he tut-tutted, "too drunk to drive. Are you too drunk for this?"

He lowered his face so that his lips were just a breath away from mine and then stopped. Taking the bait, I leapt at the chance, meeting my lips to his.

"No." He shook his head after a moment. "I guess you're not too drunk for that."

I liked that first kiss. I wanted more kisses like that.

Moving closer into his arms, I sought his lips with my own again.

For a time, he kissed me back, but even through my drunken haze I sensed that he was more distant this time, that he was somehow removed.

And then he drew away, studied my face.

"You know, Baby, I really would like to show you my bedroom right now. I'd like to take you in there, remove every stitch of clothing you have on, some of them with my teeth, then I'd like to kiss every inch of your body, fulfill desires you don't even know you have…"

*Take me! Take me in there!* My mind half screamed, as I tried to move yet closer into his arms again, practically falling into him. So what if I'd originally insisted on driving myself, my reasoning being it would keep me from drinking too much and falling into bed with him on a drunken whim. But I'd changed my mind about the drinking. I'd changed my mind about the bed. If there's one thing regularly drilled into women's minds, it's that it's our prerogative to change our minds.

"But I'm afraid I can't do that," he said sadly, shaking his head.

"Why? Why can't you do that?"

I wanted him to do that. Oh, how I wanted him to do that.

"Because it wouldn't be right," he said, chastely, kissing the tip of my nose. "Because it wouldn't be fair," he said, tauntingly kissing my neck.

"So be unfair, be unfair! I won't tell!"

"No, I'm afraid not. If you really are too drunk to drive, if you're too drunk to play cards with me, then I can't possibly take advantage of your condition. Tell you what, you can have my bed, I'll get blankets and set myself up on the couch."

What was with guys these days? First Biff wouldn't sleep with Hillary right away, or at least not until the fourth technical date. Now Billy wouldn't sleep with me right away. What was wrong with doing it right then? I was old enough! I had my own condoms!

"Really, Baby," he said, "as hard as it is to wait, I must resist you. We can do it when we get to Vegas. You know—Sin City?"

# 15

It goes without saying that not only did I have a champagne hangover the next day, but I also had the raging depression to go with it as I drove myself home from Billy's cottage in Westchester in the brutally clear light of a crisp autumnal morning. If I were still a virgin, the correct phrase for my state would be "still intact." But what is the correct phrase for a twenty-eight-year-old woman who can't persuade the man she desires to sleep with her, despite his professing a similar desire? There wasn't a whole correct phrase for it. There was just one correct word.

*"Loser."*

"You are so *not* a loser," Hillary said after I'd said as much to her.

Arriving home, I was surprised to find her there. I would

have thought that, at the rate they were going, they'd spend the whole weekend together.

"What are you doing home from Biff's so early?" I asked after calling Elizabeth Hepburn's house to see how she was doing; it was a daily habit now, checking up on her each morning to make sure she was still all right.

"What are you doing wearing Friday night's clothes on Saturday morning?" Hillary countered.

"How do you know these were last night's clothes?" I asked.

"When have you ever worn a black dress on Saturday morning?" she countered.

"I had a date with Billy," I said. "I drove myself there, but I drank too much and had to wait until this morning to drive myself home."

"Biff had an early golf date," she said. "I told him that true love was one thing but that there was no way I was going to start playing a sport I hated just to impress him and that I'd see him later. Besides, I missed you."

"Have breakfast yet?" I asked.

"Nah, I was waiting for you," she said. "Cocoa Krispies?" She waved the box cheerfully in my direction.

"Nah. I'll change and then we can go out."

"Out? You mean 'out' as in to a restaurant, a place with a real menu, where I can maybe get a full brunch with pancakes and eggs and bacon? A place where they maybe don't have Cocoa Krispies on the menu? But it's never your idea to go out to eat. I always have to drag you kicking and screaming. What has this man done to you?"

She was right. I was changing too quickly. I needed the security of old habits.

"Let me just hop into the shower and while I'm in there, you can pack a Ziploc with Cocoa Krispies so I won't starve."

And, while waiting for the water in the shower to heat up, I could always sit on the toilet and get a quick round of Sudoku in.

Hillary was in pig heaven as she dined on Belgian waffles topped with peaches and cream, chocolate–chip pancakes, a spinach and chèvre omelet, and about a half pound of bacon at the New England House.

"Never mind what Billy's done to me," I said, watching her shovel it in. "What's Biff done to you? You're eating like you're in training to get big enough to have bariatric surgery someday."

"I can't help it," she said, spooning in another bite of the fluffy omelet, a piece of spinach briefly adhering to her front tooth before her tongue swiped it away. "I eat like this when I'm in love. But don't worry, I burn it all right off, too. Being in love for me is like magic."

"Hill," I said, "I've known you for years and I've never seen you eat like this before."

She shrugged, snapped a piece of bacon in two, munched. "That's 'cause I've never been in love before."

"Then how do you know this time it's for real?" I asked.

"Believe me," she said, "when it's real, you can't miss it."

"Oh, so now you're some kind of expert?" I couldn't keep the cynic's half sneer out of my voice. I know it wasn't very attractive of me, but how could she be so sure? I mean, if a person has never had a thing before, then how can they know that the thing they have is that thing?

I said as much, to which Hillary replied, "You just know."

"Oh, thank you, wise swami." I salaamed her. "With circular reasoning like that, you could start your own religion."

"Okay, I know it sounds lame when I put it like that, but trust me, if it's real, you don't even have to ask yourself if it's real. You just know."

"More coffee?" the waitress offered Hillary, pointedly ignoring me.

Hey, what was I here, chopped liver?

But then I remembered the waitress's scathing look at my clothes when we'd first walked in—my jeans and T-shirt seemed perfectly clean to me, but apparently they weren't good enough for *her*—and remembered the sniff she'd emitted when I pulled out my Ziploc baggie of Cocoa Krispies and ordered an empty bowl and a glass of milk. So maybe she was worried about her tip, but Hillary had ordered enough food to feed a family of four, so she needn't have worried. Certainly, she didn't need to ignore me like that.

"Could I have another glass of milk, please?" I asked sweetly, tapping her on the arm with one hand as I waved my empty glass with the other.

Despite the chilly service, I liked it at the New England House. With its natural pine tables, Windsor chairs, exposed floors, evergreen-colored walls and faux fire in the fireplace, it was a sight more comfortable to eat my Cocoa Krispies there than it was back in our tiny ill-colored kitchen. Plus, it was nice to be spending time with Hillary, being just us two girls again.

"So," Hillary said, after Ms. Cheerful had departed to fill my milk order, "you spent the night at Billy's place. Then you slept with him?"

"Well, no," I admitted, and then I went on to explain what happened, a recitation that ended with my repeated self-pronouncement of "Loser."

"You are so *not* a loser," Hillary said.

"Then what do you call it?"

"I call it that Billy's a gentleman. I call it that he respects you too much to sleep with you for the first time when you're too inebriated to know what you're doing."

"I wasn't that inebriated! I knew I wanted to do it!"

"I call it that he wants to be sure it's what you really want, that you won't have any regrets in the morning."

"I do have regrets in the morning—I regret I didn't sleep with him!"

"I think he's just too much of a gentleman," she said again. "He wants it to be just perfect for you the first time."

Her worldview seemed at once practical and romantic, like Billy was practical enough to keep a clear head about the way he wanted things to be and romantic enough to want them to be a particular way.

Still, a part of me, the part that was used to working with Conchita and Rivera, couldn't help but channel what their reaction to all this would be:

"If he really wanted you so bad, *chica,*" Rivera would say, "he wouldn't be able to stop himself."

"He'd have that little pecker in you so quickly," Conchita would say, "you'd be spinning like an acrobat on Brazil Day."

Of course then they'd both point out to me how wrong Billy was for me.

"Do you think Billy is wrong for me?" I asked Hillary.

"It's not important what I think." She stabbed a cream-enshrouded peach with professional conviction. "It's important what you think."

"I'm not asking you for psychologist-speak," I said, exasperated. "I want your honest opinion. As my friend."

"I've never really talked to Billy, so how can I honestly say?"

"Well, I've never talked to Biff, not really, but I can tell he's right for you. I've never seen you so happy. You're right, you must be in love."

"And are you in love with Billy?"

What a ridiculous question! Hillary was like the scared person seeing shadows everywhere, only in her case she was the romantic in-love person seeing love everywhere. Still, I thought about it. I certainly wanted to be in his company again. It was thrilling to be in his company, to be the object of that glow he gave off. And, too, I wanted the chance to show him that I was the kind of woman who was as much fun outside of the casino as in it, the kind of woman who was worth jumping heedlessly into bed with, practicalities be damned.

"I just don't know," I said.

"Then you're not," she said, amending, "at least not *yet*." Then she glanced at her watch and quickly knocked back the rest of her coffee, rising from her chair even as she did so. "Gotta run."

"So soon?"

"Biff said he'd only play nine holes this morning. If I rush I can be back at his place just in time to meet him at the door in my nightie."

So much for the modern career woman—a psychologist, no less—refusing to cede her personal identity by subsuming it in service of a new relationship and becoming a cliché.

"Aren't you going to finish your waffle?" I called after her. But she was gone.

"Check?" Ms. Cheerful materialized at my side.

Considering I'd only had two glasses of milk, twenty-five dollars seemed like a lot to pay for breakfast, but I paid it and even tipped well. The doctor, being Hillary, may have been out, but while she'd been briefly in at least she'd convinced me that I was so *not* a loser.

"Only losers have nothing better to do than go visit their aging dads on a beautiful Saturday," my dad said when he finally answered the door.

I'd been pounding for five minutes. His car was in the drive, so I knew he had to be there; Black Jack Sampson never walked anywhere, not even down to the mailbox. As minute after minute of pounding passed without him answering, I'd grown concerned. What if something bad had happened to him? What if he'd had a cardiac episode, like Elizabeth Hepburn, only in his case he had no live-in Lottie to call for help on his behalf? What was the last thing I'd said to him? I couldn't remember.

So it was particularly insulting, having passed through that crucible of worry, to be greeted so rudely.

"What took you so long?" I said. I took in his disheveled hair, so atypical of him, took in his bathrobe. I'd never seen him wear a bathrobe in the daytime. It was a nice bathrobe, plush crimson, but still… "Only losers wear bathrobes in the middle of the day," I said, trading insult for insult. Hillary would probably say I was exhibiting hostility as a means of repressing the concern I'd been feeling a moment before. Then I wondered: when most people wear bathrobes in the daytime, it's because they're either sick or depressed. Black Jack didn't look sick. He looked too healthily annoyed at my being there to be sick. So maybe he was depressed? Maybe he'd been on another losing streak, one so bad it had caused him to retreat into the depression of plush velour? "What's wrong?" I asked, all concern now.

"What do you mean, what's wrong?" he challenged, still not letting me in.

"It's just that you're wearing a bathrobe in the middle of the day," I said.

"Oh. That. I have to go to work in a little while—" 'going to work' was the euphemism Black Jack always used for 'gambling' "—so I figured, why change twice?"

Why, indeed.

"What are you doing here?" he asked. "Don't you have anything better to do with your weekend than spending it with me?"

What was with the hostility?

"Can I come in?" I asked.

"Well, no, I mean, oh, why the hell not?" He held the door open.

"Gee, thanks."

"I was just going to grab a quick bite before getting ready for work," he said. "Cocoa Krispies?" he offered, waving the box at me. Black Jack never ate them himself, but he did keep a box on hand for me.

"Well, no, I already…" Then I stopped myself. In order to counter his hostility, I figured it was important to be as companionable as possible. Besides, who can't eat a second bowl of Cocoa Krispies? "Sure, why not?" I said.

Black Jack poured me a bowl, then popped some toast for himself into the old toaster as he waited for his coffee to brew.

"So," he said, "how long are you staying for? You never said why you're here."

I munched my dry cereal. It was really good.

"Did you ever notice how much time people spend just eating and talking? Sometimes, it feels like that's about all we people ever do."

"Is that what you came by for—to offer me your philosophical analysis of the banality of human experience?"

"Do I need a reason?"

"No, you don't. But what is it anyway?"

"I just wanted to spend a little time with you. I missed our regular get-together on Monday night—"

"We never got together *every* Monday night."

"—and then when I tried to see you on Thursday, you said no to that, too. I just missed you, Dad."

"Aw, that's sweet."

"Plus, I figured that, while I was here, maybe we could play a few hands of cards. Maybe you could show me—"

"That's a terrible idea!"

*"What?"*

I didn't get it. Sure, I'd been at loose ends, but mostly I'd stopped by to give Black Jack a mercy gamble. True, when I originally told him I wanted to start gambling, he'd been resistant to the idea, but I'd never heard him turn down a chance to play in all my years growing up in his various houses. And, hey, wasn't I one of the boys now?

I said as much.

"I just think it's a bad idea to overdo a thing, Baby, that's all," he said.

*"What?"*

I knew I was beginning to sound like a broken record,

but what was this fresh insanity of which he spoke? Black Jack had overdone things for as long as I'd known him. Overdoing things was how Black Jack came to be known as Black Jack. What was stopping him now?

"C'mon," I said, "it'll give us something to do other than talk and eat. We could just play a hand or two—"

"I said *no*, Baby." He gulped the rest of his coffee. "Now I really do need to get ready for work. Why don't you show yourself out?"

I finished my Cocoa Krispies, took my bowl to the sink, rinsed it out. I was fully intending to obey his instructions to show myself out—I swear, this was the last time I'd pay a mercy-gamble visit unannounced!—when I decided to tidy the kitchen up for him a bit, so I washed his dishes, too. Over the sound of the running water, I could hear his voice talking in the bedroom. I turned the tap off.

"Did you want something, Dad?" I called.

"No," he shouted back. "I was just on the phone. You're still here?"

I dried my hands on the dish towel, straightened up the newspapers in the living room. He'd probably been studying the football spreads. My dad needed a woman to help straighten things out around here.

"You're still here?" he said again, entering.

"I was just..." I stopped, then gasped, "*What* are you wearing?"

He had on navy-blue pants, a white shirt and navy-blue tie. His black shoes shone and his navy-blue hat with the badge on the front sat perkily on his hair. Even his mustache looked freshly combed.

"I told you I had to go to work, didn't I?" he said grumpily.

"Yeah, but as *what?*"

"Stop looking at me like that, Baby. Haven't you ever seen a security guard before?"

Oh, crap. Black Jack must have finally lost everything.

When I got home, the answering machine was blinking red that there had been one call. Even though it was just one, that blink was somehow very insistent. When I hit playback, I heard The Voice.

"Baby, it's Billy. I have to work tonight and I was hoping you could come with me. I figured I could swing by your place on the way and we could ride in together this time. If you're there, pick up… Oh, well. Guess I'll just have to hit Foxwoods without you, see how I can do on my own without my talisman. I'll call you tomorrow, let you know how I made out."

*Click.*

Later that night, lonely at home without Hillary, I fell asleep in front of the TV, empty Jake's Fault Shiraz glass and unfinished fiendish Sudoku puzzle close by. I woke the next morning to two sounds: The Yo-Yo Man commercial on the television and Billy Charisma's voice leaving another message on my machine. Too groggy to register what was going on, I watched the one while listening to the other.

How could someone who loved being a yo-yoist as much as Furthest Guy keep dropping his yo-yo all the time? I idly wondered.

"Baby, are you there? It was lousy last night without you. Without you, I'm nothing anymore. I lost…a lot. Are you there?"

"I'm here, Billy," I said, picking up the phone. "I'm here."

"Let's set a date for the Vegas trip," he said. "Let's really do it. With you by my side, I know I'll clean up. We both will."

"Okay, Billy." It felt good to be the one to make him feel better. "We'll set a date. I'll go with you."

A part of me wanted to have a normal relationship with him, the kind that Hillary was having with Biff. I wanted to go to the movies together, hold hands, go out to dinner together, do more than hold hands, play Frisbee together in the park, have sex—I really wanted to have sex together— and fall in love; I wanted him to see the sides of me he couldn't see in a casino and I wanted to see the same in him. But the other part of me said that somehow that could all be achieved by going to Vegas with him. Oh, maybe not the Frisbee-in-the-park part—I wasn't sure they even had parks in Vegas—but certainly the rest could. I'd go with Billy, I'd be his talisman so he could win again, and I'd finally win enough to buy my Jimmy Choo Ghosts.

# 16

But before jet-setting off to Sin City, I had some living to get through. True, the casinos offered incredible air-hotel-chips package deals to anyone foolish enough to think they could beat the House, but it still cost too much to book air with less than twenty-one-day notice and I needed to save some cash for my stake.

"I'll pay your way, Baby," Billy said. "I'll put it on my credit card."

"No." I turned him down. "I will not be a kept talisman." I had to remain firm about some things. "Either we do this my way, or we don't go."

"What will we do in the meantime?"

"Date?"

"Ah, more foreplay. Well, I suppose I could just manage

that." I wasn't sure if he was being dry-wit British witty or if he meant to convey it'd be a trial and was unsure if I really wanted that resolved so I kept silent.

Putting off the trip until October meant that I had yet to become Delilah Sampson, Exciting Casino Girl and was still simply Delilah Sampson, Boring Window Washer. This meant assuming the position at Stella's beck and call as per usual.

"Not Mr. Clean!" I shouted, when Stella informed me whose house we'd be doing that day.

"Yes, Mr. Clean," she insisted. Then she shook her head like a Himalayan cat shedding water. "I mean, Mr. Johnson. How do you always get me to call my customers by the ridiculous names you make up for them?"

"I don't know." I shrugged. "It's a habit I picked up from my dad. He always has nicknames for people. He's Black Jack, he calls me Baby, we used to have a neighbor he called The Man In The Rubber Shoes, his bookie was Two-Dollar Sollie, his best friend was Two-Brew Jew, one of his sisters was Slats, the other was Gold Star, if he met you you'd be—"

"I don't care what kind of bizarre names your relatives have for people." She cut me off. "Just stop doing it with my customers. I swear, one day you'll get me so confused I'll do it to a customer's face. I'll call Mr. Johnson 'Mr. Clean' or I'll call Mrs. Smith 'The Bitch' and then we'll all be screwed."

*Sheesh.* That's what a person got for trying to make the workplace more colorful.

"Hey," I called over the back of my seat, "how come you two are so quiet today? We've been in the truck for a half hour and you haven't even insulted me once yet. Is something wrong?"

"Shut up, *chica*," Rivera said.

"Yeah, mind your own business," Conchita said.

*Sheesh*. That's what a person got for trying to make the workplace a more colorful place to be.

"Fine," I said, "I won't even tell you what kind of great nicknames my dad would come up with for you."

"We already know, *chica,*" Rivera said. "He'd call us The Girls From Brazil. Just like you."

"Yeah," Conchita said, "you are just so clever."

He would not call them that. I folded my arms across my chest. My dad was a creative man. He'd come up with something much better than that.

"Yeah," Rivera said, "you and everyone in your family are just so clever."

Stella glanced over at me and I raised my eyebrows right back at her. Translation: "What gives?" The Girls From Brazil had always sniped at me, but they'd never been so sour before. Stella shrugged. Translation: "Who knows?"

Oh, well, I sighed. We'd figure it out later.

"So," I asked Stella, "what do I do when Mr. Clean follows me around from window to window?"

"When *Mr. Johnson* follows you around from window to window, you let him."

"And what do I do when Mr. Clean wipes out the

window wells a second time after I've already made them spotless the first?"

"If *Mr. Johnson* wants to wipe his window wells all day long, you let him. They're his window wells."

"And when Mr. Clean—"

"Look, Delilah, I don't care how eccentric Mr. Clean is. He's got a little problem, okay? But he's a good customer. He always pays his bills the same day—never makes me wait for it like some do while they're on some kind of round-the-world cruise, as though the window washer doesn't need to eat, too, while they're eating round-the-clock buffets—and he even pays double because he understands that he expects a lot from us."

"How can he miss it?" I snorted. "We always do him and his neighbor the same day. They have identical houses and his neighbor's takes only half the time."

"So? The man has got a problem," she said again. "He just can't help himself. I would think that you, of all people, would be a little more charitable."

The problem, the way I always saw it whenever we did his house, was that Mr. Clean's problems were mostly my problems.

True, at the beginning of each trip to his house, he'd spend a few minutes following Stella and the others around as they set up on the outside.

"Did you remember to bring the ladder mitts?" he'd ask each time, as though Stella could possibly forget his particular needs. "Did you remember the ladder mitts for all the ladders?" he'd ask anxiously, squinting up into the sky as Stella propped the twenty-eight-foot extension ladder high enough she'd be able to hop off and do his skylights; give Stella credit, when it came to heights, the woman had balls. "You know," he'd say meekly, "I just don't want to get any scratches on the paint job."

Personally, I always thought the yellow-orange rubber ladder mitts made those noble aluminum ladders look neutered, their proud masculine edges compromised, not unlike a guy in a condom: a necessary evil, true, but still. As far as Mr. Clean was concerned, though, even if Stella washed down the ends of her ladders with soap and water right before his very eyes, there was just no way those ladders were flying commando.

Then, once he had them set up outside, the real fun started.

Mr. Clean, who was well over six feet, balding and with a slight paunch, would start trailing my work on the inside. Keep in mind, most of our regular customers had day jobs that took them out of the house, as did Mr. Clean, but the others were more than content to leave a key discreetly hidden on the property. Hey, we were fully insured and bonded. There was nothing to worry about. But not Mr. Clean. Mr. Clean's appointments always needed to be carefully scheduled so he could take the day off. I guess watching someone wash your windows was so damn much fun, he didn't want to miss a thing.

Of course there's nothing fun about watching someone wash windows. I mean, after you've seen the first, they're all pretty much the same, although like with Olympic gymnastics, there are degrees of difficulty, like the windows over kitchen sinks or the ones over the tubs in these giant bathrooms everyone seems to be installing. But it's still hardly exciting stuff. And I don't think even Mr. Clean found any of it exciting; if anything, it was probably his most nerveracking activity of any season and he put himself through it in both fall and spring.

He just couldn't help himself.

"Here," he said, "you can leave your sneakers outside." I hated climbing my stepladder with stocking feet.

"Here," he said, bringing me a sheet that was still warm from the dryer as I set up my little stepladder in his living room. "The ladder won't slide on the floor and it'll pick up any fluid splatter."

I was tempted to huff at him that I never splattered. He should know that by now. But I knew there was no point. If I resisted, his anxiety level would only rise.

I reached for my can of Stella's Magic Spray and waited to hear the pitter-patter of his stocking feet leaving me in peace. But of course *that* wasn't going to happen.

So I just went ahead and did it. I just sprayed.

And then I picked up exactly three wadded-up sheets of paper towel and started to wipe…

"What about the squeegee?" Mr. Clean stridently yelled at me. "Aren't you going to use the squeegee?"

I sighed.

A part of me was tempted to explain to Mr. Clean just how I'd won my Golden Squeegee Award, an honor that was awarded for both perfection *and* speed. Over time, I'd come to realize that once we had done a job, removing sometimes years of neglect in the form of grime, so long as the customer had us back regularly, I could do just as good of a job—I would argue, better—by simply performing the tried-and-true procedure of spraying and wiping. Magic Spray, in its cheerful blue-white-and-silver canister, was a product made in window-cleaner heaven. Foaming on contact with the glass, it left no streaks; and, as good as I was with a squeegee when compelled to use one, it always left some streaks that needed to be wiped away. So right-handed I can't even scratch a mosquito bite with my left, I could still push a spray nozzle with it. Spray with the left, wipe with the right: with Magic Spray in my life, I was a two-armed cleaning bandit.

But now, just like he'd neutered Stella's poor ladders, he wanted to neuter me.

"It'll actually come out better this way," I started to say.

"Oh, no." Mr. Clean shook his head. "There'll be dirt left in the corners."

How, I wanted to ask, could there be dirt left in the corners, when there was no dirt to begin with?

"Really—" he nodded his head emphatically, as though he'd just won an argument with himself "—I'd feel much better if you used the squeegee."

"But—"

I was thinking to point out that it would go quicker my way and then he'd have my grubby little self with my dusty little sneakers out of his way that much sooner, and wouldn't that be a good thing? But he never let me finish.

"Please?" He was practically begging now, I swear I saw sweat popping out on his domed forehead. "Use the squeegee?"

"Well, if you insist…"

And so the next hour passed.

Mr. Clean wasn't a bad guy. Believe me, we had plenty of evil customers and he wasn't one of them. In fact, deep down inside, no matter what I said to Stella, I *liked* Mr. Clean. I felt sorry for him, pitied him. The only problem was, every time I was with him, I worried we were two peas in a pod. He was such an odd guy and every time I was in his house, we each had to get used to the other all over again.

I knew a little bit about Mr. Clean from previous visits because, once he did get used to me, Mr. Clean—a man people probably tried to avoid talking to whenever possible—was quite a talker. I knew he worked in some kind of investment capacity in the city (I'll bet the train ride in just killed him, despite that Metro North had spruced up some of their train cars), I knew his first marriage ended in divorce (I'll bet his first wife wanted to kill him), I knew he had a habit of…collecting things.

Mr. Clean had a sunroom that housed a plant collection to rival the Botanical Gardens. Okay, maybe not that grand, but you get the picture. And he treated them each as lovingly as other people treated their kids or pets. Now, don't get me wrong. I like plants as much as the next person, unless of course the next person is Mr. Clean, and it's not as if I go around deadheading rosebushes willy-nilly, but it seemed to me he took his horticultural love a bit too far when he gave his plants names: the spider plant, I heard him murmur "Cassandra" to, the fern was "Sally," which seemed like an odd choice of name for a fern. Not that there's a right name for a fern, but you had to wonder, why "Sally"? It got even odder when he got married for a second time earlier that year and his second wife's name turned out to be Sally. I mean, when he said "Sally," did the right living thing know which he was talking to?

"Sally," I heard him say now, but when I turned I saw he was talking into his cell phone, so I figured he was talking to the wife. "Ophelia—" that was the ficus "—is looking peaked. Do you think you could pick up that special plant food she loves on the way home? I'd get it myself, but I'm stuck here with the window washers all day."

"RAHRUHRUHRAHRAH!" I heard shouted through the cell phone. I had no idea what Sally The Person was saying, but I knew she was shouting it because I could hear her sounding like the teacher from those old Charlie Brown specials all the way on the other side of the room.

"I know it's out of your way," Mr. Clean said, "but I really think Ophelia won't last the night if we don't make her feel special. Come to think of it, Sally's not looking so hot, either."

"RAHRUHRUHRAHRAH!"

"*I* can't leave now!" Mr. Clean shouted, or at least he shouted as much as a meek person can shout. "The window washers are here! I *can't* leave the window washers all by themselves, alone with the—" he lowered his voice here "—windows."

But he needn't have lowered his voice. Discreetly, I moved off to another room. It was just too painful to listen anymore.

Unfortunately, the next room was one of Mr. Clean's hobby rooms, this one being the one where he kept all his model cars, each one of which he'd glued together with such precision you couldn't even see any remnant glue left around even the tiniest pieces. All that painstaking small work, thinking of him sitting alone with the plastic and chrome pieces of his models spread out all about him and his airplane glue—maybe he'd sniffed too much?—and no doubt worrying all the while about smearing any of it. That made me sad, too.

And the thing I heard next made me saddest of all: Mr. Clean saying, "Okay, dear, but if you could just pick up that special plant food on the way home" into the phone as he came into the room to check up on me, and realizing that Mr. Clean's second marriage would go the same way as the first. His obsessions would get the best of him, Sally The Person would get sick of his obsessions even while Sally The Plant thrived under them, and before long, he'd be alone again.

Sometimes, it just didn't do to let obsessions rage out of control.

★ ★ ★

"I finally found out what was wrong," Stella said in hushed tones as we were loading up the van side by side; Conchita and Rivera were still folding up their ladders.

"Yeah, you're telling me," I said. "Mr. Clean is fucking nuts."

"I didn't mean that," she said. "I mean about Conchita and Rivera."

"What's going on?"

"For the first time ever, they're both dating other people...exclusively."

"Oh, man," I said.

"Exactly. Each is upset about what the other is doing, each insists she has the right to do it herself."

"It's like a mammary nightmare," I admitted.

"What?"

"Never mind. I was just being small-minded."

"Like, when aren't you? But I've got a business to run here. I can't have them acting like this in front of the customers. Earlier today, Conchita punched Rivera so hard she nearly fell through a window. Thank God, Mr. Clean was too busy inside with you to notice what was going on."

"Yes, thank *God* Mr. Clean was with me. Really, what would I ever do without him?"

# 17

The weeks preceding the Vegas trip passed quickly, even if I was often solitary. Hillary now spent so much time with Biff that if it weren't for the fact that there were still two refrigerators in our home, you'd swear I lived there alone. Elizabeth Hepburn had put off my overtures to visit, saying she was recuperating nicely and that she was so busy reading Chick Lit and enjoying her Jimmy Choos, she didn't have much time for chat, adding that Lottie had been just barely tolerable lately ("She may want me to hurry up and die," she said, "but I don't think she's putting arsenic in my food…yet."). Conchita and Rivera were engaging in a silent war, both supposedly in love with other people, both acting more miserable than you'd think two people in love would act. Stella was unusually quiet and seemed wrapped up in her own mysterious preoccupation, although she still did have enough time to harass me ("The sun is your harshest critic, Delilah. I can see streaks on that window. Whatever happened to The Golden Squeegee?").

Of course, The Golden Squeegee had her own preoccupations, being simultaneously obsessed with Billy Charisma and blackjack. The former called her every day and said he couldn't wait to see her again; he even took her—that would be me—on a few dates, but they were always dates that ended chastely with Billy saying he wanted to hold off on the grand event until Vegas. As for the latter, in the hopes of hitting the jackpot in every way with Billy in Vegas, I'd been trying to enlist my dad's aid, but he kept pleading off, saying he had meetings to go to, saying he had to work. I still couldn't believe he'd taken a job as a security guard. Finally, in desperation, on the Monday before I was scheduled to fly west for my big adventure, I showed up on his doorstep unannounced, intuiting that if I called first, he'd only say no again.

"No," he said as soon as he saw me, after I'd once again pounded on the door for what seemed like minutes.

"I haven't even said what I'm here for yet," I said.

"I know what you're here for," he said, starting to close the door in my face. "And the answer is no."

"God, Dad," I said, quickly inserting my Nike into the breach so he couldn't close the door all the way, "you're acting like I'm trying to sell you Girl Scout cookies."

"You're trying to sell me something worse than Girl

Scout cookies," he said, still pushing the door against my foot as though he might push right through it. "You're trying to sell me the road to hell."

"What are you talking about? I have good intentions!"

"I'm not going back to that life, Baby. I'm finally out. I won't let you drag me back in again."

"Crap! Who *are* you? Al Pacino? And what have you done with my dad? Where's Black Jack?"

"I'm not Black Jack anymore."

"What? What are you talking about?"

"I'm Jack. I'm just Jack."

"Wha—"

"This hasn't been easy for your father," a voice said, a very feminine if throaty voice, I might add.

Then the door swung open and I saw behind my dad, who was dressed in his security guard's uniform, a pretty older woman, about ten years younger than him, with auburn hair and sparkling blue eyes. Oh, and she was wearing the velour robe my dad had been wearing the last time I visited.

Uh-oh.

"Who are you," I asked, "and why are you wearing my dad's robe?"

"It's my robe, actually." She thrust out a confident hand for a shake and I took it dumbly. My dad was sometimes wearing some woman's robe? "Vanessa Parker. And I know who you are. You're Baby. Your dad talks about you all the time."

He did?

"Come in," Vanessa said.

I entered, still dumbly, feeling odd to be invited this way into my dad's home as though she lived there and I was the guest.

"Something to drink?" she offered. "Diet Pepsi Lime? Jake's Fault Shiraz?"

"I see he has been telling you a lot about me," I said.

"Michael Angelo's Four Cheese Lasagna?" my dad offered, hopefully. "If you're hungry, I can whip some up in six minutes, tops."

"Thanks, no," I said. "I seem to have lost my appetite."

"I'm sorry, Baby. I kept meaning to tell you, but the time never was just right."

"You could have called, you could have sent a letter. It's not exactly like I'm the hardest person in the world to get a hold of. Tell me what, by the way?"

Vanessa took my dad's hand as though one of them needed support for the announcement they were obviously about to make.

"I've been living here," she said defiantly.

"Well, apparently," I huffed. "My dad's been wearing your robe."

"I knew she'd be upset," Vanessa said, turning to my dad. "I told you that even if she is twenty-eight years old, she wouldn't like the idea of someone taking her mother's place, not after having you to herself for ten years."

"Nobody's replacing anybody," my dad said. "You and

Lila, you're like those apples and oranges. She's dead. You're here. That's hardly what I'd call replacing."

"I don't care about that!" I interrupted their little tête-à-tête. I mean, I *did* care about it, just not right then. "What I care about—" I looked straight at my dad, ignoring That Other Woman "—is that for weeks now, I've been trying to get a hold of you, I've been trying to get your help with something I desperately need your help with—" it was true, for while I might have been Billy's talisman, I felt as though my dad was the talisman I needed to win enough to impress Billy, or at least I felt as though I couldn't take on the mecca of Vegas without the benefit of my dad's expertise "—and you keep being unavailable—"

"I can't be available for you in that way anymore, Baby. I'm sorry. I'm giving all of that up."

I looked at Vanessa. "What kind of witch *are* you?"

"A good witch," she said, "a very good witch who loves your father."

"Don't talk about the woman I love that way, Baby," my dad admonished.

It really was too much.

"I met her at Debtors Anonymous," my dad said.

"Bettors Anonymous," Vanessa corrected. "And we didn't meet there. Remember?"

This was just getting worse and worse.

"She's right," my dad said. "We met in the supermarket. She made those cherry tomatoes look like just so many cherry tomatoes."

"I invited him out for a drink."

"I said yes."

"I had a strawberry milkshake."

"For me it was the coffee."

"One thing led to another."

"She found out what I did for a living, what I *used* to do."

"I told him he couldn't have both me and the gambling, that he had to pick between the two, that I didn't mind living in a tiny apartment with him for the rest of my life but I'd be damned if I'd ride the emotional-financial roller coaster of bouncing back and forth between apartment and mansion, apartment and mansion."

"So I promised I'd go to Debtors Anonymous meetings with her."

"Bettors Anonymous. I used to be a gambler myself."

"And now we go together, a couple of times every week."

"You're evil!" I said to Vanessa.

"Stop that right this minute, Baby."

"But don't you realize how bad the timing *sucks* for your…your…your…your *conversion?*"

"Hey, I'm never too old to learn a new trick."

"But I'm going to Vegas this weekend!"

"Vegas? You want to talk Vegas?" Without comment, he left the room.

"Where's he going?" I asked.

"Who knows?" Vanessa shrugged. "He's your father."

A minute later, he returned, his hand clutching several small slips of paper.

"Here," he said.

"What's this?" I asked.

"That's Vegas," he said. "You're holding Vegas right in your hand."

"Gee, it doesn't look like an oasis with casinos and neon lights in the middle of the desert. Who would have thought that Vegas was just a bunch of little white slips of paper?"

"Believe me, that's Vegas. Read 'em and weep."

I looked at the slips of paper. They were dated receipts from ATM machines.

"I bring them to meetings with me," he said. "They're a reminder of how sick I am."

"I'm still not sure what I'm supposed to be seeing."

"Every ATM receipt tells a story," Vanessa said oh-so-helpfully.

"Thank you, Rod Stewart," I said, "but I still don't—"

"It's a record of my last trip to Vegas with Dan The Man," my dad said.

"Dan The Man is Jack's football bookie," Vanessa said.

"I know who Dan The Man is," I said. "Believe me, I've been hearing about Dan The Man for a lot longer than you have."

My dad grabbed the receipts back from me, studied them. Sure, it was rude for him to just grab like that, but at least he wasn't admonishing me again to speak nicer to Vanessa. As for Vanessa, I didn't really mind that my father finally had someone to fill the vacancy my mom had left—*much*—but I minded a lot that she was keeping him from fulfilling his duties to me, his only child and blackjack heir. Color me selfish, but I had Choos to win.

"No wonder you couldn't figure it out," he said, shuffling the order of the slips of paper. "They weren't arranged properly so a person could read the story in order, kind of like a book that jumps all over the place. Here, try again." He handed the papers back to me.

But I guess he still didn't trust me to be smart enough to figure it out on my own, because he stood beside me, pointing with his finger so I wouldn't miss a thing as he narrated his tale.

"This is Saturday afternoon, at two-fifteen. We'd arrived late the night before, so all was good up to this point. I started out winning right off the bat, nearly doubled my stake before packing it in for the night. But the next morning, who knows what happened? First the losing started in dribs and drabs, or five-dollar chips and ten-dollar chips, but then by the time I hit the ATM for the first time, my stake was gone."

The first receipt was for one hundred dollars. What's a hundred between friends? But hadn't Black Jack always said you should walk away if you lose your stake?

"What's a hundred between friends, right?" he echoed my thoughts. Then he shuffled to the next slip. "But as you can see," he said, "six hours later, having multiplied my hundred as high as a thousand, it all disintegrated and I was back at the ATM."

This one said two hundred dollars.

And from there on, the slips decreased in time intervals while increasing in withdrawal amounts. The last, for five thousand dollars, was on Sunday afternoon.

"That was right before heading for the airport. It's amazing how quickly you can blow through five thousand dollars in chips at the high-stakes tables."

"Wow," I said. If I'd been doing the math right, he'd lost ten grand in a single weekend. Sure, he'd lost more in the past. But he'd also had more to lose in the past.

"Oops, one more," he said.

This one, time-stamped four-eighteen, was at the airport ATM and was for fifty dollars.

"Parking at the other end?" I asked.

"Nah, it was for the airport slots. I was hoping to at least recoup a little while waiting to board, but no such luck. At the other end, I had to borrow from Dan The Man to get my car back from extended parking in White Plains."

"How'd Dan do?" I asked, vaguely curious.

"Oh, his ATM story was even worse than mine. But you know Dan. He's got the book behind him, so he can afford it."

True.

"So," the man formerly known as Black Jack Sampson sighed, "that's how I lost the house."

"Wait a second. Back up. What do you mean you lost the house?" I studied the slips. "You didn't *lose* the house on this trip. You lost the house last year. These slips are dated a little over a month ago. Besides, ten thousand dollars isn't exactly a house. Not since around 1950, it's not."

"True, but I'd been planning on winning the house back. Well, not the same house, but at least *a* house. I had it all planned out. If I kept doubling my money over the course of the weekend, by the time I left I'd have enough for a down payment on a new place, a place that would make you proud to come to see me."

"I'm always proud to come see you, Dad."

"Fine. Then I haven't been proud to have you see me like this. I wanted to do better. But instead I lost everything."

"You didn't even have the money to bail your own car out of extended parking. You were rock bottom."

"Exactly. It was the next night, while doing the grocery shopping with the little money I had under the mattress, that I met Vanessa in front of the cherry tomatoes."

"My hair clashed," Vanessa said, "but Jack didn't seem to notice."

"She talked me into getting a job as a security guard and going to Debtors Anonymous—"

"Bettors Anonymous."

"—and the rest is history."

"Fine. Great," I said. "I'm really happy for you that you've found each other and that you're living here together in bathrobe heaven. But I'm still going to Vegas this weekend. I still need Dad to help me out just one last time. After this, I promise I'll stop. I promise I won't ask anymore."

"But that's what everyone always says, Baby," Vanessa said with great sadness. "Everyone always says they want just one last time, that that'll be it. And then they go back."

"Vanessa's right," my dad said. "I just can't do it. Look what happened to me."

"Look what happened to you? You got the girl!"

"I'm sorry, Baby," Vanessa said, "Jack just can't participate in your ruin."

"Yeah," he said, "I can't participate in your ruin."

Vanessa kissed him on the head. "I'm going to go take my shower now," she said. "It was nice meeting you, Baby. Maybe next time we can have a real dinner together and I'll even wear real clothes."

"What does she do for a living?" I asked once she was gone.

"She's the head counselor at Debtors Anonymous."

Of course.

"Look, Dad, I just need—"

"Shh." He held his finger to his lips. Then, cocking his ear and hearing the sound of the shower drumming in the bathroom, he tiptoed into the kitchen and got a locked box down from the top of the fridge.

"What's in there?" I asked as he opened it.

"Didn't I just say 'shh'?" he whispered. "It's got my insurance policies and birth certificate in it, stuff like that."

Why was he showing me this now?

"Is something wrong with you?" I asked. Maybe he'd taken up with Vanessa to have one last fling before meeting up with the Great Croupier In The Sky.

"Nothing like that," he whispered. "I just keep all my important stuff in here, plus a few things I don't want anyone else to see…like this."

It was a slim paperback, vaguely familiar in cover design.

"*You* read *Blackjack Winning Basics,* by Tony Casino?" I was shocked.

"Shh! I don't want Vanessa to know I kept it."

"But why would you need to read—?"

"Listen, Baby, all the greats need some help, a little re-minding, every now and then. Do you think every time Beethoven sat down to play *Ode to Joy,* he remembered all the notes?"

"Well, actually, y—"

"Never mind that now. Really, there's nothing I can teach you that isn't in that book. And, anyway, I'd lose Vanessa if I *did* try to teach you."

I studied the cover of the book as if it contained the mystery of the sphinx: *Blackjack Winning Basics,* by Tony Casino.

I couldn't believe that, instead of helping me, my dad was giving me *a book.*

"You're on your own, Baby."

I was on my own.

What do you do on the eve of your trip to Las Vegas, when your best friend is sleeping over at her boyfriend's place because you didn't want to ruin her good time by letting her know how important this is to you, when your dad has taken up with a redhead who won't even let him talk gambling anymore much less do it, when the two Brazilian girls you work with aren't speaking to each other let alone anyone else, when the fact that your boss was never your friend anyway rules her out, when the guy you're going with is the last person you should be revealing your anxieties to? You go see the fading Hollywood star who's slept with everyone who's anyone, plus more, which is exactly what I did.

"How did you know it when you were in love?"

"Who are we talking about?"

We were in Elizabeth Hepburn's bedroom, a pink affair with frilly curtains, flattering lighting, round bed with white fur bedspread—fake fur, I was almost sure—and round mirror overhead. If only that mirror could talk, I wondered what tales it had to tell. I was seated in a chair beside the bed and Elizabeth Hepburn had put down her Chick Lit book just long enough to offer me the sage advice I needed, the sage advice I couldn't find anywhere else.

"I don't know," I shrugged. "Any of them."

"Well, if we're talking about Errol Flynn, it was the sword."

"Yes, but wasn't he—"

"If we're talking about the Sultan of Brunei, it was the money."

My eyebrows shot up. "You've been to Brunei?"

"If we're talking about Frank Sinatra, it was the voice."

"Not the eyes?"

"Hey, Paul Newman had blue eyes, too. Sometimes the eyes *don't* have it."

"Um, don't you mean *ayes?*" I said, raising my hand.

"We're not talking about voting here, Delilah," she said with uncommon snappishness. "But if we were, I could tell you a few things about Roosevelt."

"You were with Franklin Roosevelt?"

"Who said anything about Franklin?"

"But wouldn't Teddy have been too far before your time? Just how old are you?"

"Who said anything about Teddy Roosevelt? I'm talking about Joe, Joe Roosevelt, the guy who serviced my Packer back in the forties. He used to fix elections and my engine like nobody's business."

"I see."

"What gives? What's with the love questions?"

I explained about my dad hooking up with Vanessa. A part of me was glad he had someone other than me and Dan The Man to spend time with now, a part of me worried she might not be good enough to fill my mother's penny loafers. Already she was changing him.

"And all this is about your father?" she asked.

I nodded.

"Excuse me for saying this, Delilah, but horseshit. People don't visit little old ladies at night to ask about their father's love life, not unless of course they want to fix the little old lady up with their father. How old did you say he was again?"

"I didn't, but he is kind of taken right now."

Which would be worse, having Elizabeth Hepburn for a stepmother, the woman who liked to pretend she'd done

Dallas before Debbie? Or having Vanessa Parker for a step-mother, the woman who was currently neutering my dad from Black Jack to just plain Jack?

"Bummer," Elizabeth Hepburn said. "If he was free and we got married, maybe I'd be able to fire Lottie The Ghoul."

Just then The Ghoul walked in.

"Do you need anything else tonight, Ms. Hepburn?" The Ghoul asked. "Isn't your visitor leaving yet? I could get you some tea after she goes…"

"No, thanks. I'll make my own in the morning."

Once The Ghoul was gone, Elizabeth Hepburn whispered, "I used to not worry that she was poisoning me, but lately I sense a certain desperation around the edges. The other day she suggested I get my bedroom repainted a darker shade of pink. At first, I was tempted, but then I remembered what happened to Clare Booth Luce."

"Clare Booth Luce?"

"When she was ambassador, she started getting a weird kind of sick." She nodded sagely. "Then they found arsenic in the paint that was used to redo her bedroom."

"You don't think Lottie would…"

"I'm not saying nothing," she said, going all James Cagney on me. "All I'm saying is, I'm not eating anything, I'm not drinking anything, I'm not sniffing anything, unless I pour it, cook it, paint it myself."

"Have you ever cooked a meal in your life?"

"Hey, I can make toast when I want to. And don't forget my cookies. It was how we met, remember?"

"But if Lottie's so bad, if you're worried she might be out to *kill* you, why don't you just fire her?"

"I've tried to tell you before, you have no idea how hard it is to find good live-in help."

"What's so good about live-in help that wants to kill you?"

"Hey, at least she's not boring."

"I guess." Then I thought of something. "I'm going to ask Stella if she'll keep an eye on you while I'm gone, maybe pop in occasionally. You know, just to be on the safe side."

"You're going away?"

"Yes, I—"

"Oh, good, I like Stella. In that uniform of hers, she reminds me exactly of Dean Martin, except she's not a man, has blond hair and I don't think she sings."

"No," I said. "Stella doesn't usually sing."

"Rats. It's that guy from Foxwoods, isn't it?"

"Excuse me?"

"The guy who has your knickers all in a twist. It's that guy with the blond hair and his own tuxedo and The Voice, isn't it?"

I admitted as much, explained that we were leaving for Vegas the next day just as soon as I got off work, how Billy and I were going away together for four days, how I'd persuaded Stella that Columbus Day was a holiday I truly did need to have off for observance.

"You're not Italian," Stella had said.

"True," I'd replied, "but I do eat a lot of Michael

Angelo's Four Cheese Lasagna, plus all those Amy's Cheese Pizza Pockets."

"Oh, brother," Elizabeth Hepburn said now. "I would not trust that one as far as I could throw him."

"Um, I don't think you could throw him at all." I sighed. "The Girls From Brazil, Stella, Hillary, *you*—nobody seems to trust Billy. What's up with that?"

"The guy hangs out at casinos, he wears a tux in the daytime and his name is Billy Charisma. How many reasons do I need?"

"You're saying I shouldn't go?"

"Are you kidding me? And miss the chance to be with that blond hair, that tuxedo that's never been worn by other bodies, even if he does wear it in the daytime, too, and The Voice?" Her own voice turned conspiratorial. "Hey, wanna sell me your ticket?"

"Then you're saying I should go?"

"Hell, *yes.* Just be careful."

"How so?"

"Well, don't do anything I wouldn't do."

That certainly left the field wide-open.

# 18

I got my first foreshadowing that all would not go perfectly well on the trip to Vegas on the plane ride out.

Billy had made all the arrangements. We were to fly out of White Plains with layovers in Chicago and St. Louis.

"Isn't that a little insane?" I asked. "Isn't it a little too much stop-start to land in Chicago and then just basically land on the other side of the state again before heading off to your real destination?"

Billy shrugged. "They're both hub airports. I think they just like to get you to spend as many tourist dollars in the gift shops as possible."

Apparently, he'd done more traveling than I had. Me, I'd mostly done none.

"Yes—" I still resisted "—but wouldn't it be more normal to have just one layover each way?"

"Ah, but that would depend on where your destination is, plus you wouldn't get the added pleasure of flying Flaps Airways for only fifty-nine dollars round-trip."

"Will we have to fly holding on to the wing the whole time?" I asked him.

"Oh, come on, Baby," he said, stowing the olive-green garment bag that no doubt held his tuxedo in the minuscule overhead bin, "it's not that bad. It'll be an adventure."

Some adventure.

In truth, though, it wasn't the primitive aircraft that made me feel unsettled as we took off.

"If you grip the armrests any tighter," he said, "you'll punch an ashtray hole through the screwed-over metal where one used to be."

Nor was it that he still wouldn't tell me what hotel we were staying at.

"I want it to be a surprise," he said.

"Will it be a surprise like Flaps Airways is a surprise?" I asked, still gripping those armrests.

"No, I think you'll like this surprise. I want to take you somewhere fit for a queen, somewhere where it'll be the perfect natural setting for your special talents to flow forth."

"I'm going to be washing the windows at The Mirage?"

"No, Baby," he laughed.

It wasn't even that he seemed to laugh at me a lot.

It was the food.

So far, with the exception of the night I'd spent in Billy's bed sans Billy, I'd only taken day trips away from the comforting habits I'd cocooned myself in for years. True, I'd probably be able to scare up a glass of Jake's Fault Shiraz somewhere, but what was I going to do for four whole days and three whole nights without my beloved Cocoa Krispies, my beloved Diet Pepsi Lime, my beloved Amy's Cheese Pizza Pockets and my beloved Michael Angelo's Four Cheese Lasagna? Sure, I could fake it for one or two meals here and there, but this really was too much.

"What do you think they'll give us for dinner?" I asked.

"Where?"

"Here. On the plane."

"You're joking, right? You'll be lucky to get a stale package of pretzels." He thought about it for a minute. "I'm pretty sure they've given up serving peanuts because of all the people who suddenly have severe nut allergies these days. We'll grab a bite on the run, if you're hungry, when we stop in Chicago. Hey, if eating is the most important thing for you about this trip, we can eat again in St. Louis, too."

I pictured what the hub airports would be like, with all their chain restaurants. I'd starve. The good news was, by the time the trip was over, I'd be skinnier than I'd been in years. If I wasn't dead from starvation.

And, no, I guess it wasn't the food, either, although that was certainly a preoccupation. It was everything. It was leaving behind all the comforts of home, not just the food. It was leaving behind the security of family, of friends, of *routine* to fly into the unknown with a man I had yet to spend more than several hours with at a single go.

"You seem so tense, Baby," Billy said. "Just remember one thing." He covered his hand with mine. "Whatever happens in Vegas, *stays* in Vegas."

Oh, brother.

"Welcome to Vegas, Baby," Billy said, gallantly handing me out of the limousine he'd hired to speed us out from the airport.

Nothing had prepared me for the surrealness of the city as I'd gazed down at it from the airplane, the sudden nuclear glow of neon bursting out of the darkness of the surrounding desert.

"Wait until you approach it like that from the ground," Billy said. "It's the oddest driving experience in the world. You're driving along in the desert and suddenly—boom!— bright lights, minicity."

"You actually drive outside of the city sometimes when you go there to gamble?" I was shocked. My dad had mentioned many times over the years that there was plenty to do in the Vegas area—hiking, the Hoover Dam, chopper flights to the Grand Canyon, tours of the Ethel M Chocolate Factory and the Liberace Museum—but that he'd just never bothered to do any of it.

"Of course not," Billy said. "I've just seen it like that coming in from the airport."

If Billy had skimped on the airline, he certainly hadn't

skimped on anything else. Not only was the limo a white stretch with full bar in the back and liveried driver, but the hotel…

"It's beautiful!" I jumped up and down, gazing up at its gold-toned monolithic twin structures. "I can't believe we're staying at THEhotel at Mandalay Bay!"

"You mean you've heard of it?" Billy sounded surprised.

"Well, no," I admitted, "but I do like the eccentric way they spell the name, THEhot—"

"C'mon," he said, grabbing my hand. "We'll let the bellhop grab our things. Let's go inside."

"It's beautiful!" I oohed again.

The lobby was indeed impressive, and not at all Las Vegas-y, what with its black walls, subtle lighting and overall eschewal of glitz. Not to mention…

"Is that a real Andy Warhol painting?"

"Try not to gape, Baby. Yes, it is. And that's an authentic Jasper Johns, too. You didn't think I'd take you to a dump, did you?"

I don't know what I'd thought. My dad had always said that since you spent all your time in the casinos in Vegas, the room didn't matter.

Suddenly, I wanted to see the room.

"Let's go." I tugged on his hand, tugging him toward the elevator banks.

"Let's go see the casino first," he said, distinctly tugging me in the other direction. "Don't you want to see the casino first? It's one hundred and thirty-five thousand square feet.

Can you imagine how big that is? They have twenty-four hundred slot-video poker machines, they have one hundred and twenty-two table games—"

"Please?" I said. "I need to settle in first. There'll be plenty of time for that later."

His expression softened.

"Of course, Baby," he said, "if you need to warm up to the place first." He patted my hand. "Anything you need."

"I *love* this room!" I said, flopping down on the cream-colored bedspread. It was huge! THEhotel at Mandalay Bay was an all-suite hotel and not only was there a giant plasma TV in our bedroom area, there was even one in our bathroom, as well! And the sitting room…which had a third TV…

"I could stay here all day," I said, "or at least all night."

He removed his tux from the garment bag, hung up the bag.

"Yes, well," he said, "if we start *that*…" He went off to the bathroom, presumably to change. But who knows? Maybe he was going to watch some TV.

Prior to the trip, we hadn't gone into the specifics of the sleeping arrangements. All I knew was that Billy had over-ridden my protests about paying my own way, saying, "Don't be ridiculous, Baby. My talisman doesn't pay her own way. What kind of person would I be if I expected you to accept such terms? And you needn't worry about owing me a tit for my tat. Anything that happens between us in that regard is purely your decision."

But of course as I'd seen firsthand that night at his cottage, it wasn't my decision, not if when I made my decision he could easily say no to me.

"I don't mind at all taking the couch in the sitting room," he said, adjusting his black bow tie as he emerged from the bathroom. "It's plenty long enough for me."

"I just assumed…" I said.

"What?" He looked up. "That I'd booked two separate rooms?" He shrugged. "Well, it is a bit pricey."

"No, I mean, I thought…"

"What? That we'd share the same bed? Look, why don't we wait and see how things develop, shall we? I'm sure that, after a night down in the casino, well, anything might happen."

He was right, wasn't he? Hadn't I come here to finally win enough for my Jimmy Choo Ghosts?

Still, something was stopping me.

"I just don't feel…ready," I said. "It was such a long flight, what with the layovers and all. I'm just worried that if I play now, I might…lose."

I was thinking about the sad story my dad's ATM receipts had told. And he even had an ATM machine with money in it to back him up! At least until he lost it all. I didn't even have that. If I lost my stake the very first night, I'd be stuck here until Monday with no money. Certainly, I'd feel foolish asking Billy for money.

Apparently, he could be made to see reason, though, or maybe there was something in the word *lose* I'd used, because he surprised me by saying, "Oh. Well. We can't have that."

"Thank you! Thank you!" I said. I was so relieved I threw myself into his arms. "I'm sure that by tomorrow morning I'll feel—"

"Yes. Well." He gently peeled my arms off. "I think at the very least we should go downstairs and look at the casino, don't you? That way the layout won't be completely unfamiliar to you tomorrow morning. I mean, it can't hurt you to just look, right?"

Of course, he was right. And he'd done so much for me already, paying for the trip, putting up with all my little idiosyncrasies without too much teasing. Why, he'd even had Diet Pepsi Lime on hand when I'd gone to visit him! When I thought about it, I realized he wasn't really asking for very much.

"Just let me throw some water on my face to freshen up," I said.

Then I noticed he looked antsy.

"Tell you what," I said. "Rather than holding you up, why don't you go down now, I'll put my own things away so they don't wrinkle any more than they have already, and I'll meet you down there in a few minutes?"

"How will you find me in one hundred and thirty-five thousand square feet of casino?"

"You'll be the man in the tux by the blackjack tables, right?"

*Ka-ching!*

It was difficult to tell, from the sound of the slots, whether more people were winning or losing. One thing was for certain: a lot of people were going to have sore right arms in the morning.

As I passed through the ocean of one-armed bandits and the roulette tables into the blackjack area, I craned my neck to find Billy among the multitude of gamblers. Despite that there were so many people crowded into the room, it being Friday night which was no doubt a hot time in the old town, I figured it wouldn't be that hard to find a man in a tux. After all, America had long since gone the way of down style, so that most people dressed in jeans or khakis in places where formally you would have only found black tie or some other form of formal dress, meaning that with the exception of the pit bosses, Billy would be the only one in jacket and tie and his tie was even a bow tie, and not an old-fashioned bow tie like Tucker Carlson's, but a really cool bow tie, a fuck-you bow tie. But what I hadn't counted on was that the crush of people, combined with my own tiny stature, would make the task as difficult as finding a free chip on the floor. I mean, who drops a chip in a casino without noticing?

"Mine!" a man shouted, knocking me over as he insinuated himself between two gaming tables and stamping his foot on the ground just within bounds of the pit.

"I believe that is the House's chip, sir," a pit boss said, ringing the man's ankle with his hand and stopping him cold.

"It's mine, I tell you," the man said. "I just dropped it."

"Ohh, *really?*" the pit boss said, with a little more sarcasm than I felt the situation warranted. And, hey, wasn't anyone going to help me up off the floor here? Crap. I guess I was going to have to do it myself...

"Then tell me," the pit boss said, "what denomination is the chip?"

The man tried to wiggle his foot so he could see underneath it, but the pit boss held firm.

"It was a twenty-five," the man said, a bead of sweat breaking out on his brow. "Yeah, that's it," he added. "It was a twenty-five."

The pit boss lifted the man's foot and with disdain set it down next to the chip.

"Sorry, sir," he said, picking up the chip and not looking sorry at all, "but it looks like the chip you didn't lose was a hundred. Perhaps you should have aimed higher? Better luck next time."

"Crap," the man muttered to himself. "Whatever happened to 'finders keepers'?"

"Whatever happened to 'you knock the lady down, you help her up'?" I countered with my own mutter.

"What did you say?" The man turned to me and now I could see him clearly for the first time, how disheveled he looked with his shirt half hanging out of his pants, a porkpie hat jammed on his head.

"You knocked me over." I stood my ground.

But apparently my problems were secondary and I was incidental.

"Did you see what that jerk just did?" he said to me, muffling his angry voice enough so the pit boss wouldn't overhear him. "He stole my chip!"

"Well, actually, I think he fairly successfully proved, even if he was a bit rude about it—"

"That was my chip! My last chip!"

"Oh, I'm sorry, but—"

"I was going to use it to stage the biggest comeback this town has ever seen!"

"Well, yes, I'm sure it would have been—"

"Hey, have you got some cash on you? You got a spare chip?"

"Well, no, I don't have any chips. I just got here and—"

"What about the cash then?" He snapped his fingers. "Come on, come on."

"Are you trying to *mug* me in the middle of a casino?"

"Mug? What are you talking about? I just figured, since it was your fault I lost my chip—"

"*My* fault? *Your* chip?"

"Of course." He looked a combination of shocked and hurt. "If you hadn't gotten in my way, I would have seen the exact denomination of that chip I lost and then that shyster could never have stolen it from me. I'll bet he goes out for drinks after work tonight…on me."

"I'm sure there must be rules that govern what a pit boss has to do when he finds a chip—"

"Come on, come on. Are you going to give me that fiver to make up for screwing up my night?"

"When did we agree on a fiver?"

"You're not going to just give me a handful of change, are you? I suck at the slots."

I was in a quandary. A part of me, the part with gumption, wanted to tell Mr. Porkpie to go scam someone else. But another part of me, the betting part, admired the idea of someone who could actually believe that all it would take would be five dollars to rebuild his fortunes and stage the biggest comeback Vegas had ever seen. Really, it took big balls to be as big of a jerk as this guy was being and it merited some kind of reward.

Reluctantly, I reached into my bag, located my purse. Then I opened it just the tiniest of cracks, for fear that if he saw what I had inside it, he'd be hitting me up for something bigger than a fiver.

"Thanks," he said, with apparent relief when I handed over the bill. Now that he had what he wanted, the tension in his expression eased as though we'd gone from being sort-of adversaries to being sort-of friends. "You know," he confided, "it really was my own damn fault."

"That's right," I said righteously, glad he was finally admitting it. "If you hadn't created so much bad karma by knocking me over—"

"What the fuck are you talking about? Get over it already! I meant I should never have forsaken my cardinal rule."

"Which is?"

"Always keep a fiver in your sock and you'll always have something to start over with."

"But what if you lose that fiver? That's what you're going to do now, isn't it, gamble some more?"

"Details. And, anyway, who said I was going to lose?"

"Well, you could."

"And all I'm saying is, missy, you should always stash a fiver in your sock and no matter what happens, somehow, you'll be okay." He glanced down at my feet, took in my Momo Flats. I'd worn the shoes for luck and, inside them, I was sockless.

"Oh," he said. "I guess it doesn't apply to dames."

"Who calls women *dames* anymore?"

But he ignored me. "Just put a fiver in your bra, missy, and you'll always do okay."

He was an odd person to be taking advice from, but it didn't seem prudent to be ignoring obvious omens and as soon as he walked off to stage his comeback, I hightailed it to the nearest restroom and stuffed a fiver in my Victoria's Secret. Hey, it didn't pay to be too careful, I thought, jiggling my shoulders around a bit as I tried to get used to the feel of the crisp money scratching against my boobs before hitting the casino again.

Where was Billy?

"Would you care for a drink?"

No, the speaker wasn't my purported date for the evening. It was a cocktail waitress in full casino mufti: towering heels, bustierlike leotard, hooker makeup and a feather or two.

"How do you walk in those things all night?" I asked, looking at her feet.

"Honey, if my bunions could talk, they'd say, 'Cut it out,

bitch,' but lucky for me, they can't talk or I'd be out of a job. Every time I turn around, they'd be flipping off some bozo or another."

I giggled. "Can toes flip someone off?"

"Believe me, when toes have been abused as much as mine have, they become capable of just about anything."

"Then why do you do it?"

"Are you kidding me?"

I shook my head.

"Well, let's see…" She consulted the high ceiling, perhaps reading the smoke signals from all the cigarettes. "Medical school lost my application, being a call girl might involve some daytime work and I hate to work a split shift, and I'm not smart enough to take the dealer's course."

"If you're smart enough to remember who gets which drink, I'd think you'd be smart enough to remember the basic rules of blackjack from the dealer's standpoint. It's pretty easy—draw to Sixteen, stand on Seventeen, if the player gets Twenty-one you pay back three to two and if the cards in the chute get low, reshuffle."

"Too many numbers." She shrugged. "Besides, it's not like I really remember everyone's drinks."

"You don't?"

"Hell, no. Oh, sure, I listen as well as I can, but mostly I just count how many people give me orders, then I order that many drinks from Charlie the bartender. And if Mr. Gin & Tonic ends up with Mr. Rum & Coke's drink, who's there to complain?"

"You mean the customers don't mind?"

"Nah, so long as it's a guy and he hasn't lost too much, I just wiggle a feather or two at him and he takes whatever I give him."

"But the women do mind?"

"It all depends." Another shrug. "Some do, some don't. I think some of the ladies like the feathers, too."

"Have you seen a gorgeous guy in a tux? Tall? Blond hair? Talks with a slightly British accent?"

"You mean Mr. Club Soda?"

I had no idea, but it sounded like Billy, at least when he was gambling.

But how did she remember *his* drink when she couldn't remember anyone else's? Oh yeah, that's right: Billy's charisma *was* memorable.

"Okay," I said. "That's him."

"Last time I saw him, he was down that second aisle over there—" she pointed "—third blackjack table on the left."

"Thanks."

"So, do you want that drink?"

"Sure." I thought about it. "Can I get a diet cola with lime squeezed into it."

"I don't see why not. Just don't be upset if I come back with a Seven-Up with lemon in it. Or if I don't find you again. That sometimes happens, too."

As she went off to maybe get my drink, I looked for Billy down the second aisle at the third blackjack table on the left. But Billy wasn't there.

Where was Billy?

I circled the entire blackjack area, weaving in and out between the tables, but I couldn't find him anywhere. Maybe, I started to think, I kept just missing him? Maybe, as I was desperately searching to find him, he was desperately searching for me?

That's it, I thought, coming to a stop with my back to the blackjack table that was most centrally located. I would just stand there and wait until he showed up. The Native Americans, formerly known as the American Indians, used to say that if you stayed in one spot long enough, eventually the whole world would come by. I didn't actually believe this was true—I mean, what were the chances that the Dalai Lama or the Pope or Tom Jones was going to just walk by?—and I wasn't even sure the Native Americans had ever really said or believed that. It was just something I'd read in a book. All I knew was that despite the fact that I wasn't burdened with the towering heels of the cocktail waitress, and even though I was wearing my gloriously comfortable Momo Flats, my dogs were tired after a day of travel and now a night of standing. Surely, if I just stayed in one spot and didn't move, surely if Billy was looking as hard for me as I was looking for him, the man of my dreams would find me right where I was standing.

"Delilah?"

Well, that wasn't Billy. Billy never called me by my given name. But it was obviously someone who knew me. I put together the surprising and the inevitable even as I whirled around and saw…

"Chris!"

It was Furthest Guy from the Yo-Yo Man commercials, aka Chris Westacott, only he was looking like I'd never seen him before. Rather than the scruffy hair and clothes I expected upon recognizing his voice, based on his appearance in Atlantic City, his hair had been recently trimmed so that all of the wave I remembered was gone and he was attired in the same outfit as the dealers: black pants, shiny cummerbund, white shirt with blouson sleeves. But before I could ask the obvious question of "What are you doing dressed like that?" he came at me with one of his own.

"What are you doing here?" he asked.

I looked pointedly around me: at the casino in general, at the blackjack tables in specific.

"Oh. Of course," he said, seeming disappointed.

"It's just a short trip," I said. "I'm here until Monday. But what are *you* doing here?"

"I work here," he said. "This is my day job. Well," he laughed, "except for the fact that I do it at night. But I'm just getting off duty. Want to have a drink?"

"I'd love to, but I'm—"

"Just one," he said, "and it doesn't even have to be an alcoholic drink. I've got to get home and practice."

"Practice?"

"Yeah, you know, practice? My yo-yoing."

"Oh, of course, but—" And then I stopped myself. I'd been about to say thanks, but no thanks, that I was waiting to find the friend I'd come with. But then I realized how silly that was. I'd been looking for Billy for how long now? My feet were so tired I needed to sit down, but if I sat down at one of the tables, I'd have to gamble and I just wasn't ready to gamble yet. So what was so wrong about having a quick drink with a sort-of old friend and resting my dogs for a bit? I could always go back to not finding Billy later.

"Sure, why not?"

"Great, I'll just go change real quick. Don't want my bosses to think I'm drinking with customers while on the job. Don't move."

I obeyed the instructions not to move, which gave me a few more minutes to wait for Billy, but by the time Chris returned in jeans and a light blue button-down shirt, Billy still hadn't come back.

"Ready?" he asked.

He took me up to the Mix Lounge, which had wall-to-wall black leather with red lighting.

"Mmm," I said, "it's very, um..."

"Cozy?"

"Well, maybe in a sadomasochistic way."

"True," he laughed. "But it's as far away as I can get from work and still be in the same building."

"Do you think they have Diet Pepsi Lime here?" I asked.

"If they don't," he said, "I'll make sure they do such a good job of imitating one, you won't know the difference." And when the bartender asked what we wanted, he made a persuasive case for the bartender to do just that.

"I heard Tom Jones is supposed to be here later on this weekend," he said, raising his voice to shout over the sound of music that had suddenly started to pound, "but tonight we're stuck with the DJ."

Ha! I knew if I stayed in one place long enough, eventually Tom Jones would show up. Maybe the Dalai Lama and His Holiness were soon to follow? *Not.*

"Can I ask you a question?" I asked.

"Sure."

So I asked him the same question he'd asked me just a short time ago. "What are you doing here?"

"Having a drink with you."

I playfully punched his arm. "Besides that. I mean, what are you doing working here?" I remembered what the cocktail waitress had said earlier. "Did medical school lose your application? Would being a call girl eat up too much of your daytime hours? Heels too tough on the feet to be a cocktail waitress?"

"Something like that."

"Huh?"

But he ignored my duh moment in favor of some introspection. "Sometimes," he said, "I hate all this."

"DJ music?" I said. "Well, I suppose it would be more fun if it were Tom Jones."

"I don't mean that. I mean working in a casino."

"Why?" For myself, I couldn't see it. I'd started to really love what used to be my father's place of business. Sure, all of the smoke was a bitch. But there was that constant edge of excitement. It was addicting, which was maybe one of the reasons I was hesitant to start playing again.

"Did you see some of those people down there?" he said.

"I saw a lot of people down there."

"Did you see the ones with that desperate look in their eyes, like everything that has to do with happiness in their life rides on what card they'll turn up next?"

"I guess I saw a few of those."

"I hate that. And did you see the guy who kept trying to find chips on the ground? What a character! The one in the porkpie hat scrounging around for just one chip?"

"Him I *definitely* saw."

"That's what I mean. Some of them are just so pathetic. And I hate being a part of all that patheticness. Some nights, I feel like what I do is no better than a crack dealer selling people cocaine."

"People have free will," I pointed out.

"Not much," he snorted.

"Then why do you do it?"

"Some nights I'm not altogether sure. I think I do it mostly because I was born here. This place is in my blood. What else do I know?"

"Yo-yos?" I suggested.

"Well, that's the dream, isn't it?" he conceded. "I guess that's the real reason I do it. The job here gives me my days free so I can work as much as I want to on my craft."

His craft? Wasn't he laying it on a bit thick now?

"It's great," he said. "Every day I yo-yo for several hours

and then I get to do local gigs, exhibitions like at parties and libraries and stuff, or work casinos in other states on my vacations like you saw me doing in Connecticut."

"Must be great," I said. I wasn't sure if I meant it or not— would it be great to pursue one's dream, even if that dream was to be a yo-yoist?—but it seemed like the thing to say at the time.

"Why don't you just quit," I said, "if that's how you feel, and devote your time to being a full-time…yo-yoist?"

"Because this place really *is* in my blood." He sighed. "And, yeah," he said, as though conceding something else, "it's exciting, being around people who could at any second become princes or paupers."

Speaking of which…

"Oops, gotta run," I said.

"But you haven't finished your diet cola with lime in it yet."

"I know and I wish I could stay," I said ruefully, "but I need to go find the friend I came with and see if he's turned into a prince or a pauper yet."

Where the fuck was Billy?

Search the casino as I might, though, he was nowhere to be found. At last concluding I was chasing my own tail around in circles like a dog and that my tail didn't want to be caught, I headed back up to the room. Once there, I changed into one of the pretty teddies I'd brought with me—it was lilac lace and required a blueprint to get into it—and crawled into bed to watch some Jon Stewart, hoping to still be awake when Billy returned. With apologies to Shakespeare, there was a long overdue consummation I was devoutly wishing for.

But by the time Jon Stewart finished his fifth Bush joke, my spirits and my teddy gave in at about the same time, the former sagging from lack of sleep with the latter sagging from the heat because I'd been too lazy to turn the AC on earlier, and off I went to sleep.

"If only you'd been there, Baby," Billy said.

"Huh?" I blinked against the light of the room.

"I kept looking for you everywhere," he said, removing the jacket of his tux and throwing it with disdain over the back of a chair.

"But I was looking for you, too!" I protested.

"Every single second?" he accused.

"Well, no," I admitted, thinking of Chris, "I did have to leave the floor at one point. But I looked and I looked—"

"I really could have used you by my side tonight, Baby," he said.

"Why? What's wrong? What happened?"

"I lost." He yanked his bow tie off. "I lost big-time."

Oh, shit.

"Promise me you'll gamble with me first thing in the morning? Earlier, you said you would."

"Shh, sleep now," I soothed. "You can even take the bed and I'll take the couch. You've had a tough night."

# 19

But the next morning, I didn't feel any different. I was still reluctant to gamble.

"Let's go to Red Rock Canyon!" I announced, between taking turns in the bathroom.

"Why would we want to do that?" Billy said.

"While you were in the shower, I looked through this brochure here, *Things to Do in Vegas Outside of Gambling.*"

"And, again, I ask, why would we want to do that?"

"Well, you did say you lost a lot last night…"

"Right. So the best thing to do would be to win it all back and then some first thing this morning."

"But we can't hit the casino first thing in the morning!"

Billy gave me a look that said that of all the stupid things

I'd said, and his expression implied that I'd said a lot of them, this was the stupidest yet.

"And this is because...?" he prompted.

I had a flash to our time together in Atlantic City, how we'd spent all day and night in the casino, how Hillary and Biff had spent their time differently, seeing all the sights and falling in love.

"It just seems," I said, "that if we've come all the way across the country, we should also do a few...other things."

"Why would we—"

I stopped him before he could question my sanity again.

"Look," I said, letting myself get all enthusiastic. "Let's just try it my way. We'll go to Red Rock Canyon this morning, see something we couldn't see back home, and while we're there I'll charge up my talismanic powers. Honest. By the time we come back, I'm sure I'll be ready to win. Big-time."

I must have buried the magic words in there somewhere, because after cinnamon French toast and huevos rancheros in The Café—you can guess which one of us had which, but let me just say that the cinnamon was enough to make me only barely miss my Cocoa Krispies—we were off to find a rental car dealership.

"Can you believe how that guy tried to rip us off?" Billy said, keying the engine of the subcompact, a sickly green not normally occurring anywhere in nature, and driving out of the city toward the desert. Well, really, it was all a desert.

"What are you talking about?" I said, fiddling with the

radio. Anything but Dido, I prayed. It wasn't that I had anything against Dido per se, but if I had to go down with that ship one more time, I'd switch my passage for the *Titanic*.

"Mr. Smarmy back at the U-Can-Drive-It place. First saying if we wanted something bigger than this toy car, it would cost three times as much, then making me give him that hundred-dollar deposit and trying to sell us that extra insurance."

"Oh—" I pooh-poohed "—that's probably just the way they do things around here."

"Right," he said grumpily. "Bilk the tourists."

"No, I don't mean that. It's just that, if they didn't take some self-protective measures, they'd probably be inundated with drunken people deciding to get married and then at the last minute disappearing with the cars after deciding to get married somewhere with a little more finesse."

"Huh?"

"Hey, did you ever see the Vegas two-parter of *Friends?*"

"Huh?"

"Never mind. I'll just navigate."

I'd never been good at navigating while driving and I proved no better at navigating without driving.

"How can we be lost already?" Billy said.

"I'm as shocked as you are," I said. "This is the desert and there are supposed to be some canyons out here made of red rock. How hard can that be to find?"

"We should have stayed back at the casino."

"Trust me, this'll be great. Just keep driving until you see something poking out of the desert and that's bound to be it."

But after getting us twenty miles lost in the wrong direction—it's tough when you're always used to living east to go west and then have to realize that it's possible to go still further west—it took another hour to get us back to where we wanted to be. Or to where I wanted to be, at any rate.

"We should have stayed back at the casino," Billy said.

"Wow, this is great," I said, overriding him as I got out of the car. I tried to imagine what people like Hillary and Biff would talk about if they were there. "Look," I said. "Isn't it amazing? Visitors can hike, picnic and view plant and animal life under three-thousand-foot-high rock formations!"

"We could be gambling right this minute, probably win a bundle."

"The strata exposed reveal more than five hundred million years of geological history! The canyon is a bed of an ancient deep sea, where, over time, sediments washed in and the water evaporated!"

"If you wanted to see something different so badly, we could have gone to see the Bonnie and Clyde getaway car. That wouldn't have taken us all morning."

"It would have taken longer," I pointed out. After all, who here was the one who was familiar with the brochure? "That's forty miles from our hotel. This is only twenty miles."

"Yes, but you got us lost, so I'll see your twenty miles and raise you the forty we covered in doubling back and your sixty still beats my forty, which is not a good thing."

"The boulders and pinnacles range in color from deep sandstone-red to white! The red color is the result of weathered iron composites! Isn't this fascinating?"

"Or we could have stayed right at the casino and seen the shark reef they have right there. Do you realize that? There's a shark reef right in our very casino. If nature was what you wanted, we could have seen some without all this fuss and bother, without ever leaving our hotel."

"Visitors can explore the park on a thirteen-mile-loop road that winds through the canyon and reveals rock formations that cannot be seen from outside the park! Picnic areas and hiking trails also can be accessed by the loop! Isn't it fascinating?"

"Fascinating would be the anchor seat at a table where the dealer can't deal without busting himself to save his life."

"A visitors' center at the park's entrance displays trail maps, plant and wildlife information and a history of the area!"

"I really think we should—"

"A few miles south of Red Rock Canyon is Bonnie Springs. There you can get a real taste of Old Nevada, an 1880s western mining town reproduction and Spring Mountain Ranch State Park. It—"

"Baby." Billy effectively stopped me by putting his hands on either side of my face, his lips on mine. "I want to go back."

"But we just got—"

"I've seen enough."

"But we haven't seen—"

"Enough, Baby," he spoke softly, but if that instant bulge in his pants was anything to go by, he was carrying a big stick. "I want to go back."

Shit. I was pretty sure that this wasn't how things would be going if we were Hillary and Biff.

"Aren't you having even a little bit of fun?" I asked.

"We're in a desert and, oh, I don't know, there are some *rocks* here. Frankly, I hadn't pegged you as being the Mother Nature type."

"What? You don't think I can be earthy? I can be earthy."

"Oh, I'm sure you can. I just figured that if you were interested in rocks at all, they'd be diamonds, you know, the kind one special person puts on another special person's ring finger. C'mon, Baby—" and here he most effectively nibbled my ear "—let's go back to the casino and see if I can't win enough to buy a pretty rock to put on that pretty finger of yours, shall we?"

How could I resist an offer like that?

My mind raced: had Biff proposed to Hillary yet? Did he follow her out to the desert, even though he didn't really want to go, and then get so carried away with the setting that he started promising her diamonds?

Screw Mother Nature! I was going to head back to the casino!

And all would have gone perfectly, or at least all would have had more of a chance to go perfectly, had it not been for the man back at the U-Can-Drive-It place.

"It looks to me," he said, tut-tutting as he examined the front passenger bumper with a magnifying glass, "like you can't drive it."

"What are you talking about?" Billy said. "I didn't hit anything."

"Sometimes," Mr. Car Dealer Cheat said mysteriously, "you can hit things without realizing you are hitting anything."

"I told you," Billy said, "I didn't hit anything."

"Of course you would say that," Mr. Car Dealer Cheat said. "But tell me," he added, leaning in to whisper, "how far did the body fly?"

Ever since we'd met him that morning, I'd been trying to place Mr. Car Dealer Cheat's accent. It wasn't quite Middle Eastern, but almost. And now I had it. That last line he spoke, he sounded just like the John Belushi character in the old *Blues Brothers* movie when, in a fancy restaurant, he leans over to a very proper family of strangers and intones, "How much for the little girl?" He sounded exactly like John Belushi saying that. Come to think of it, he even looked like John Belushi!

*"What?"* Billy said. "There was no *body*."

"Ah," Mr. Car Dealer Cheat said, "the victim just crawled off into the desert to die."

"There was no victim!"

"It's a shame you didn't sign for the extra insurance I offered you earlier." Mr. Car Dealer Cheat sighed. "So, how do you plan to pay for this?"

"I'm not paying for anything! That…that…I can't even

call it a dent…that…*ding* must have been there when you leant it to me."

"You are accusing me of being a cheat?" Mr. Car Dealer Cheat drew back. "Here, let me show you something." He produced a sheet of paper, at the bottom of which was Billy's signature. "This is an affidavit showing what condition this car was in when I most trustfully loaned it to you. See? It says here, 'Puke-green subcompact in impeccable condition.' It says absolutely nothing here about the front passenger panel being caved in."

"It's not caved in! It's a *ding!* You need a bloody magnifying glass just to see it!"

"Perhaps I should call the cops?" Mr. Car Dealer Cheat stroked a nonexistent beard.

"Yes," Billy said, nodding emphatically. "I think that's an excellent idea."

"Of course," Mr. Car Dealer Cheat said, "no matter who is right and who is wrong, I am sure it will take the police the entire day to sort this out, possibly the rest of the weekend." He shrugged. "You know how public servants are. And in this heat, they move soooo sloooow…"

"Fine," Billy said. "*Fine.* How do *you* propose we resolve this?"

"Well, if you had only signed for the additional renter's insurance—"

"Yes, yes, I know about all this. Can we speed this up somehow?"

I could see Billy's wheels spinning and the direction they

were spinning in was toward getting us out of there and back to the casino as quickly as possible.

"I think," Mr. Car Dealer Cheat said with more absent-beard stroking, "that if you let me keep your one hundred-dollar deposit—"

"I'm not going to let you keep my hundred dollars! Not when I'm sure you're going to just turn around and rent this car, *as is,* to the next poor unsuspecting person who comes along."

Mr. Car Dealer Cheat shrugged. "The decision is yours. You can let me keep the hundred dollars that is my due or we can wait around debating this until the cows come home or the casinos close, whichever comes first."

"I don't think there are cows around here," I said, feeling the need to say something. "Can cows even live in a climate like this!"

Another shrug. "Then the casinos. We'll wait here until the casinos close."

"But I didn't think the casinos ever closed," I said.

"Which is exactly my point," Mr. Car Dealer Cheat said. "As I'm sure your friend well knows…"

"Ohh, fine," Billy said. "Keep the blasted hundred dollars. I'll win that back in a minute."

"Ooh," Mr. Car Dealer Cheat said. "Big man. Big talk."

"Come on, Baby." Billy grabbed my hand. "Let's get out of this…*insane* car dealership."

"Good luck at the gaming tables!" Mr. Car Dealer Cheat shouted after us. "And please do come again!"

Once we were out on the blistering pavement, Billy turned to me, somehow less solicitous than he'd seemed when he proprietarily grabbed my hand back in the shop.

"You know, Baby," he said, "you're turning out to be not quite the talisman I'd envisioned you being."

And it was then I realized that it was time to put up or shut up.

# 20

People will tell you that there's no such thing as "put up or shut up," that right up to the last minute—of anything, really—you can still change your mind.

People, generally speaking, can be full of shit.

Sure, it's true, in theory, that a woman can say "yes" she's going to do something twenty times leading up to the thing and at the last minute change it to "um, no," but try doing that too often in real life and see what it gets you. And, for some reason, it's a lot more acceptable to change "no" into "yes" than it is to change "yes" into "no."

I'd sworn, if not on a stack of Bibles then at least through action and resulting inference that I would in good faith come to Vegas with Billy and in good faith be his talisman. And yet, ever since we'd arrived, it seemed as though I was willing to do anything but that one thing. True, he could have been a better sport about spending a few hours doing something else, but I could see where he was getting annoyed with me and I couldn't honestly say I blamed him. And I could also see that, if I didn't do something drastic soon, I was going to lose him completely.

"I know!" I said, as soon as we got back to the room, the sweat from being outside still adhering my shirt to my body. "Let's go down to the casino!"

"Oh, stop toying with me." He flopped down on the bed, shielded his eyes with his forearm, making him look not unlike a male Greta Garbo.

"I'm not toying with you!" I said, grabbing his hand and pulling. "I want to go."

"No," he said, still resisting my tug. "You'll just get me down there and I'll get all excited, only to have you announce we're going to see the shark reef."

"I'm not kidding, Billy!" I said. "I want to *gamble!*"

"Or maybe you'll drag me to see the Bonnie and Clyde getaway car this time."

"Come *on,*" I said, grabbing his tux down from off the hanger. "Put this *on!*"

"You mean…you mean…you mean you're not joking?"

I shook my head and, before I was even through shaking it, he was sweeping me up into his arms.

"Oh, Baby," he said, "you've made me the happiest man in Vegas!" Which made me feel great. Really, it did. There was just one problem: what if I'd used up all my good luck on my previous trips to Foxwoods and Atlantic City? And what if I was now destined to fail?

But then I remembered that I was as prepared for this as I'd never been prepared for anything. I was Black Jack Sampson's progeny, even if he no longer went by that name and even if he'd lost more than he'd won; I had digested every word of *Blackjack Winning Basics,* by Tony Casino, and had even understood most of them; and I had a five-dollar bill crinkling between my breasts. As my old friend Hamlet would say:

*The readiness is all.*

*Ka-ching!*

The readiness was soo all.

Billy and I hit the casino in THEhotel at Mandalay like Mickey Mantle grabbing a mantelpiece and whaling the hell out of a baseball.

Or something like that.

Actually, I was doing most of the whaling, pulling Billy along in my wake.

I sat down at the first table we came to.

"Are you sure you don't want to walk around for a bit?" Billy asked. "Perhaps check out the lay of the land? See how the cards are running for each dealer?"

"No," I said. "I feel hot."

And I was.

In no time, I'd picked up a few hundred, while Billy had picked up a few thousand. Then, abruptly, I rose.

"We're not going already, are we?" Billy asked.

"Not at all," I said. "We're just switching tables."

"But this is the table right next to the one we started at. I mean, it's not very *scientific*."

"I know what I'm doing."

And I seemed to. Again, in almost no time, we were way ahead of where we were when we sat down.

I rose.

"Switch?" Billy inquired, more calmly this time.

"Aren't you going to ask if I know what I'm doing?" I said.

"No," he said. "I can see that you do. I totally trust you. I am in your hands."

Switch, switch, switch, switch, switch.

By now I'd worked my way down one side of an aisle and was turning to make my way down the other. Afternoon had turned into early evening, something I could tell from looking at my watch since you couldn't tell anything about the outside world from inside. And by now I had a little chip caddy to ferry my chips from table to table; the casino had helpfully provided that and one for Billy, as well.

"Wouldn't it be easier," Billy asked, "to just exchange some of our chips into cash at the bank?"

"It might be easier," I said with confidence, "but it would jinx things."

"How so?"

"It would make me feel as though I'm partially giving up.

So long as I'm hauling all these chips around, I feel as though I'm still on my streak."

"Yes, I suppose I can see that, but it does make it difficult to keep count…"

But I won that argument.

And I kept winning at the tables, too. And, along with every one of my wins, Billy won, too.

It would be nice if I could say that my string of luck infected the others at our tables, too, but such was not the case. With the exception of we two, the other players at our tables lost and inevitably dropped out. Certainly, the dealers kept losing to us, but they couldn't just drop out. So, as we hit table after table, we were building something of a following, a following that was there to observe, rather than play with. And the pit bosses were keeping an eye on us, too. Not to mention the dealers.

"Let's skip this table," I said, halfway down another aisle.

"What do you mean, skip? Why should we skip it?"

"I just thought maybe we should shake things up a bit, maybe play at every other table from now on."

"Oh, I see, well, yes, I suppose that could work just as well… Oh, hello! Don't I know you from somewhere?"

Obviously, Billy was no longer talking to me.

I turned to see who he was talking to, and came face-to-face with the reason why I'd suddenly decided to skip a table, employing the "now I just want to play at every other table" ruse.

Billy snapped his fingers at the dealer.

"I know *you,*" Billy said. *Snap, snap.* "I *know* you. You're that chap who I keep running into everywhere, the one who's always dropping his yo-yos all over the place."

Of course it was Chris.

"Come on," I said to Billy. I was standing behind Billy, so that hopefully Chris couldn't see me.

"You cut your hair, right?" Billy asked. "Didn't it used to be shaggier? And, of course, it's not so easy to place you right away without your yo-yos."

"Come *on,*" I hissed.

"No, you come on, Baby. We've played it your way all day. Now let's play it my way. And just think how much fun it'll be to play against someone you sort-of know?"

Actually, I didn't think it would be fun at all, but I couldn't say that. Besides, Chris was doing a great job of maintaining a professional mien. He'd barely nodded once at Billy and once at me, before resuming his job of sliding cards out of the chute.

As we sat down at Chris's table, I felt as though we were doing something illegal. Shouldn't there be rules against a dealer dealing to people he knew? Weren't there laws against doctors operating on kin? Sure, we weren't kin to Chris, but didn't the same principle sort of apply?

The pit bosses who zoomed to stand behind Chris before our butts had even raised the warmth level on our leather seats certainly made me feel that way, but then I realized how twisted my reasoning was. How could the casinos prevent families and friends of dealers from sitting down at their tables to play? And where was the need? From all the security cameras overhead, not to mention the Capo-Regime-like pit bosses, there was no way a dealer could cheat to favor anybody. Plus, the dealer's own play was governed by strict rules. And dealers made idle chitchat with players all the time, responded to questions from players too. ("Been enjoying your stay here?" "How long have you been dealing?") So the only problem would be if the dealer got too chatty with the players or if the players got too chatty with the dealer, thereby disrupting the game and the constant flow of cash into the casino's coffers. The former didn't look as if it would be a problem, since after that brief nod Chris barely acknowledged us except to ask if we wanted a hit or to stay. As for the latter…

"You're not much better with the cards than you are with those yo-yos, are you?" Billy asked, as Chris's own cards revealed a hand that was a loser to both of ours.

Billy's smile was genial enough, and yet to my ear there was something off there. But then I decided that what I was hearing was a by-product of my own reluctance to play against Chris. And why was I so reluctant? After all, as Billy said earlier, it should have been fun. I mean, I liked Chris, so why wouldn't I want to play at his table?

As the play drew on, though, and the other players dropped out as they had at other tables, I became lost in the cards, lost in the winning. I lost sight of Chris.

Billy leaned in for a whisper as the dealer shuffled the decks. "Have you counted your chips lately, Baby?"

I blinked out of my haze of cards and looked down at the caddy before me. It was getting full on one side. I tried to do the math, and couldn't. All I knew was one thing: recalling my original intention, back from when all this started, I realized that I now had exactly what I'd wanted. I had enough money to buy my Jimmy Choo Ghosts. Hell, I had enough money to buy pairs for every day of the week and then some.

"Omigod, Billy!" I said, leaping up. "I did it! I did it!"

"What did you do, Baby?" Billy asked.

"What did you do, Delilah?" Chris asked at the same time.

"I just…won a lot," I finished off lamely, not wanting to say. Had this really all been just about a pair of shoes?

"Yes," Billy said emphatically. "Yes, you did."

"I did, didn't I?" I was suddenly unsure. "I really did?"

"Absolutely," Billy said. "And while I'm hesitant to stop when we're on such a roll, I would hate to overuse my talisman."

"Is it possible to overuse a talisman?" I raised the rhetorical question.

Hands on my shoulders, Billy had gently spun me around, so my back was to Chris and Chris was once again out of the picture.

"Baby Sampson—" Billy looked at me fondly, as he held a fake microphone up to my lips "—you've just won me more money than I've won in one afternoon all year. What are you going to do for an encore, go to Disney World?"

I shook my head.

"No? Then what about heading off to see the Shark Reef here at the hotel? I understand they have a forty-million-dollar aquarium covering more than ninety thousand square feet that holds more than one and a half million gallons of seawater and one hundred species of animals. You love all that nature shit. You know. Remember Red Rock Canyon? Sounds right up your alley."

I shook my head again.

"Ah! I know! You want to do some more *gambling!*"

I shook my head a third time, hard. I was starting to make myself dizzy.

"Then, what? What is it you want to do now, Baby, to celebrate?"

I stood on tiptoes and whispered shyly in his ear.

"Oh, my, Baby," he said. "You *are* an ambitious girl."

Back in my high-school days, when it came time for the prom, I'd hear guys in the cafeteria complain about how hard it was to put on a tux. Yeah, right, like it's so easy for girls to cram themselves into stockings and strapless bras, to starve for weeks in advance so they can wear a dress one or two sizes smaller than usual, to have their hair pulled back so tight into a sophisticated style that they wind up with a migraine, to have so much makeup on that the black mascara spiders its way into their eyes thereby creating an ultra-painful reaction when it gets trapped behind their contact lenses. But I suppose people only know what they know and that whatever the worst pain a person ever has is, that's it for them. So I'd take the guys' word for it, that putting on a tux sucked. But I'll tell you one thing: a tux may suck going on, but it sure comes off easy.

"*Oh,* Baby," Billy said into my neck as I removed his cummerbund.

"Oh, *Baby,*" he said, when the crisp white shirt and bow tie followed, both removed by *moi.*

"Here," he said, pulling away, "let me do you now."

Do me now? Well, if not exactly an artful synonym for making love, it had been such a long time I guessed it was okay. But then I saw what he meant: he was going to take my clothes off for me. Normally, this was a moment that, while experiencing the passion with one half of my being, had the potential to throw the other half into sheer terror. *What would he see when I was naked? Would he notice that I was nothing like the celluloid, glossy-magazine embodiments of female perfection that men and women are constantly being bombarded with? How could he not notice?*

And yet, I was so caught up in the excitement of the day, so caught up in the winning and the moment, my usual insecurities fell like so many thongs off the back of a Victoria's Secret truck overturned on Route 66.

"You are," Billy said between kisses and clothes fumbling, "you are so…I mean, you are…Baby, excuse me, but did a five-dollar bill just fall out of your bra?"

"Never mind that," I said, kissing him forcefully on the lips before pushing him down on the bed and climbing on top.

"Oh, my," he said, as I kissed him some more. "But, speaking of money, don't you think we should do something with the chips first?"

"Like what?" I said. *Kiss, kiss.*

"Like maybe bring them down to the bank and exchange them for cash, then put the cash in the safety deposit box here?"

"No," I said, undoing the clasp of his tux trousers.

"Then perhaps we should at least put the chips into the safe? You know, so they don't get lost or something here, or in case we run out afterward and forget all about them, or something like—"

"No," I said, sliding down his zipper.

"Oh…oh, my, Baby, whoever knew that *no* could be such a wonderful word?"

And then as Billy quickly resumed his role of Gentleman while I continued in my current role as No Lady, and my *no*es turned into a string of yeses, all at the behest of his expert hands, tongue and, er, "big bet," I recognized one thing for sure.

When it came to making love, Billy Charisma had The Rat and The Weasel beat by a tuxedoed mile.

I gazed up at the ceiling afterward, experiencing bliss. Is this, I wondered, what Elizabeth Hepburn felt like when she lay with Frank Sinatra, with Errol Flynn, with Jimmy Hoffa and Winston Churchill? No, it was probably better….

"I must say, Baby," Billy said, stroking my hair as I lay with my head against his naked chest, "you are indeed full of surprises. That thing you did with your tongue? It was almost as good as drawing a hard Eighteen to a dealer's soft Seventeen."

"Mmm." All I could do was purr.

"But now," Billy said, "I think I'd like to do something for you."

"I think you just did." I purred some more.

"I'm not talking about that," Billy laughed. "Although that is very nice. I want to take you shopping."

"Shopping?"

"Yes. I mean, the clothes you usually wear are nice enough, but wouldn't you like something, oh, I don't know, *zippier* for when we go back to playing later?"

I thought about him in his tux, me in my usual okay clothes. He did sort of have a point.

"And it would give me great pleasure to *buy* you things, Baby."

"You want to buy me things?" No man had ever said that to me before. Usually, they asked me to buy them things—another beer, a burger and fries from the drive-through—before summarily dumping me.

"Oh, yes. I mean, I have to take good care of my perfect little talisman, don't I?"

"Um…okay!"

Retail shops in casinos are designed with winners in mind. No Gap stores, either regular or baby or geriatric. No JCPenney's. No Sears. Instead, it's all designer clothes, upscale foodie places like The Chocolate Swan, and price tags to break the bank.

"I can't accept this," I said to Billy, as he picked out an outfit for me that was a formfitting silver cocktail dress.

"Of course you can," he said. "It looks marvelous on you and it'll look great next to my tux. Besides, the color reminds me of the top you had on the first night I met you at Foxwoods. You remember. The first night we won together."

No one had ever told me I looked marvelous before.

"I can't accept this," I said, referring to the pure-white dress he picked out next.

"Of course you can," he said, "although I do think we'll be saving that one for later."

*Later?*

"Now," he said, deep in thought, "I do think you'll need the right jewelry to go with that…"

"I can't let you buy me jewelry."

"Oh, yes, you can. If it weren't for you, I wouldn't have so much money to pay these credit-card debts with when they come due. I think the diamond earrings will be lovely. Maybe the bracelet, too? No? All right, then, I can see where the clinking around of those stones would be distracting when you're at the tables. Now, then, before we leave, let me just ask the nice jeweler a question about, um, insurance while you wait outside…

"Shoes!" he announced as he emerged from the store. "I know you're pretty attached to those blue-green things I always see you wearing—"

How could he refer to my precious Jimmy Choo Momo Flats as "those blue-green things"?

"—but I don't think they'll go properly with the silver dress. Or with the white one, come to that. So the only thing for it is to…"

And then he bought me silver stilettos to go with the cocktail dress and pure-white pumps to go with the white dress, which was more of a sexy suit really, not unlike a skirted version of the one Bianca wore when she married Mick Jagger all those years ago.

"What do you think?" Billy asked, obviously still full of energy. "Have we covered everything?"

"More than," I said, a little overwhelmed by it all.

"Are you sure about that? Perhaps a negligee? No, perhaps not. One more trip like the last to the gaming tables and I won't want anything to get between me and that body of yours."

His words set my body all atingle, and I let my body fall into his, imagining us running back up to the room.

"Well, there is one more place," he said.

I wondered what he had in mind, since we'd already ruled out the need for lingerie, but it wasn't long before I had my answer.

"The Sunrise and Sunset Chapels at Mandalay Bay?" I was incredulous. "We're getting married?"

"Well, yes. I mean, I figured, why wait?"

Why wait, indeed?

"Look," he said. "The interiors of the chapels are open

and airy with a tropical feel. Bamboo, chandeliers and French windows create an elegant ambience."

"Yes, I can see that."

"And we can have our choice. The Platinum Skies package includes video recording of the ceremony, a garter, pianist, bouquet, boutonniere and a bottle of champagne and champagne flutes—you'd look great in a garter. The Opal Shores package includes photography with complete coverage of wedding party and immediate family, video of the ceremony, pianist, a bottle of champagne and a custom wedding certificate holder—well, I suppose the immediate-family part is out, since we don't have anyone here with us. The Crystal Waters package offers a bridal garter, bridal bouquet, pianist, bottle of champagne and a groom's boutonniere—simple, elegant, plus we'd still have the garter and I suppose the pianist would be okay, so long as it's not Billy Joel, and even though the Platinum Skies package did also offer a pianist, at least with this one we don't get to include immediate family so we won't feel maudlin about not having any. And the Diamond Lights package includes a bridal bouquet, groom's boutonniere, maid-of-honor bouquet, best man's boutonniere, garter, photos, video, unity candle, deluxe fruit basket, champagne dinner for two at Shanghai Lilly, breakfast in bed for two, a honeymoon suite for one night, a pianist and a Skinklinic package—I'm afraid I don't know what the hell the Skinklinic package adds on to the whole thing, plus this one's got a whole lot of add-ons that I don't suppose either of us need. I mean, are you really so into fruit that it needs to be deluxe and in a basket?"

Dumbly, I shook my head.

"No," he said, "I didn't think so. There's nothing else for it then, it's the Crystal Waters for us, unless of course you want to go for the Platinum Skies with the added video recording. I suppose that might make a nice memento to show the folks back home."

"Wait!"

"What?"

"When did we decide this? Did I miss something here?"

"Well, we are here," he said, "and it is terribly convenient."

"But shouldn't there have been something in between?"

"Such as?"

"Such as, oh, I don't know, maybe you saying you love me?"

I couldn't believe I was actually asking a guy to tell me he loved me. I mean, how lame. But then he was asking me to marry him. Sort of.

"Of course I love you, Baby," he said gently. "How could I not love you? You're my talisman."

Every now and then, I found myself wishing he'd lose that word from his vocabulary.

"Well, then," I said, still in objection mode, "wouldn't this work better if you actually asked me to marry you first instead of just assuming—"

"What do you think I got this for then?" he asked, reaching into his inside jacket pocket.

What could he be going for? What did people wearing tuxes keep in their inside pockets? Did he have a gun in there, like James Bond? Was he going to hold his gun to my head until I said yes? Didn't he realize that such desperate lengths were unnecessary? That a simple bended knee would probably do?

But then he completed his reaching motion, at the end of which he produced a box from his inside pocket.

It was a jeweler's box.

"Here you go," he said, opening the lid.

The thing was a fucking rock. It was a diamond-shaped rock that gave out more points of light than George Bush Senior before vomiting on the prime minister of Japan's shoes.

"I picked this out," he said, "when I sent you out of the jeweler's before, when I told you I was staying behind to get insurance."

I should have known that was a ruse. Every blackjack player knows that insurance—whereby the player takes out insurance to protect against the dealer beating her with black-jack—is a mug's game, invested in by losers who don't trust their own hands and want to play it safe by breaking even.

Did I trust my own hands, the hands that had touched Billy's body such a short time ago? Did I just want to play it safe?

I reached for a piece of the rock.

And that's when Billy snapped the velvet lid shut.

"Not so fast," he said.

"But why wait?" I asked, deciding he'd been right when he said the same thing earlier.

"See," he said, pointing to the hours of operation. "It's

almost ten o'clock. The office closes in five minutes. So why don't we wait until tomorrow to do this. Haven't you guessed yet, that the pretty white suit I picked out for you is for tomorrow? Now, then, in the meantime…"

Naturally, I assumed that "in the meantime" meant we'd be going back up to the room to do the dirty deed again, now that we were sort-of officially sort-of betrothed.

And we did go back up to the room, only there was no doing the dirty deed.

"Here," Billy said, handing me the garment bag from downstairs, "put this on."

"The wedding suit? But I thought you said we weren't going to get married until tomorrow."

"Of course I don't mean the wedding suit. I mean the silver cocktail dress."

Oh. Of course.

"Great," I said a few minutes later, emerging from the bathroom, "I'm dressed."

Billy pulled me to him, so we were standing side by side in front of the mirror and I saw that it was great.

"Don't we look great together?" he said.

We did look great together now. So what if my feet, albeit pretty in sky-high silver, looked as though I'd betrayed them by wearing something on them other than my good luck Jimmy Choos?

"I'm ready," I said, letting out a breath I didn't know I'd been holding. "But what am I ready for?"

He grabbed his chip caddy from earlier in the night, handed me mine.

"We're going down," he said, "for more. This time we'll double what we have here."

On the way out the door, I grabbed my crumpled five-dollar bill and shoved it in my cleavage.

# 21

It was a hand dealt straight out of a dream: two Aces.

*What to do, what to do…*

Easy answer: the dealer had just shuffled right before dealing, so there were nearly six full decks left in the chute, all of those beautiful Jacks, Queens and Kings. Even the Tens would be beautiful and a person didn't need to be a pro at counting cards to realize that the game, for once, was strongly in the player's favor.

So, very easy answer: split the Aces.

The next decision, if not as easy, relied totally on the player's instincts: double down, or let the original bet ride? The original bet represented half of the player's holdings, but the player was feeling cocky, riding high. Besides, the dealer was showing a Seven.

Big deal.

The player looked at the dealer, a face that had become so familiar. The player looked over one shoulder, at the man standing just behind, a man who gave a slight nod of his head: approval.

Giving the matter not a moment's further thought, the player pushed the rest of the chips forward, hitting the table limit. Those chips, tens of thousands of dollars' worth of chips, represented everything the player had in the world.

Whatever two cards the dealer turned over next would decide the future fate of the player.

And so, let the real game begin…

Dream had become reality. Only the dealer in the reality version was Chris and the man standing just behind the player, me, was Billy, only rather than being behind me, in reality he was sitting at the table beside me, in the anchor chair, with his own double-down dilemma before him.

As soon as we'd hit the casino floor just a few minutes prior, Billy had made straight for Chris like a heat-seeking missile. A few hours had passed since we'd been down there before, with mind-blowing sex and a shopping spree and a shoe change filling the intervention, so Chris had changed tables. But Billy found his new table right away all the same.

Before I could demur, Billy was placing his chip caddy down next to the anchor spot.

"We had such good luck playing against…Yo-Yo Boy before," he said.

I should have stopped right then and there. I know that now. Certainly, I should have at least paused when Chris briefly met my eyes straight on, shaking his head almost imperceptibly: No. He was obviously trying to tell me something, but I was too drunk on the combined highs of Billy, of wearing pretty silver clothes, of *winning* for once in my life to pay him any heed.

And now here I was, with all my money on the table, everything I had with me except for the five-dollar bill crammed in my cleavage, waiting for him to chute out the cards that would double my money, double Billy's money, filling our chip caddies to the brink, making Billy so happy with me he'd marry me in the Sunrise and Sunset Chapels tomorrow.

Since both Billy and I were doubling down, we'd get one card for each of our two hands and that would be that. The odds were so strongly in our favors. Maybe we'd pull two Tens each and win everything with a quadruple blackjack. Or maybe one of us would win two hands, preferably him since he had more at stake, while the other would lose. Or maybe we'd each win one of our two hands, pushing…

It was all too much to think about. My mind couldn't race, couldn't compute that fast. And now here was Chris, the dealer, chuting out in rapid succession a Two for me and then a Three, followed by a Four for Billy and then a Five.

*Ka-chunk.*

*Ka-thump.*

What were the odds?

"You *stupid…cow!*" Billy said to me. He was out of his chair.

Only peripherally did I register Chris quietly taking all our chips away.

"Billy?" I said questioningly.

"Why did I ever listen to you?" he said. "You're not my talisman anymore! You're bad luck!"

Before I could say anything, he was gone.

And then I was out of my own chair. No, I didn't want to run after him, but I definitely needed to get out of there.

"Delilah!" Chris screamed after me. With the exception of his imperceptible shake of the head earlier, this was the first unprofessional thing he'd done on my behalf, but I was moving too quickly to pay that any heed, either.

*If you can make one heap of all your winnings*
*And risk it on one turn of pitch-and-toss,*
*And lose, and start again at your beginnings*
*And never breathe a word about your loss…*

Fuck you, too, Rudyard Kipling. It's just not that easy.

I spent the next half hour just riding the elevator up and down.

I didn't want to go back to the room—Billy was probably back there, packing, getting as far away from his broken talisman as fast as he could—and I didn't want to go outside. Where would I go with my stinking five dollars? Sure, I could try to use it as a stake to stage a comeback at the tables, but after what I'd just been through, I knew that madness lay in that idea.

Every time the elevator stopped at a floor, if there was a man on there with me, even sometimes if there was a woman, whoever was on would gesture for me to exit first; I must have looked that special in my silver clothes, like someone you'd always let go first. But I always declined and just kept on with my long elevator ride to nowhere.

At last, when the elevator stopped at the top of the building for the fifteenth time, I debarked.

The Mix Lounge again?

Sure. Why not.

I'll tell you why not. There was a twenty-five-dollar cover charge and all I had on me was my stupid fiver. The shopping and entertainments of Sin City are not for the losers or the poor.

But the doorman must have felt sorry for me when all I produced was that crumpled fiver from my cleavage, because he waved me on in, even waved my fiver away when I tried to hand it to him.

"Keep it, girl," he said in a Jamaican accent. "Maybe you can buy a club soda with it."

Crap. That probably meant I couldn't even afford a diet cola with a lime squeezed into it. Maybe I could at least afford the lime?

"The second show's about to start," he said, "so you might want to find yourself a seat."

I thought about sitting down at the bar, but then I realized the bartender would only come over and expect me to order something. Then I considered sitting down at a table, but figured the cocktail waitress would eventually do the same. So I walked over to the floor-to-ceiling windows and looked down on the incredible view of the Strip. All those lights. All those dreams firing up and being extinguished by those lights. Honestly, it would be a great place if only a person were winning, if only a person still had someone by her side who sparkled like Billy Charisma…even if he had turned out to be both a rat *and* a weasel.

I turned back to face the room and for the first time noticed that the crowd was scant. Who could even draw such a small crowd? If there had been a sign outside saying whom the performer was, I'd been too depressed when I walked in to notice it. Maybe everyone else in the building was so busy winning that I was one of the few people there?

Oh, well, I thought, as some introductory music started to play on a piano, their loss—or maybe their winnings?—was my gain. I'd just slip into a seat at one of the tables, just so, right when the announcer was announcing the performer, just so. Surely, the cocktail waitress wouldn't bother me while the show was going on, would she?

"Ladies and Gentlemen, Las Vegas and THEhotel at Mandalay Bay are proud to present… *Tom Jones!*"

And there he was, in his black tux and crisp white shirt, hair still thick and bushy. True, a tux wasn't totally out of place in Las Vegas on a Saturday night. I mean, wherever Wayne Newton was playing, he was probably wearing one, too. And Billy, too, come to that, wherever he was now. But somehow a tux on Tom Jones looked different. He was just so Tom Jones. He was so…*Welsh*. Plus, his bow tie was bigger.

"I'd like to open tonight—"Tom Jones seduced into the microphone "—with an old favorite of mine. But, first, I'd like to ask the question I always ask. Is there anyone here named—"

Oh, no. He wasn't going to do this…was he?

"—Delilah?"

I craned my neck around the room to see if anyone else was going to raise their hands, but it looked like I was the only one in the bunch. Timidly, I twinkled my fingers in the air.

"You?" he boomed, his bejeweled fingers grasping the thick microphone as if it was, well, something else.

And then before I knew it, he was serenading me, "My, my, my, Delilah" and "Why, why, why, Delilah?" and telling everyone how he loved me and how I deceived him and how "I felt the knife in my hand and she laughed no more."

Great, I'd been killed off in a song. At least I wasn't boring.

Before I could get over that one, he was launching into, "It's not unusual to be loved by anyone…"

*Yes, it is,* I started to think, my thoughts turning maudlin.

*It's very unusual for me to be loved by anyone. Oh, sure, I'm loved by my dad and by Hillary, maybe even by Elizabeth Hepburn. But I thought I was loved by Billy and look where that ended up.*

And then it was time for "What's New, Pussycat?" and whoever knew that "What's New, Pussycat?" was such a sad, sad song? Oh, sure, it starts out all innocent enough with all that "whoa, whoa, whoa" stuff, but by the time Tom got to the last verse and chorus— "Pussycat, pussycat/You're delicious"—I was bawling—"…you and your pussycat nose!"

I mean, who wouldn't want someone to love them enough that the lover would even love the lovee's nose? I wanted to be loved like that.

"Back in five," I heard Tom Jones say into the mic. "It looks like we've got a bit of an emergency here. I think we've got a crier on our hands."

And then he was at my little table, sitting right there with me.

"What's wrong, luv?" he said, very Welshly. "Tell Uncle Tom what's going on."

It all came out in a flooding gush.

"I don't even know what I'm *doing* here!" I cried. "I mean, I thought I knew what I was doing. I thought I came for the shoes. I thought I came for Billy. Maybe I came for the gambling? I don't know. But now the money's gone and Billy's gone…and I don't even have the shoes! I swear, I don't even know what I'm *doing* here!"

"Easy, luv, you're starting to move into what's known as

the refrain in my business. Look, you're main problem seems to be that you don't know what you're doing anymore. Have I got that right?"

I nodded.

"Here's what you need to do then. Find what you love to do and just get out there and do it. I've been singing the same songs for forty years now and occasionally some grandmother still throws her panties on stage. Honestly, it's not a bad life."

"But what if I don't know what I want to do? What if I don't know who I want to be or who I want to be with?"

He leaned over and patted my knee. Considering that the patter was Tom Jones, it was a surprisingly avuncular pat.

"Then *that's* what you need to find out, Delilah." Then he rose to his feet. "Now, then, if that crisis is over for the moment, I think I'd better go sing 'Sex Bomb.' Or possibly 'Mama Told Me Not to Come'? Who knows." He winked. "I'll decide once I get back up there."

"Mr. Jones?" I called after him.

"Tom," he said.

"Tom. Did you ever know an actress called Elizabeth Hepburn?"

"God, yes," He smiled fondly. "Everyone knows Lizzie. Sinatra introduced us."

I pushed the button for the elevator and as I was about to board, Chris stepped off. He was still in uniform.

"I've been looking for you everywhere!" he said. "I tried

to run after you, but the crowd got in the way. And by the time I pressed through, I couldn't find you anywhere. I asked everyone. Then one of the front-desk people said some woman in a silver dress had been riding the elevator up and down for a half hour, so I figured I'd ride it, too, and maybe you'd come back."

"You left your post for me?" I said. "Won't you get fired for that?"

"I don't know." He shrugged. "I've never done anything like that before. It was the first time I've ever walked off the job. Do you think they'd fire me for that?"

Stella probably wouldn't fire me for walking off on a job, but then I was The Golden Squeegee and Stella wasn't a Vegas pit boss. They'd probably break Chris's legs.

"Uh, *yeah,*" I said.

He thought about it for a minute. "If they do," he said, "it doesn't matter. Maybe they'd be doing me a favor."

"Not if they break your legs when they fire you, they won't."

"Huh? Never mind. What I want to know is, what happened down there before?"

"Well, first there were these shoes, see. It all started with these shoes."

Having told my story once to Tom Jones, sort of, I was now ready to tell it to the world.

"Wait a second," Chris said, pushing the elevator button. "Let's go outside for this. I've been cooped up in here for hours. Wouldn't you like to just go outside and get some fresh air?"

"Well, it'll probably be freshly polluted air, but sure. Why not."

Before I knew it we were on the elevator, off the elevator, across the lobby, and then…

It felt odd to be outside in Las Vegas.

Sure, I'd gone to Red Rock Canyon with Billy earlier in the day—God, that seemed so long ago now, another lifetime—but with the exception of the walk from the limo to the hotel when we'd first arrived, this was the first time I'd been outside. And despite everything that had gone wrong with the day and night, it felt terrific to escape the hermetically sealed confines of the casino. It was like being liberated.

As we walked down The Strip, Chris took my hand. It wasn't a girlfriend-boyfriend type of hand-taking, more like two gal pals linking arms in an old-fashioned storybook or maybe he could just tell I needed whatever support I could find.

"It all started with these shoes," I started to say again.

"Wait," he said. "Let me take you to my favorite spot on The Strip and then you can tell me."

His favorite spot on The Strip turned out to be the exploding volcano in front of The Mirage hotel.

"Damn!" he said, looking at his watch. "I forgot, it's after midnight."

"And that's a problem, Cinderella?"

"Well, yeah. The volcano stops exploding then. You should see it when it's going." His eyes got all excited, just like a little kid. "After a few moments of foreboding silence, the cascading water begins to churn and a low rumble emerges from the heart of the once-dormant volcano. Then, the eruption kicks into high gear as bright orange flames leap about one hundred feet above the water, illuminating the night sky. As the fire spreads across the lagoon, those standing close enough can feel the temperature rise. Several smaller explosions erupt, and eventually the volcano goes quiet once more."

"And this is your favorite spot on The Strip?"

"Well, yeah," he said again, as if his reasoning should be obvious. "It's not every day you get to see a volcano erupt in the middle of the desert."

Huh. "Well, when it is working, how often does it erupt?"

"Every night at thirty-minute intervals from 8:00 p.m. until midnight."

"So then actually you *can* see a volcano erupt every day in the desert."

"Well, no, actually you can only see it at night."

"But every night."

"Well, yeah." He ran his fingers through his hair in a gesture that said his hand expected to find more hair there. "I guess I'm not really very good at this sort of thing," he admitted.

"What sort of thing?"

"Talking, in general. Talking to damsels in distress, in particular."

I wanted to tell him he was doing fine, that all the talking about the nonerupting volcano had distracted me from my own problems, had distracted me from Billy for at least five minutes.

"Well," I said instead, "I suppose we could just stand around here and watch it *not* explode."

"Tell me about the shoes, Delilah."

"See, I was washing windows for this wealthy fading movie star—"

"Is that what you do for a living, wash windows?"

"Uh-huh."

"That's good. I was worried you might be a professional gambler. I do keep running into you in casinos. And at least you do something that makes people happy."

"Clean windows makes people happy?"

"Of course. It's almost as good as being a donut salesperson. Everyone loves a donut salesperson."

"They do?"

"Well, sure. What could be better than being the person who gives other people a dozen assorted donuts?"

"I don't know. Washing windows?"

"Exactly! Their windows were dirty, now they're clean, you're the one who did it for them. What could be better? But getting back to the shoes…"

"Right. Those shoes. Those damn Jimmy Choos. So, anyway, I was cleaning Elizabeth Hepburn's windows—"

"*The* Elizabeth Hepburn?"

I nodded.

"One time, during the years that John Travolta's career was in the crapper, my mom took me to see him do a dancing exhibition. His partner was Ms. Hepburn and even though she was already pretty old at the time, man, could she dip."

"Anyway, she gave me this Chick Lit book, see, *High Heels and Hand Trucks: My Life Among the Books*—"

"Great title."

"And I started reading the book…"

I proceeded to tell him my story, getting as far as Billy following me to Atlantic City…

"His talisman? Isn't that a little…hokey?"

I thought about it for a moment. "Well, yeah."

"And that didn't bother you?"

"Yes. No. I don't know. I mean, I was flattered. He seemed so suave, so debonair and even though most of what we ever talked about was gambling, I felt as though he was really interested in me. You know. As a woman."

"Who wouldn't be interested in you as a woman?"

The list was so long, I wouldn't have known where to start, so instead I barreled on.

"Then Billy started to pressure me into going to Vegas with him after admitting he was a professional gambler—"

"You mean to say he told you he was a professional gambler and still you kept on with him?"

"I guess that was stupid, huh?"

"Well, *yeah*. Why did you do that, Delilah? Why, why, why?"

"Because my mom stuck by my dad? Because he was exciting? Because I wanted those damn shoes?"

"Go on."

"I'd done well at Atlantic City…" I continued, ending with, "then my dad got involved with a woman who made him go to Debtors Anonymous."

"I think you must mean Bettors Anonymous."

"That's what she said. Plus, Stella was worried about Elizabeth Hepburn's evil servant, Lottie—which, truth to tell, so was I—and Conchita and Rivera weren't talking to each other anymore—"

"Wait a second. Stella? Conchita and Rivera? I don't think you've mentioned any of them before."

"My boss and the other two window washers who work on our crew, respectively if not respectfully. Conchita and Rivera are lesbians, by the way."

"Well, of course. Why wouldn't they be?"

"So—" big finish "—I finally came to Vegas with Billy and it was wonderful! At first. But then he kept wanting to gamble and for some reason I really didn't, so I talked him into going to Red Rock Canyon with me this morning, and that was a bust, and then when we returned the car John Belushi claimed we put a dent in it—"

"The real John Belushi?"

"Well, no. So then Billy said maybe I wasn't such a great talisman after all, because he had to forfeit his hundred-dollar deposit and I realized I had to put up or shut up, so we hit the casino and won big—you saw us do it—which was great and afterward he took me shopping and bought me these clothes and these shoes, which are pretty even if they're not Jimmy Choos, and he told me we'd get married in the Sunrise and Sunset Chapels tomorrow—"

"He asked you to marry him? What did you say?"

"I don't exactly remember saying yes, but I didn't say no, either. And then he said we'd get married the next day, but that first we needed to double our winnings—"

"And that's when I saw you again, when you lost all your chips."

"It was everything I had, except this." I produced the crumpled fiver from my cleavage.

"And then Billy just took off?"

"Uh-huh. He said I wasn't his talisman anymore."

"And you haven't seen him since?"

"Nope."

"I've got one question for you, Delilah—did you love him?"

"I don't know. I mean, I thought I might have. Sort of."

"'Men have died from time to time, and worms have eaten them, but not for love.'"

"You know Shakespeare?"

"Doesn't everyone? And I know one other thing, too, Billy's a creep."

"Oh, I guess we all know that by now. Me more than anybody. If the names *The Rat* and *The Weasel* weren't already taken, he'd be those, too."

"I think you need to be sure you're over him."

"How do I do that?"

He didn't say anything. He just leaned down slowly, pressed his lips gently to mine. His lips tasted just like something fresh, with maybe a hint of lime.

Oh, boy.

"It's a start," he said. "How long did you say you're in town for? When do you go back home?"

"I didn't say, but I go back on Monday. I'm stuck here until Monday with just my plane ticket back and this five-dollar bill. I don't even know how I'll eat. Not that I feel like eating."

"You have to eat. I'll talk to the guys in the kitchen, make sure room service brings up a few meals to you, on the house."

"What if you're fired after running out on the job like that?"

He shrugged. "I can always drop off meals for you myself. What do you like to eat?"

"Cocoa Krispies for breakfast, Amy's Cheese Pizza Pocket for lunch, Michael Angelo's Four Cheese Lasagna for dinner. For drinks, I like Diet Pepsi Lime and Jake's Fault Shiraz." I shrugged. "You know, the kind of stuff everyone likes."

"Done."

For good measure, he kissed me again. No pressure, just something light with a hint of promise in it.

"I can't believe you did all this," he said, "and you never even got your Choos."

"Me, either."

"What will you do with the rest of your time here?"

"I don't know." My last full day, Sunday, was already here. "Maybe go to church and watch other people get married all day."

"I've got an idea," he said. He took out his wallet and from there produced a business card. It said Las Vegas Library with an address.

"What's this?" I asked.

"Just be there tomorrow at two. Look for the Storytime Room. And dress casual."

After Chris walked me back to the hotel, giving me one more kiss just outside, I took the elevator up, made the long condemned-girl's walk down the corridor to the room I'd shared with Billy.

On the bed, so well made up by the housekeeper it looked sterile, he'd left my plane ticket and a note:

Baby,

Sorry to leave you in the lurch like this with just a plane ticket, but I'm sure you'll understand that I just had to leave town early. There's no point in me staying in Vegas when you've caused the cards to run cold on me. I'm sure that by now you also understand that our engagement is off. I simply can't have a talisman that only works for me some of the time. I'll be returning the white suit and shoes on my way out, but I suppose you can keep the silver things. Since you've already worn them, I can't imagine they'd give me my money back.

See you in the casinos! Or perhaps I should say I hope I *don't* see you in the casinos. At any rate, happy gambling,

Billy Charisma


I got the silver dress and shoes off me quicker than you can say "a natural Twenty-one beats everything else," and tossed the offending clothes in the garbage. Then I climbed into bed naked where I dreamt of nothing but Furthest Guy. Only now he was center stage and he wasn't dropping any of his yo-yos.

# 22

The Las Vegas Library looked nothing like the libraries back home. Instead of wood or brick, it was off-white painted stone, presumably protection against the desert heat, and there wasn't a Doric or Ionic or Corinthian column in sight.

I had no idea what to expect there.

I'd smiled while eating the room service breakfast of dry Cocoa Krispies that had been delivered to my door with a Diet Pepsi Lime chaser. Sure, it had been too early in the day for soda, but I'd forgotten to mention to Chris about the milk. And I'd smiled even more when lunch came at noon, Amy's Cheese Pizza Pockets, with yet more Diet Pepsi Lime, only this time there was an added treat on the tray: *Men Are Not The Only Heels,* the latest brand-spanking-new Shelby Macallister Chick Lit novel.

But now that I was in the library, finding my way to the Storytime Room, I wasn't smiling any longer because I had no idea what to expect.

The Storytime Room was brightly decorated with children in mind and had a capacity of about thirty people, judging from the seating setup. Most of the seats were already taken and I had to search for a minute before finding the last vacant seat in the middle of the third row. Seating myself between a grandfatherly man and a fiftysomething woman in a business suit who was reading a book while waiting for whatever was supposed to start to start, I noticed that in front of the first row of seats, down on the ground, were a couple of rows of small children.

The grandfatherly man had a hearing aid on the ear that was to my side so, worrying that if I asked him I might still have to shout, I leaned toward the woman on my right, started to whisper, "Do you know what the program—"

But before I could finish, a librarian type of woman wearing a laminated name tag on a lanyard made an announcement.

"Ladies and Gentlemen, Boys and Girls, we here at the Las Vegas Library are pleased to welcome back today Chris Westacott, yo-yoist extraordinaire!"

Everyone clapped politely, with the exception of the woman to my right, as Chris took the center of the nubby gray carpeting. Gone were his slick dealer clothes and while he obviously couldn't grow his shaggy hair back overnight, his whole appearance was more like the version of him I'd originally met. Instead of black pants, he now had on low-slung long khaki shorts that came to the knee. Instead of a cummerbund, he had on a brown leather belt that was barely holding up the khaki shorts. Instead of a crisp white shirt, he had on a maroon T-shirt that said Spanky Ate Here.

Chris took the microphone from the librarian and gave a slight bow to his audience.

"Thanks," he said. "First, I'm going to do a few tricks and, in between, if there are any questions, I'll be glad to answer them. Actually," he smiled winningly, "I sweat so much under these lights that if you ask me questions, you'll be doing me a favor."

And then he went to work, much of what he was doing being things I'd seen him do before: round the world, walking the dog, the two-handed yo-yo trick. But there was a difference between seeing him here and the times I'd seen him performing in the lobbies of casinos. Oh, he still lost control of his yo-yos here occasionally, but there were no Billys to heckle him and the crowd, young and old alike, were so entranced with what he was doing that no one seemed to mind if he made a few fumbles.

"Isn't he terrific?" I asked the lady next to me as he made a hot-pink yo-yo go round and round.

"Oh, that's one word for him all right," she said.

Chris finished the trick and he paused, obviously hoping someone would ask him a question. A little boy in the front row obliged.

"How many hours a day do you practice?" the boy asked.

"That's a great question," Chris said, wiping his brow. "Eight, if I can get it in. Yo-yoing, if you want to be good at it, is a full-time job."

He did another trick, this time turning out the lights and using glow-in-the-dark yo-yos so that it was like two ghouls revolving in the night.

"Can you make a living at what you do?" a little girl asked during the next break.

"It's not easy," Chris said, "but I suppose that if a person could fill their calendar with enough jobs and was willing to travel all over the country to do libraries and exhibitions and things, sure, why not? Now watch this…"

But when Chris tried to do his next trick, it turned out there was a competing performer in the room: a little girl, about five years old, with long brown hair, big brown eyes like chocolate drops, and a pink Lycra halter dress on with yellow-and-green trim, who obviously thought her half-executed cartwheels were an entertainment match for the yo-yo-meister. Even though she was interrupting Chris's show, he didn't seem to mind, and I smiled along with him as she cartwheeled in a misshapen circle around his performance area. I'd never given any thought to having kids of my own before, but watching that energetic girl, with her personality brighter than a shooting star, I suddenly wanted one.

"God," I said aloud, "I'd love to have a kid like that."

"That's *my* kid up there," said the lady to my right.

"She is?" I was surprised. The lady would have had to have

had her when she was in her late forties at least, if that was indeed her little girl.

"Not the girl," she said, eyes focused on the performance area, where Chris had started to do yet another trick. "The boy. Or, I guess I should say, man."

"The guy with the yo-yos is your *son?*"

I mean, it wasn't exactly like meeting Mary, mother of you-know-who, but it was close enough.

I looked at her more closely: steel-colored hair, matching glasses, gray eyes. She didn't look a thing like Chris and not just because of all of that. It was the suit. She looked like she'd been wearing a suit for thirty-five years. Well, maybe not the same one, but you get the picture.

"He's my son all right," she said, and I couldn't tell from her tone if she was proud or not.

"You must be very proud of him," I said.

"You think? I just thought I'd come here today to see how he was doing. I don't get to see him perform very often. Usually, he does it too far away or it's during hours when I'm working, but this time it was right at home… Of course, I couldn't get his father to come."

"You must be so proud of him," I said again, eyes glued on Chris and realizing how much I meant it. "You and your husband must both be so proud."

"Why?" she asked earnestly, as if she really didn't know.

"My God," I said, "look at him." I gestured. "Look at *them*." I pointed to the rows of kids, each face enraptured by whatever the heck it was Chris was doing with that oversized yo-yo. "Your son creates real *joy* in the world. He makes other people *happy*. I mean, I don't think those kids could be any happier if he'd given them each a dozen donuts and I don't think the adults could be happier if he'd washed all their windows."

"Huh?"

"Think about it," I said. "He's smart. He could have been a doctor or a lawyer or a businessperson—"

"Which is exactly what his father and I wanted him to be."

"—but instead, he does something that brings genuine happiness into the world to everyone he performs for. Well, so long as it's not in casinos. Honestly, what better job could he possibly ever have? He makes people *happy*."

"Huh."

Before leaving for the airport the next day, I tossed my copy of *Blackjack Winning Basics,* by Tony Casino, in the trash.

# Epilogue

From Shakespeare we learn that tragedy ends in death, while comedy ends in marriage.

Has anyone died here?

People have surely been dying all over the place while I've been telling my story—from disease, from accident, from war, from evil and from sheer stupidity—but I don't think anyone has died here. On the contrary, not only is there one marriage of sorts looming on the horizon; there are several.

Conchita and Rivera have realized that they are each the better other half of the other.

Stella is giving up Squeaky Qlean for good in favor of becoming Elizabeth Hepburn's live-in companion, enabling Elizabeth to give scheming Lottie the sack.

Black Jack Sampson has permanently laid down his

312 LAUREN BARATZ-LOGSTED

nickname and will go back to being simply Jack Sampson for all time on the day he marries Vanessa Parker. As Jackie Mason would say: *mazel tov.*

Hillary Clinton will go the whole traditional route, marrying Biff Williams in a white satin gown with red roses and baby's breath threaded through her hair. Old habit will make her toss the bouquet to the woman who will stand closest to her during the Episcopalian service and then she will need to rethrow it since her best friend is not her maid of honor, but rather her matron of honor, since her best friend—drum roll, please!—is already married.

Two years after the Vegas debacle—Sin City!—Chris and I tied the knot. In the interim, he persuaded me to finish my degree and I am now, like my mother before me, a teacher of English, only in my case I teach Shakespeare to senior high-school students who show more interest in sex than sonnets. Still, it allows me to channel my obsessive nature into something I love since, while teaching, I get to read my beloved Shakespeare over and over and over again.

As for Chris, he is now a full-time yo-yoist who travels all around the country for his work. This means that I do not get to see him as much as I would like, but being married to someone who is content is far preferable to being married to someone who is miserable.

We got married on a mountain in Maine in the autumn, our less sturdy family and friends needing to ride the ski lift up. When it came time to exchange rings, he had an extra surprise for me that he'd had Biff, his best man, carry up the slope. Out of a backpack he pulled a shoe box, within which was a pair of Jimmy Choos: the Ghost. Then he took out a high-heeled sandal, copper-colored, more pink than bronze, with diamond-shaped sapphire-colored stones encrusted with crystal stones across the toe strap and more sapphire and crystal bejeweling the intricate mesh of chain around the ankle with three straps of chain anchoring it to more copper leather at the back. I swear, when he slipped that gorgeous shoe on my foot, I felt as though my mother was kissing me on the cheek.

And on our honeymoon in Saint Croix, where we didn't leave our hotel room for a solid week? Chris didn't drop his yo-yos. Not once.

We now live in our own house in Danbury, where our cabinets are stocked with organic cocoa-flavored cereal, our freezer stocked with almost every organic product Amy's has ever made. We're still addicts, but we've learned to compensate, to make our addictions work for us rather than hurting us, and I've learned to forsake Diet Pepsi Lime and Jake's Fault Shiraz for the nonce because—second drumroll here, please!—I'm pregnant with our first child. And, with a little luck, I won't become so addicted to having babies that I turn into The Old Woman In A Shoe.

# Lee Nichols

Brigid Ashbury is the best accident reconstructionist in the
country. Only problem is, a personal car crash has left her with
a phobia about cars. Not exactly great for her career. Out of
work for almost a year, she gets a call from her former boss. A
millionaire's daughter, Jody Hulfinger, has crashed her car off
the coast of Maine. Her father, Small Hulfinger, wants to know
what killed her. As the case progresses through accident
reconstruction, a false kidnapping, misidentified bodies and
family turmoil, Brigid struggles to overcome her fears and
find the murderer.

# Reconstructing Brigid

"Nichols is one of chick lit's brightest lights."
—*Publishers Weekly*

# Melissa Senate

A *New York Times* article lists fifteen questions couples should ask before marrying. Ruby Miller and her fiancé, Tom Truby, have questions one to fourteen *almost* covered. It's question fifteen that has the Maine schoolteacher stumped: *Is* their relationship strong enough to withstand challenges?

Challenges like…Ruby's twin sister, Stella. The professional muse, flirt and face reader thinks Ruby is playing it safe. And that the future Mrs. Ruby Truby will die of boredom before her first anniversary or thirtieth birthday, whichever comes first.

Challenges like…sexy maverick teacher Nick McDermott, Ruby's secret longtime crush, who confesses his feelings for her at her own engagement party.

## Questions to Ask Before Marrying

"Senate's prose is fresh and lively." —*Boston Globe*

**Available wherever trade paperbacks are sold!**

## RED DRESS INK™

# Carole Matthews

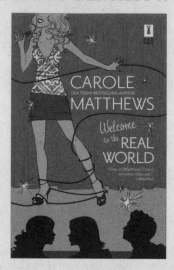

During one crazy week, aspiring singer Fern Kendal lands
a spot on the reality-television talent show *Fame Game*
and a glam new job as personal assistant to world-famous
singer Evan David, leading to an adventure of a lifetime—
both onstage and off!

"With a lovable heroine, a dashing hero, and plenty
of twists and turns, Matthews' new novel has
all the right ingredients."
—*Booklist*

## Welcome to the Real World

Available wherever
trade paperbacks
are sold!